Made in the USA
Middletown, DE
22 July 2024

SPILLING the BEANS

a novel

ALSO BY STEVE ZOUSMER

"Famous" with Richard Liebmann-Smith

TV News Off-Camera

Galapagos: Discovery in Darwin's Islands, with Dr. David Steadman

You Don't Have To Be Famous: How To Write Your Life Story

How To Write For The Big Guy

Falling Into The Mob

The Phantom Songbird of New York

a novel by **STEVE ZOUSMER**

NEW YORK, NEW YORK

Copyright © 2024 by Steve Zousmer

All rights reserved. No part of this publication, or parts thereof, may be reproduced in any form, except for the inclusion of brief quotes in a review, without the written permission of the publisher.

Library of Congress Control Number: 2024911978

   Steve Zousmer, author
      Spilling the Beans / Steve Zousmer
      New York, New York; Zousmer Books
      ISBN: 979-8-218-45217-9 (paperback)
      ISBN: 979-8-218-45218-6 (ebook)

Cover Design, Lon Kirschner: www.kirschnerdesign.com

Printed in the United States of America

DEDICATION

I've dedicated books to my parents, both wives, both kids, my Labrador Retriever, and a woman I met on a train. I didn't get her name but our conversation inspired my novel about falling into the Mafia.

This book, probably my last, is dedicated to the people who taught me to write. It's a long list starting with my parents, who were both writers. Next come some excellent teachers: William B.T. Mock in high school, and at Stanford, Blair Fuller, Richard Scowcroft, Wallace Stegner, and my all-time favorite teacher, Nancy Huddleston Packer.

[The Apollo 11 astronauts] are like people who have gone into the other world and have returned, and you sense they bear secrets that we will never entirely know, and that they will never entirely be able to explain.

—ERIC SEVAREID, *CBS News*

STEVE ZOUSMER

CHAPTER 1

April 8, 1948
McGill, Ohio

My memory of the day starts with a gasp, the sharp collective gasp as we emerged from the church with the organ music floating us out the doors, the first funeral of my young life coming to an end.

At first I couldn't see what people were gasping about. I was a tall girl for my age (seven) but height-deficient when packed into a crowd of adults. I waited for my parents to explain what was happening, but they didn't. Then someone moved and I could see for myself.

It was a crowd of black folks. I'd never seen so many in one place. Journalism training later in life taught me that it's tricky to estimate crowd size but it's safe to put the number at well over fifty, maybe closer to a hundred. Men, women, and children.

They were standing solemnly, respectfully, wearing their Sunday best (on a Thursday), and even I could tell they were ill at ease because in 1948 it was begging for trouble to cross the tracks and form a crowd on the white side of a far from racially enlightened Ohio town. In those times (has it changed today?) white folks got twitchy and dangerous when blacks did anything that jiggled the usual balance of things.

What're *they* doing here?—that whispered question raced around among the whites. Whatever soft emotion had been stirred by HB Taylor's farewell quickly stiffened into consternation and alarm.

I never knew there was so many of them.

Don't they have any respect for Mr. Taylor's funeral?

Don't they know enough to keep to themselves?

My grandmother, Mary Louise Taylor (known by her nickname, Sportie), stepped forward. She was petite and gracious, still beautiful in her mid-sixties. A brave woman, widowed for only three days. She crossed the distance between the church steps, where the whites were bunched up, to the pavement where the blacks were tightly gathered, and approached Robert Deems.

Robert Deems was a tall and dignified black man in his seventies who if clad in striped tie and tails could have passed for an ambassador. In fact you could say he *was* the ambassador between the town's black and white communities, well-liked by everyone. Generations had grown up riding to school on the yellow bus he drove, later entrusting him with their own children. He was unfailingly kind and courteous, exempt from the town's simmering prejudice.

Robert Deems towered over Sportie. His face was deep with sympathy.

"Mrs. Taylor, we are here to pay our respects."

Sportie said, in an accent I think was Virginian, "Robert, what a lovely surprise. And you brought so many friends. You are all welcome."

"That's a matter of opinion," came a distinctly white growl.

"Would I be permitted to say a few words?"

"Of course, Robert," Sportie said, standing back as Robert Deems stepped forward.

"I'll be brief," he said.

"Not brief enough," came that growling voice again.

Sportie turned and snapped, "You shush up and mind your manners, Earl Bridgewater. Please continue, Robert."

But her scolding of Earl Bridgewater turned the tension up another notch.

My mother, hands on my shoulders, pushed me forward so I could hear.

"This may come as a big surprise to you," Robert said, his eyes sweeping the white faces, "but Tuesday nights as long as I remember, Mr. Taylor would travel over to our side. He would sit down at various kitchen tables and open that smart-looking leather briefcase of his, pulling out a nice bottle of Haig scotch whiskey which he'd share with us. Scotch was a rare and special taste for us given its cost.

"Our community leaders, mainly businessmen, would come in and wait their turn to consult with him. They would often bring along their account books. HB was a certified public accountant and he scanned those books with an eagle eye. If called for, he made sharp comments.

Then he'd listen keenly as the men told him about problems or business ideas they were cooking up and he would offer advice.

"He was a good-hearted enjoyable fellow, quick with a witticism, but he was blunt and brooked no nonsense. He saw right through it if someone was blowing hot air or telling tales or rhapsodizing about dreams with no chance of coming true. He would acquaint us with needed tax documents and permits and whatnot and how to deal with various legalities and how to stay right with the town and the state and the bank, because on matters like these we didn't know our tail from a teakettle.

"What you have to understand is that we didn't have nobody else to get leadership from, you know? *Nobody else*. And this white man was the former treasurer of Ohio Bell Telephone. He put in the accounting system used in much of the entire American telephone system. How about that? He was a member of the State Tax Commission and he served as our McGill village clerk for twenty years. A man of this distinction, with nothing to gain for himself, came to help us. He spoke to us like men. He addressed our women as 'Mrs.,' not 'girl.' He knew our children's names. And when he went home, things always seemed more hopeful. And hope was just as rare in those dark years as that fine scotch whiskey."

"Why didn't he come to our houses too?" came a white woman's voice. "God knows we could have used the help."

"He *did* give you help, Connie," Sportie shot back. "He never said no to anyone needing a helping hand. If you've forgotten that, what in God's name are you doing at this funeral?"

The white folks seemed puzzled and distressed by what they'd heard and chewed it over for a while. HB was held in high regard but there was something suspicious about a lone white man circulating in the black side of town and not getting beaten up and robbed and in fact being genuinely liked and admired. It seemed he'd taken a crazy chance that made no sense unless the motive was illicit.

I didn't know what to make of the agitated stirring around me, but I understand now that what the white folks were asking was: had this good man, HB Taylor, been a secret traitor to the white race? Was he a—I don't want to spell out this horrid term, common in those years, but it was hyphenated with the first letter beginning with "n" and the second word being "-lover." This was the meanest, most scabrous label that could be put on you. It was a horrible stain on your good name. It won you no points whatsoever with the small high-minded community and made you a target of scorn from the much larger ignoramus community. HB had one of the best reputations in town. Why would he put it at risk?

"I don't want to jabber on," said Robert. "We just thought we should venture over here today, welcome or not—"

"Not," came Earl Bridgewater's voice. "Not welcome."

"—And say the right thing because we owed it to him. We have a debt to him. Oh, and look who's here: do you see that pretty young blonde girl in the blue dress? She was the apple of his eye, his granddaughter Charlotte Whistler—everyone calls her Lake—who is here today with her mom and dad, Kate and John Whistler from New York City. Kate grew up in McGill and used to ride my bus."

"Wave, Lake," my mother whispered.

I held up a hand, timidly.

"We'll be on our way now," said Robert, turning away. "Thank you for your kind attention."

The crowd was dead silent. Faces were stony.

Sportie took a step after Robert and said for all to hear, "Robert, come to dinner tonight at 614 (the Taylor home at 614 Cambridge Street). And make sure to bring Lucille."

"Oh now that's pushing it," roared Earl Bridgewater, and there were murmurs of agreement that Sportie's invitation was a step too far. It was bad enough that HB had visited black homes; it was shocking that blacks were welcome in a white family's dining room. Robert Deems sensed the thin ice of the moment and deftly defused it by humbly declining the invitation. (Sportie understood Robert's tactic and telephoned him later to renew the invitation, which he accepted.)

Robert's backing out of the mixed-race dinner at 614 was taken as a display of blacks knowing their place, which eased the discomfort of the whites. But then Sportie sent the tension rising again as she stepped past Robert to greet and thank HB's black cronies who stood in the front rank of the black folks.

"Are you inviting them *all* to dinner?" Bridgewater shouted.

This brought snickers and a few outright jeers from some whites. Bridgewater knew what they were thinking because he was thinking the same thing: had *all* these black people been sneaking over to 614 to socialize equally at the Taylor dinner table? Had they *all* violated the invisible border in the dark of night, trespassing in one of the town's nicest and whitest neighborhoods?

Tempers were starting to boil. Muttered objections were audible around me and not just from this one crank, Bridgewater. For the first time in my life, I felt a radiating tingle of jeopardy. I looked up at my parents for guidance. My dad pressed a finger over his lips, signaling me to not speak, to wait for an explanation at a better time. It was all he could do. We were hemmed in. He must have been concerned about defending me and my mother and Sportie if things got out of hand. And whatever form "out of hand" would take, from an exchange of threats and curses to an all-out melee, it would poison race relations in the town for years to come. For decades to come.

Luck intervened. A nasty public incident requires an instigator, a fired-up figure whose fervor incites reckless abandon. But on this day only one candidate for leadership asserted himself and that was Earl Bridgewater, who was rabble but ungifted as a rabble-rouser.

Nearly everyone in town recalled distasteful run-ins with him or his ornery family and no one would follow him for even a brief cathartic purge of racist bile. And there were no other volunteers for the leadership role.

Earl's unworthiness saved the day for McGill. Not that he didn't give it a try. Evidently assuming that his day for greatness had arrived and that fellow bigots would join a charge behind him, he ran at our car as we climbed into it, cursing and waving clenched fists. Just as he realized he had no plan and no fired-up troops behind him, he encountered a real soldier in front of him. My dad, an ex-marine who'd fought in the Pacific during the War, got out of the car and stood up to him, and Earl Bridgewater came to a sputtering stop, dropping his fists. His embarrassing trepidation was universally noted.

To make it worse, he then let himself be smacked down by my grandmother.

He shouted at Sportie, "Mrs. Taylor, we wouldn't have come out here today if we'd knowed you was going to pull *this* on us," and she icily replied, "I didn't *pull* anything, Earl. And, by the way, your behavior is beneath contempt."

Beneath contempt. That was a new one for Earl. He was used to far more vulgar disparagement. The elegance of "beneath contempt" left him uncomprehending. As my dad later said with amusement, "He was okay with being called riffraff or other names but 'beneath contempt' seemed to be a demotion to an even lower level, too subtle for him to grasp." And, especially coming from a respected elder like Sportie with many people observing, it was a breathtaking stab to his heart. His fat round face contorted in a mix of pain and rage. But more pain than rage. He gave us a half-hearted middle finger and turned away.

The whites and blacks drifted home. It had been a memorable moment, a close call, in which respect for HB Taylor just barely transcended the town's instinctive racism. Everyone was relieved there'd been no violent surfacing of emotions that would forever upset the delicate balance of race relations in their town.

Earl's behavior was inexplicable to me as a seven-year-old, but it made a deep impression. It was the first time I'd seen the sorry stereotype of bigoted rage in its rawest state. When I saw it again as a reporter, I always thought of Earl Bridgewater.

* * *

Riding home my mother was giving me a sermon on racial equality and how the white people at the church should have applauded HB as a brave and principled hero instead of fretting that he'd betrayed the white race.

Sportie gently interrupted. "Lake, you'll remember this day all your life so let me help you get it right. HB was no race hero. He didn't want credit for doing good. In fact he kept it secret because he knew it would confuse people and rile them up. If he could help you, he would help you. It's as simple as that. That's how you should remember him."

After a moment's silence my mother asked Sportie if she anticipated trouble.

"No, dear, I don't, other than people giving me the evil eye when I'm in the market. Maybe there'll be some shouted curses out of cars speeding past 614 in the middle of the night or empty beer bottles thrown on the lawn. We used to call it moonshine courage. But I don't expect it. These people wouldn't dick with HB and they won't dick with me. Pardon my *français*."

* * *

The night before all this happened, HB was laid out in an open casket in 614's sunroom. He was the first dead person I'd seen.

I recall alarming the adults by declaring my intention to spend the night sleeping on the couch in the sunroom. My thinking was that it would be HB's final night at 614 and he shouldn't be alone, dead or not. This idea met with parental resistance, but I was adamant. To avoid a squabble, the adults gave in. When bedtime came, a blanket and pillow were provided and I was tucked in on the couch.

But not long after the grown-ups had gone upstairs, I started feeling spooked about being alone with a corpse. A lamp had been left on and HB's face was dimly illuminated as I bent over his casket and tried to find words to say goodbye. I touched the two-inch vertical scar on the right side of his neck, a childhood farming injury which he always teased me about, saying it happened in a knife fight with Sitting Bull.

HB was not a big man, but he was formidable, even in his casket. He was slightly yellow and waxy, of course, but his face was strong with definite features, a prominent nose and cheekbones, and a firm jawline. It looked like it had been chipped out of the granite of Mount Rushmore.

I fell asleep on the couch and later someone came and carried me upstairs and I would never see HB again.

Well, not for thirty-one years.

CHAPTER 2

September 2, 1979
Amanituck, New York

I hadn't thought about HB's funeral in years but here it was, coming back in a burst of memory. And it intruded with the worst possible timing: I was having sex.

In the years since I'd been abruptly returned to the singles market, I'd had alternating periods of promiscuity and chastity, neither of which I recommend. For a number of summers, I'd been among eight or ten weekend renters in Brendan Leary's old house in the Long Island beach town of Amanituck, which is close to the Hamptons in everything but per capita affluence.

Sexual hijinks are part of the implicit promise of such arrangements but nothing much happened in our group until one especially boozy season-ending Labor Day Weekend celebration when Brendan Leary and I wound up in my upstairs bedroom.

We were friends with little in common except that we were both unmarried heterosexual New Yorkers. Brendan was an ex-cop, now the owner of a New York saloon with a blue-collar clientele. I was approaching forty, he was slightly past it. We could have repeated the sex in Amanituck or back in the city but neither of us wanted to dilute our sexual chemistry by stretching it out for more than one great night per year. If we extended beyond that, we felt, our differences would doom a nice relationship. So it became a strictly annual tradition which we looked forward to, joked about, and enjoyed with libertine gusto.

At the moment when imagery of HB's funeral flooded into my mind, Brendan and I were neck-and-neck thundering into the homestretch with me in an unladylike position, which I will leave undescribed. I tried my best to ward off the distraction of the funeral memory—loss of focus at a moment like this violates the unwritten rules of fornication.

But my attention had been hijacked beyond recovery. Brendan sensed it in an instant. Years of tending bar and policing had equipped him with superlative antennae.

Slowing down he asked if I was okay, if anything was wrong.

"No, no. Brendan. I'm sorry. Would you mind…"

He flopped on his back, awaiting my explanation.

I said nothing. What can you say to a man at a time like this?

I was face-down, looking away from him, catching my breath.

"Hey, it happens, Lake," he said.

"You're a good sport," I said.

He stroked my back and waited for something more.

I said, "Everything was going great, really, and then, ka-boom. It was like I was suddenly watching an old home movie. Although why the projectionist showed a movie of my grandfather's funeral in 1948, I'll never know. Let me clear my head for a second and we'll get back to business."

"Sure."

I replayed it in my mind.

"Brendan, when we were doing it, did you hear something strange? Or feel something strange? Like a tone or vibration or something like a little ripple in the air?"

"A ripple in the air? What the hell is that?"

"I don't know. It felt weird."

The heat of the sexual moment was gone and I felt a chill as the night air met my flesh. I sat up and felt around for my T-shirt, found it, and pulled it over my head. My hair must have been chaotic.

"Tell me more about the dream and the ripple."

"I don't know. It was weird. I feel like a teenager using the word 'weird' but that's what it was."

And not the first weird thing of the day. Earlier, at the beach, we'd watched an astonishingly supernatural-seeming sunset as a colossal mountain of purple clouds towered over us, reaching upward into the heavens and streaked by every color in the spectrum. It was one of those moments that gives you a shiver, a reminder of what pipsqueaks we are under the magnitude and mystery of the cosmos.

"I have to look out the window," I said.

"The window? Why?"

"I don't know."

"There's nothing to see out there. It's dark, you know."

I got out of bed and carried a pillow which I clutched over my breasts as I crept warily across the dark room to the window, feeling Brendan's gaze on my rear end. The window was knee-high with no curtains. An Irish bachelor like Brendan never got around to amenities like curtains.

I should make clear that Brendan's house was far from fancy. It was old and drab, located on a quiet street in a working-class neighborhood, untouched by Amanituck's luxury enclaves where Brendan aspired to sell real estate. He hadn't gotten his foot in that door so far, but his Irish charm and rugged good looks had won us invites to some Gatsby-like pool parties where we rubbed shoulders and shared intoxicants with the rich and famous.

I peeked out the window.

Brendan was correct about darkness, but my view panned around to a streetlamp which dropped a circle of light downward to the sidewalk. In that circle, to my surprise, was a man who stood motionless, his face tilted up as if he were looking directly at me.

I was slightly shocked to meet his gaze.

"There's a man out there."

"At this time of night? Hold on while I grab my Glock."

I turned around to see if he was kidding. You never know with cops. But I could tell he was amused. He wasn't taking this seriously. He got out of bed, stepping into his jeans and zipping up as he joined me at the window, looking over my shoulder.

The man, seemingly middle-aged, wore a natty summer suit, straw-colored. A matching fedora was pulled down at a smart angle over his forehead. Old-world elegance. He was compact and had a serious-man posture.

"Voyeurs aren't usually so dapper, even in Amanituck," said Brendan.

"He sees me."

"He can't see you, you're in a dark room."

But he could see me. He was looking up, a hand shielding his eyes from the brightness of the streetlamp. With his other hand he waved to me.

"Oh, God," I said. "Should I wave back?"

"Nothing good can come of it. My professional instinct is for you to get back in bed. We have better things to do."

"I need to go down and talk to him," I said. "See what this is about."

"Are you nuts? Why the hell would you want to talk to him? What's going on with you, Lake? Some older gentleman stands outside your window at five thirty in the morning so you feel some magnetic pull and want to go running down to see what he wants? And have you forgotten that you're not wearing pants?"

It was true that I felt a hard-to-figure magnetic pull. It was also true about the pants. I found my red shorts and pulled them on.

Brendan said, "Okay, skimpy shorts and tight T-shirt, the ideal outfit to run out and meet a stranger on a dark street."

"I'm going."

"If you gotta go, you gotta go. I'll be right behind you. I'll be in the same position when we come back."

"No, stay here. Please, Brendan, I don't know why but just stay here."

"Okay, if you say so. My years on the job tell me this guy isn't dangerous. But if anything gets hinky, I'll come running. Fix your hair or you'll scare him."

I took a few swipes at my hair as I went downstairs hoping my steps on the creaky stairs didn't wake our housemates, though probably everyone was sleeping deeply after the merriment of our summer-ending party. In bare feet I walked across the dewy lawn toward the streetlight.

* * *

I knew who he was.

Knew it, but rejected it. Emphatically. Your long-dead grandfather or a topnotch facsimile thereof appears in front of you and you're supposed to say, "Hi, Grandpa"?

No no no no no. Ridiculous. No.

I decided I was simply mistaken. My memory of HB's funeral had somehow bled over to thinking I was seeing HB Taylor instead of a stranger who just happened to be taking a near-dawn stroll.

With just a few steps between us, he tipped his hat. We stared at each other.

"I thought a lot about what my first words to you would be," he said, in a slightly gruff voice. "But now everything slips my goddamn mind."

"Please don't tell me you're HB Taylor."

"Good for you. Yes, that's me."

"I have tragic news for you."

"What's that?"

"You're dead."

He smiled. "Yes, I'm aware of that, believe me."

"You died in 1948."

"What year is it now?"

"1979."

"Thirty-one years. I was gone for thirty-one years?"

In my New York apartment I have a bookshelf of family photos including one of HB (the photo used in his obituary—"Well-Known Citizen Dies"—which my mother scissored out of the McGill newspaper). The face in that photo was unmistakably the face I was looking at now.

But I fought it. One thing I knew with absolute certainty was that dead people do not return.

He stood there in a serious pose, his hands thrust downward into his suit jacket pockets, hat brim shading his face. He wore eyeglasses whose wire frames were probably ordinary in 1948 but stylishly retro three decades later.

"I can't get over seeing you all grown up," he said. "You're taller than your mom but you were tall as a girl. And that beautiful blonde hair. I remember Sportie braiding it."

"How do you know about Sportie?" I asked, stupidly.

He smiled. "I was married to her for forty years."

I think it was bringing dear beloved Sportie, who was very real to me, into this that really unnerved me. I handled the situation with an extreme absence of dignity. I turned and looked up to the bedroom window where I knew Brendan was watching. I motioned for him to raise the window and when he did, I shouted, "THIS IS BULLSHIT!"

It came out loud enough to wake the neighbors. My voice did not sound like my voice.

It was angry verging on unhinged. And then I made it worse by repeating the scream, trying to sound even angrier, but the second scream amplified a note of falseness. It exposed my bewilderment and a sense of acute embarrassment as if the whole world was watching as I was bamboozled, tricked, scammed, hoaxed, duped, or made a fool of in a cruel practical joke.

His calmness made it worse. He said, "I'm thinking of a summer evening when your mom and dad and Sportie and I were having G&Ts on the porch and Sportie was braiding your hair and she said you were as blonde as Veronica Lake, the movie star. You were so small at the time and had no idea who Veronica Lake was or even what a movie star was. We started teasingly calling you Veronica and you were furious because you couldn't pronounce it—you said Wavonica—and insisted on being called 'Lake' instead. So we did. And it stuck."

I'd heard that anecdote many times and told it many times myself so it was not something that only he could have known. He could have heard it or dug it up in research and worked it into his scam. But the nostalgic affection in the way he told it seemed authentic.

"I always preferred Lake, despite the jokes about going fishing or swimming in Lake Whistler," I said. "Charlotte is awful. I hated it."

"Charlotte was my mother's name. You were named after her."

"Sorry," I said. "I don't remember that."

"She hated it too. We called her Charlie."

We almost shared a laugh over that.

This exchange relaxed me for a millisecond. I was cold, goose-bumped from head to toe. I was appalled by my behavior. I'd been foul-mouthed and flustered. I'd been painfully uncool, not getting the joke or catching on to whatever this was and not liking it one bit.

The screen door slammed and I heard Brendan hurrying out to help but I signaled him to stay back.

"Lake," said HB, "I understand this is difficult to believe. In your shoes, not that you're wearing shoes, I wouldn't believe it either."

I said, "One small detail that keeps me from believing you is that I attended your funeral. I saw your body in your casket. I touched your face."

"I bet I was the first stiff you'd ever seen. Was it a good funeral? Did Robert Deems bring his people over? Theotis Ames, Marlon Jenkins, Herb Witherspoon, the Barneses and all the others? Robert told me they'd come. I pleaded with him to make them stay home. People could get hurt."

"They came," I managed to say. "All of them."

"Was there any trouble?"

"No one got hurt. A guy named Earl Bridgewater tried to stir up trouble but nothing happened."

"I remember Earl. Not a model citizen. His dad, Earl Senior, was worse. Jim Farraday hauled him off to the hoosegow on numerous occasions. I'm relieved nobody got hurt."

Brendan, standing next to me now, was overhearing this. His presence stiffened my resistance. I dropped back from almost believing to wiseassed skepticism.

I said, "Why don't you tell me you looked down from heaven and watched the whole funeral?"

"That's not how it works. There's no looking down from heaven."

"Well, there's a helluva headline," I said sarcastically. "NO LOOKING DOWN FROM HEAVEN. People have been wondering about that forever, but you've just cleared it up. But there apparently is some sort of afterlife because that's where you've been all these years."

"Yes."

"There's another headline! AFTERLIFE EXISTS. You're telling me all this big stuff with a straight face. Are you going to charge me for hearing it?"

"Money? Of course not."

I knew it was an offensive question and scolded myself for asking it but I put it down to my natural journalistic suspicion: if this was a scam there was probably a money angle.

I wasn't sure where to go next. I felt myself fumbling.

"You seem to know how death works," I said.

"Just the rudiments. Newcomer level."

"There are *levels*?"

"Levels might not be the best word. Maybe *depths*. But I don't know anything about the depth below mine."

"One revelation after another! Could you discuss this on television because billions of people would be extremely interested?"

"Television? I remember talk about television. I never saw it."

"You never saw television?"

Brendan interrupted, asking, "Does God exist?"

"Brendan, shut up. Don't tell me you're taking this guy seriously. You were a cop. You own a bar. You've heard all the bullshit in the world. But a guy tells you he's back from the dead and you're asking him if God exists?"

"I'd like to know. I was raised Catholic in the Bronx."

HB chuckled.

"I've had enough of this," I said. "If there's more to this joke, get on with it but if not, I'm going back inside."

HB said, "Lake, dying doesn't mean you get an introductory lecture on how death works, any more than a newborn child gets a lecture on how life works. There are things I know about death and a lot of things I don't know."

I was shivering. Brendan put his arm around my shoulder. A couple people from the house, awakened by my screaming, stood on the front porch watching but cautiously keeping their distance.

Daylight was breaking.

"Are you okay, Lake?" asked Brendan.

"Have you figured out, Brendan, that this man not only claims to be back from the dead but claims to be my grandfather?"

"The grandfather you were dreaming about? And two minutes later he shows up outside the window?"

"That's how it works," said HB. "I guess it's to refresh your memory."

Then he offered his hand for a handshake. Brendan hesitated, then shook.

"I'm Brendan Leary. I think we need to know exactly what you're up to."

CHAPTER 3

At that moment an Amanituck police car pulled up, roof lights blinking.

A very young officer rolled down his window.

"We've had calls of a disturbance. A woman shouting profanity."

"Who the fuck could that have been?" I cried.

Just when I thought I was getting a grip on self-control, I was losing it again. I saw myself as this cop must have seen me: standard middle-of-the-night messed-up floozy, physically and emotionally disheveled, difficult and disgusting. There was wine on my breath and my hair was a mess from sex. I was shivering and my nipples were erect from the chill, perking through the material of my T-shirt which, to make matters even worse, I realized I'd put on inside-out. And I was presenting this total loser image to three men: a cop who looked like a teenager, a sex partner, and a man claiming to be a dead relative I'd been raised to revere.

Brendan stepped forward, addressing the cop as "Luke" and assuring him everything was under control. Brendan is buddy-buddy with the local police. He explained that I was a summer renter, he'd known me for years, I was a respected TV writer, and he'd never seen me lose my cool.

Luke the cop said, "And who is this gentleman?"

"I am HB Taylor, deceased."

"Come again?" The cop looked at HB, then Brendan.

"That's HB without the periods. The initials don't stand for anything. I had a brother named AB and a sister named CB."

Brendan said, "He appears to be sober. Maybe a tad wacko but not criminal. No problem, really."

"The rumors of my death are not exaggerated," HB said, with a smile. "And by the way, those flashing colored lights on your car roof are glorious. We had nothing like that in my day."

"I'll have to see some identification," the cop said impatiently. "Driver's license."

"I have no identification. I never drove a car. Got by fine without one for seventy-two years."

"You don't look seventy-two," the cop said.

"Tonight I'm fifty-five, but I was seventy-two when I died. You can come back at whatever age you want. You get a choice."

"Is this some kind of screwball comedy act?" said Luke. "What's going on here, Brendan? I figured this would be a drunk and disorderly thing but you all look fairly sober."

"Which is regrettable," HB said.

Some neighbors, apparently feeling safe because of the police car, were coming out in their bathrobes to see what was going on. Dawn was in full swing. Birds were chirping.

The cop had no idea what to do so Brendan said, "There won't be any trouble here, Luke. I can handle it."

Luke shrugged and said, "Enjoy your stay in Amanituck," and drove off.

"I'm freezing my butt off," I said. "Can we go inside?"

"Speaking of alcohol, I'd love a scotch," said HB.

"At this hour you want a scotch?" asked Brendan. "I'll pour it on your Cheerios."

* * *

HB and I took places at the kitchen table as Brendan stood at the stove cooking a sizzling breakfast. The other houseguests gave us room, going back to bed.

"I'm joking about the scotch," said HB. "I'd love one but I couldn't taste it and it wouldn't do anything for me. I won't even be able to taste your scrambled eggs, Brendan, though I appreciate the hospitality. There are no physical sensations for me. No taste, no smell, no appetite of any kind."

Brendan said, "Okay, but if you change your mind, I could make you some tasteless waffles."

HB laughed. Then there was silence.

"Maybe I should do some explaining," HB said. "I'll start with what I'm *not* here for. I have no mission or purpose. I can't do anything that alters the flow of life among the living. I can't finish painting the front porch or shoot the president. I can't right wrongs or get revenge or intervene among warring tribes, that kind of thing."

I said, "But you can affect people. If I was really your granddaughter, wouldn't I be affected by you suddenly showing up?"

"I suppose, but that's incidental. You should understand this. This is not something out of the movies. I'm not a personal angel sent to guide you or impart wisdom. I'm here for me, not you. As I understand it, it's sort of a last look at what life was like, based on seeing you. Oh, look out there, the boy on his bike. Doing his paper route."

HB was looking out the window with an expression of delight. The boy tossed a folded-up newspaper onto Brendan's front lawn.

"Lake, I remember when your mom was trying to teach you to ride a bike and you took a bad spill and you both came in with bloody knees. It was a hot summer day and Sportie bandaged you up and gave you lemonade."

I remembered that. I'd refused to get on the bike for a week after that. This was not an oft-told anecdote. It was highly unlikely that an impostor could have known about it.

HB said, "So you're wondering why I've come back today instead of any other time in the last thirty years. The answer is that when you're dead you get the offer to come back when there's only one significant person from your family or close friends still alive. For me that's you, Lake."

"Really. So that means that every significant person in your family is dead now except me, and somebody else must have just died to make me the last one?"

"Yes. You're not told who it was. I don't want to know. But you're my last link to the life I led. When there's no one left, my existence as HB Taylor is finished and I'll sink into the death of the forgotten. I don't know what happens there. But for now I get to spend some time, but not much time, with you."

"You said you get an *offer* to come back," I said. "Can you reject it?"

"Yes. Most people start to leap at the offer but after a little thought they reject it. For a million reasons. They realize they'll be alone in a changed and different world where all they can do is lonely sightseeing. Maybe they don't want to see how things have changed or how little it mattered that they lived or died. Maybe they died as babies and have nothing to remember. Maybe their lives were nothing but misery, fear, disease, cruelty, starvation, and so on. Maybe they don't want to remember what bastards they were or how lonely they were or how guilty they feel. Do you think Hitler would have wanted to come back? I don't think he'd have gotten a warm welcome."

I said, "I'm thinking about whether I'd make the choice to come back. I don't think so. I'd have no one significant to come back to."

"HB, can't you get in trouble for blabbing about this stuff?" asked Brendan, ever the rule-enforcing lawman. "I mean, are you *allowed* to divulge the secrets of death?"

"I don't think they're secrets, Brendan. They're just not known. If you can't find your blue socks is that a secret of the universe or do you just not know where your socks are?"

Brendan replied, "But are you saying you can tell everything you know about death? And are you saying everyone who dies gets an offer to come back and presumably this has been going on forever, is that right? So a helluva lot of dead people must have come back. So how come everything hasn't been revealed? How come no one's spilled the beans?"

HB smiled. "Oh, I'm sure the beans have been spilled many times, but do living people *believe* the beans? What if it goes against their religion? What if they just won't listen? If some dead guy pops up in a village in China and starts telling everything he knows, how are people going to react? They won't believe him. Maybe they'll try to hush him up because he's making their family look like lunatics or witches or because he scares people. And what he says won't reach more than a few people anyway. Also, these bean spillers are like me, they've only gone through the entry years of death. They haven't seen the whole shebang."

"And nobody who's seen the whole shebang comes back to talk about it?"

"Correct. There's only one chance to come back."

"Okay, so this is your chance," I said. "What are you going to do while you're here?"

"Spend time with you. Look around."

"With me? I live in a small apartment in New York. There's no room for you. You'll have to sleep on the couch."

"I don't sleep. I won't be in the way."

"I have to go to work every day. I can't show you around."

"I'll be fine."

"How long does this go on?"

"I don't know. Just a wink in time."

"How long is a wink?"

"I think about a week. I don't know. I don't think it's exact."

Then a long silence.

"Brendan," I said. "I'm tempted to try this. My life really needs a little shake-up.

Something a little different."

Brendan said, "A little different? Like letting some unknown man who says he's your dead grandfather move into your apartment for a week? That's just crazy."

"Sometimes you have to take a chance."

"My advice is to shake hands with Mr. Taylor or whoever he is and send him on his way. He seems like a fine gentleman, but this cannot be for real. Don't fall for this, Lake."

I turned to HB. "What if I say no? If I say I don't want you here?"

"I disappear. Right now," he said, snapping his fingers. "I vanish forever."

A true con man would have been ready with a bunch of reasons why I shouldn't say no.

But HB said no more.

"This's your chance, Lake," said Brendan. "Say no and he vanishes and this whole thing is over. No harm done."

I looked hard at HB, searching for a decision-tipping signal. And I found one: the nearly faded scar on the side of his neck.

"HB Taylor used to tease me with a tall tale about that scar," I said, pointing to it. "He told me he got it in a knife fight with a famous person. Can you name that famous person?"

He laughed. "I told you it was Sitting Bull."

CHAPTER 4

I announced my decision: HB could stay but before we drove back to Manhattan I needed some sleep. HB could kill time by strolling on the beautiful beach which was only a ten-minute walk from Brendan's house.

"Excellent idea," he said. "I was kind of a landlocked Ohio guy. Haven't seen much of oceans."

Brendan followed me upstairs. He seemed bothered that I was declining his advice about HB, but he joined me in the sack and before falling asleep we consummated our unfinished annual business. I didn't want him feeling cheated out of sex by a highly implausible supernatural event.

Two hours later we awoke to the sound of laughter from downstairs. HB had gathered our housemates around the table in Brendan's sparsely furnished dining room and was entertaining them with stories from the old days. He had a gift for entertaining guests at dining room tables. I remembered him holding court at the big round dinner table at 614, pouring drinks nonstop as gin rummy or cribbage was played, the best yarns were told, and voices were raised in table-slamming political debate. His guests included civic leaders, judges, the newspaper editor, schoolteachers, and his good friend, Police Chief Jim Farraday. It must have been the place to be in McGill, the town's unofficial power center with HB at the center of it.

I jumped into my clothes—jeans, black sweater, pink tennis shoes—and went downstairs.

The housemates—two married couples and two single women—seemed delighted by the presence of a lively raconteur in their midst though naturally perplexed by his unconcealed identity as a visitor from the kingdom of death.

As I entered the room and took a seat, HB was launching an anecdote about an event at the Hotel Bellavia in Cleveland in 1908.

Business leaders had assembled to hear after-dinner remarks by the president of the United States, Theodore Roosevelt.

"After the talk I repaired to a small men's room off the lobby. The room had two shoulder-high urinals (old-fashioned even then) and two adjoining sinks. While I was conducting my business at the urinal, another man came in and assumed the usual stance at the second urinal. He was a burly fellow and I could sense his dynamism but I did not glance at him directly—men standing at urinals carefully avoid eye contact. I finished first and moved to the sink, removing my glasses as I washed my hands and face. He followed me to the other sink and did the same.

"We were both bent over the sinks when, in a booming voice, he asked, 'How'd you like my speech in there?' And it was then that I realized he was Teddy Roosevelt himself. I was momentarily taken aback but recovered and told him it was a damn good speech. He liked that. He was glowing with success.

"'Sometimes I get going really good,' he said.

"We straightened up, toweled off, put our glasses back on, and looked at each other.

"I introduced myself. 'I'm HB Taylor, treasurer of Ohio Bell Telephone.'

"He said, 'I'm Theodore Roosevelt, president of the United States.'

"I looked into his big round smiling face as we shook hands. He had a helluva grip.

"'Mr. President, I'm honored to meet you but I'm foreseeing a dilemma: how am I going to tell my young daughter that I took an elbow-to-elbow piss next to the president of the United States?'

"He laughed at that, such a loud eruption of heartiness that it alarmed his bodyguard who was waiting outside the men's room. The bodyguard pushed the door half open—one hand reaching into his suit jacket, possibly to draw his firearm—but T.R. waved him away.

"'Why not just tell her you met me but omit the urination aspect,' he said. 'Tell her you had a chat with the president. That ought to impress her.'

"'I'm not sure about that,' I said, and I could see his face darken quickly at what seemed like an insult. 'She's one year old and doesn't give a rip about politics.'

"It took a moment for him to catch the humor but then he exploded in another booming laugh. 'Tell you what, HB,' he said. 'I suspect you'll be telling this story for many years and it will sooner or later reach her tender ears with all the details included. And maybe embroidered. So don't worry about it. Good luck, young man.'

"With that, he gave me a manly clap on the back and departed."

Everyone at the table seemed pleased by the story except Artie Southway, who had taken the seat at the head of the table next to his wife, Elizabeth. Southway had always been a cranky presence among Brendan's houseguests. He was a high-ranking official in New York City's budget bureaucracy who frequently expressed bitterness that his progress to greater glory had been stymied by superiors who envied his Harvard degree, which he flaunted relentlessly in conversation along with his wardrobe of Harvard-branded leisure wear.

"That's a good tale, HB," he said. "But I'm trying to figure out what your angle is here. You're obviously a slick conversationalist and your stories sound believable *except* you tell us you've been dead for thirty years until this morning when you traveled down to earth and landed here at Brendan Leary's house in Amanituck, Long Island. And that, my friend, is preposterous," said Artie with a small unamused smile. "Too stupid to be worth talking about with educated people."

His voice was rising as he spoke. Elizabeth patted his arm, trying to calm him.

"So, HB, what if I sat here and told a story about taking a piss with Abraham Lincoln? Right after the Gettysburg Address. Abe and I walked into the woods and took a whiz together. Would you believe that?"

"No, sir, I would not," said HB.

"How about taking a pee with Christopher Columbus off the heaving bow of the Santa Maria as it crossed the Atlantic in search of the New World?"

"It's a fine image, but I wouldn't believe it," said HB.

"I know we're just a few folks sitting around a table in a summerhouse and what gets said here makes no difference to mankind but you're bullshitting us. You know what I smell? I smell a snake-oil salesman, like they used to say."

HB smiled. "Well, if it's what they used to say, I probably said it myself."

Somebody laughed.

Brendan came down the stairs buttoning his shirt.

"By the way," said HB, "I didn't travel down to earth. That's not how it works."

"Oh? So where'd you come from? And where did you spend three decades being dead? Heaven or what? Outer space? Pittsburgh?"

"That's a fair question and I can't give you a good answer," confessed HB. "But I was there and it was *somewhere*. My thinking is that when you die a tiny particle comes loose from your mind and you breathe it out on your last breath, and your whole afterlife exists in that particle. I don't know where it's located."

It was a surprising concept that seemed to merit some thought, but Artie gave it none, pouncing on HB's mention of his mind. "Ah! Your mind, your *imagination*. Maybe that's where this afterlife takes place. Maybe you were in a mental institution all these years and this imagined death story was your evolving central fantasy. And then you got out and saw it as your meal ticket and you made a run at your only living relative, Lake Whistler, and tried to pull some sort of con job on her."

"I think your imagination is working harder than mine."

"Listen, I lost my sister last winter. I had to confront her death, and death is the most serious thing there is. The most profound. The darkest, saddest, most final—"

"—Humbling," said HB.

"Okay, humbling. Yes."

"—Enormous," added HB.

"For sure," said Artie, his chain of thought disrupted by HB's interjections. But he regained it. "Death is the most serious thing there is, and yet you sit here making a farce of it. *Disrespecting it*. Joking about it. And I resent it, Mr. Taylor."

"I'm sorry about your sister," said HB, unruffled. "But I've lost *everyone* I ever cared about. My wife, my daughters, friends, and family, everyone but Lake. All dead. And of course I've lost my own life as well. These things are not amusing to me, and I'm not joking. As for where I live, I don't know but it's not Pittsburgh."

Artie said, "I believe when you die, that's it. Hobbes said death is like a great leap in the dark. You're nowhere. You're totally deleted. End of story." His voice was tightening. Then he added, "No coming back to visit your granddaughter."

"I believed that too," said HB. "Incorrectly."

"Well, it's the truth and there's not a bit of learning or science or any kind of proof that says I'm wrong."

"Or that you're right. And lots of people think you're wrong. Mainly religious people. I attended the Episcopal Church in McGill, Ohio, for many years. I was not the most devout worshipper, but I bet most of the people in that congregation would disagree with you."

"Fine, but that's faith. I'm okay with that. If people have a need to believe there's an afterlife, I have no problem with it. And if they need to believe they'll be reunited with their dead mother Geraldine or take country hikes with their dead grandfather and his dead Labrador, that's okay, too. Let them have that comfort."

"Because they're weak-minded morons?" I asked. "Is that what you're saying?"

"I'm saying they can believe anything but that doesn't make it true."

"Honey," said Elizabeth, trying to cool him down. The others had gone silent.

"Truth is what's provable and your story doesn't make the cut. It's not provable."

HB said, "I wouldn't be so sure that provability is always a test of what's true. And sometimes the proof is wrong. The proof that the earth is flat didn't turn out to be so accurate, did it? And sometimes we just aren't ready or able to do the proving."

"I think you're a faker, Mr. Taylor. You're an insult to our intelligence."

"Look, I can see I've made you hot under the collar. If I've insulted anyone, I apologize. I understand how you feel."

"I doubt it. A con man doesn't understand."

"Con men succeed because they *do* understand, but I'm not a con man. I have no angle. What I've told you is true, including meeting Teddy Roosevelt in a hotel john. We met, we peed, we laughed."

"Very funny. I bet you have a lot of crowd-pleaser stories about famous people you've met."

"No. Aside from Roosevelt, the only famous person I met in my life was Napoleon Lajoie, the baseball star." HB was about to begin an anecdote about Lajoie, but Artie angrily waved a hand to cut him off.

"Artie, I think you're being rude," said Brendan.

Minnie Horch, one of the single women, entered the conversation.

"Lake, you work on that morning TV show. You ought to put HB on it."

"Fat chance of that," I said. "Unless the network wants to be laughed out of business."

"He could tell the Teddy Roosevelt story."

"I'm afraid not. You can rule that one out."

Then Minnie had a question for HB.

"HB, when you're dead do you meet famous dead people? Like Goethe, maybe just gliding by and stopping to talk? He's the one I'd like to meet. I wrote a paper on him in college."

HB chuckled. "I'm sure Goethe would be flattered."

Minnie had another one, "When you die do you meet God?"

"Jesus Christ," Artie blurted in an exasperated head-shaking snarl.

"I believe she asked about God, not Jesus Christ," said HB, but Artie was too pissed off to catch the humor, pushing back his chair noisily en route to a fuming exit.

Howard Horton, who was a dean of an upscale private boys school in the city, cleared his throat to deliver a lecture he'd undoubtedly inflicted on generations of students: "I think we have to pause at this point and remind ourselves to be respectful of different viewpoints, no matter how far-fetched. We have to be open to different stories and different experiences. We—"

"Oh, blow it out your ass, Howard," said Artie, scowling. "Save the tolerance homily for your little rich boys in their little blue blazers."

Artie was heading for the door. Over his shoulder, he said, "Brendan, I'm sorry the season had to end on this note. It's very disappointing."

Brendan said, "Nothing's forcing you to come back next summer."

Elizabeth, glaring at Brendan, rose to join her husband. "You know what they call this in Pig Latin? *Ullshit-bay.*"

"HB, we've got to get going," I said. "We've got a couple hours of driving."

I fetched my suitcase and hustled him out of there, passing Artie and Elizabeth on the front porch. I flipped Artie the bird and accentuated it with a slap to the inner elbow to add verve to the gesture.

I backed out of Brendan's driveway and saw Artie and Elizabeth still glaring at me. I rolled down the window and yelled, "HARVARD SUCKS."

That felt so good, I added, "Yale, Princeton, and Stanford are better. NYU is better. Oneonta State Teachers College is better. Fuck yourself."

I can't describe how great that felt. Artie and Elizabeth were frozen in shock. Brendan, coming out to wave goodbye, doubled over in laughter. I floored the accelerator and we shot off with squealing tires.

But the manic pleasure of the moment was short-lived. As I came down from it, I realized I was genuinely angry at Artie Southway, despite the possible merits of his argument. I further realized that my allegiance was to this man who called himself my grandfather. This allegiance came from some deep place and was strong enough to override my skepticism, at least in the heat of the moment. If, in the next week, there were moments when sides had to be taken, I would be on HB's side whether I believed him or not.

However, I quickly added a cautionary thought: if I were to somehow be the manager of HB's time back in the world, it might be prudent to steer clear of situations where his story might cause blow-ups like Artie's, or worse. There could be a multitude of reactions to it. Some people might be very disturbed. Things could spiral out of control.

I mentioned this to HB and after a moment's thought he nodded agreement. "I didn't mean to cause a ruckus. There are a lot of touchy emotions involved with this, aren't there? I'll try to keep it in mind."

* * *

I'd loaded HB into my ancient Saab along with another passenger, Minnie Horch, for whom I often provided rides back to New York City because she was pleasant though birdbrained company, even if it meant that I had to spend an extra hour driving her way down to Greenwich Village before heading uptown to my place on the Upper West Side.

Her presence put a damper on a foundational relationship-building conversation HB and I might have had while driving. I had her in the back seat, with HB in the passenger seat, but this separation didn't lessen her chatterbox impact. She seemed remarkably unfazed by being in a car with a man who was either dead or pretending to be dead.

Sometimes, driving back to Manhattan, I see things the way a foreign visitor might see them riding in for the first time from one of the NY airports. Dreary street businesses and apartment buildings are all you see and the traffic is dense and aggravating. The visitor would think, "I've just completed my journey to the most exciting city in the world but all I'm seeing is more like the grungy side of my town back in Milwaukee or Belgium or wherever."

"This is Queens," I said. "Not Manhattan."

"My only time in New York City was in 1942," said HB. "Sportie and I came by train to greet the new baby, meaning you, Lake. You were the one bright spot in dark times. The War was on and there was no guarantee we'd win it. Your dad had to stand in long rationing lines to get fresh fruit and vegetables for you. It could take an hour to get a goddamn banana. Later your mom had to stand in the lines because your dad went into the service and got shipped out to the Pacific."

I said, "It must have been a hard time for mom."

"Yes, we exchanged letters every day. She was a wonderful writer. You probably got your writing talent from her."

"Did you visit the Statue of Liberty?" asked Minnie.

"Yes, we took a guided-tour boat around Manhattan and saw the statue and later walked around everywhere. Had lunch at the Horn & Hardart automat. Went to a game at Yankee Stadium.

"But you know what I remember most, Lake? One night your dad had to go out late to an all-night pharmacy to get some pills for you. I went along to keep him company. We had to take the subway to get to the drugstore. Coming home, it was a warm night and we sat down on a bench and had a few smokes and a few nips from my flask. I think it was the first time I'd ever talked with your dad with no one else around.

We had a dandy of a conversation. It's a great memory. We learned things about each other that we didn't know. I forget what, exactly, but I remember thinking, goddamn it, my daughter married a fine young man. And, oh God, please let him make it through the war."

"My dad was in the navy," Minnie said. "He was a cook on a troop ship. When he got home, he refused to ever set foot in our kitchen, he was so disgusted with cooking food."

HB was lost in thought. Mentally he was still in 1942 while peering out at 1979.

Minnie said, "If I ever come back from death, I'll spend the whole time having sex. I can't imagine how horny you must get after years of being dead."

HB and I exchanged glances.

HB said, "The sex drive goes away when you're dead, Minnie. So does every other drive. They're just not relevant anymore."

"Bummer," said Minnie. "So I better get it while I can."

I said, "But maybe it's a relief to not be thinking about sex all the time."

HB explained, "On these visits back, we're not equipped for debauchery. I'd guess it's to make us be serious and not behave like sex-crazed sailors on shore liberty in some exotic port."

"Are you a ghost?" Minnie asked.

"Nope. Not a ghost. Don't confuse me with ghosts."

Minnie said, "Okay, so here's another one. Since you're from Ohio, I have to ask you, have you ever been to Wapakoneta?"

"Wapakoneta? I know where it is, northwest of Columbus. I don't remember ever going there."

"It's the hometown of an American hero. Neil Armstrong."

HB seemed to search his memory but gave up, shaking his head.

"The astronaut," said Minnie.

HB said, "I'm not clear on what an astronaut is."

"Neil Armstrong was the first man on the moon."

"A man on the moon? No! How could that happen? Is this a fictional guy we're talking about?"

"No, a real guy. He went up on a rocket ship and landed on the moon."

"You're pulling my leg."

"No. For real." Minnie went into an eccentric narrative of Armstrong's time on the moon that seemed to baffle HB, so I stepped in and gave a capsule description of the Apollo 11 mission, astronauts, and subsequent landings.

"I'll be damned," HB said. "That takes the cake! That's the goddamnedest thing I ever heard. What did they find up there?"

"Rocks, mainly."

"That's all?"

Minnie said, "The reason I remember Wapakoneta is because I remember Walter Cronkite seemed to love the name and kept saying it over and over again as if it was a poem, sort of belching out each syllable. Wappa-ko-neta. Wappa-ko-neta O-hi-o."

"And Walter Cronkite was who?"

"The anchorman."

I tried to explain about anchormen, though it came back to me that HB had never seen television. "I'll show you what television is tonight and we can watch Cronkite when we're back at my apartment," I said.

Minnie said, "The moon thing was very exciting, HB. It's hard to believe you don't remember it."

"I was otherwise occupied."

Stop—had Minnie tried to trap HB? Had she tried to get him to be aware of something he couldn't be aware of because he'd allegedly died before it happened? But no, not a chance. Minnie was guileless as well as clueless. It seemed like a lesson to me that Minnie was the opposite of Artie Southway. For every rational (and hostile) skeptic like him there would be good-hearted innocents like her who heard HB's story with no skepticism and the most idiosyncratic reactions ("When you're dead can you meet Goethe?"). There would be vulnerable, gullible souls who embraced his story unquestioningly and people who wouldn't tolerate it for a moment because it was out-of-the-question impossible.

HB said, "When I was alive the thought of putting men on the moon was fantasy. It couldn't possibly be done. I can hardly believe men were on the moon."

"We can't quite believe men can come back from the dead," I said.

We entered the Queens-Midtown Tunnel and emerged in Manhattan.

CHAPTER 5

It's a clue about the barrenness of my life without my husband that in all my time in my apartment, I'd never had company. Well, maybe a few visitors stopping by for drinks and a few guys who stayed the night and left early, but never a real guest.

Hosting does not come naturally to me and I was apprehensive about it as we drove back from Amanituck, but visitors from the afterlife present fewer hosting duties than normal guests. HB arrived with no luggage, he brought no gifts and had no agenda—no sights to see, friends to visit, or events to attend. He had no food needs or alcohol needs or laundry needs. His natty summer suit (which he called his "death costume") was impervious to dirt or wrinkles, a miracle fabric. He never even used the john. This was a blessing because it spared me the embarrassment of him seeing the bras and panties I'd left hanging from the shower rod.

After dropping Minnie in Greenwich Village, I turned uptown and, though it was not my style, attempted to act as a tour guide, pointing out this and that about Manhattan. HB showed polite interest but I didn't get the point until, passing Lincoln Center, I saw an empty parking space that was too good to be true and pulled into it. We got out of the car and walked around Lincoln Center which he admired without being overly impressed. "Quite grand but it's the kind of thing you'd expect in a metropolis of any advanced civilization," he said.

The point was that HB was not here as a tourist. Nor did he care about catching up on historical events or cultural changes he'd missed in thirty-one years. He made few comparisons between then and now.

I was lost in thought as I drove up to my neighborhood. Central Park West above Eighty-Sixth Street in those days was a neighborhood in transition from run-down to desirable, but it had not yet fully arrived at desirable. It was in-between Harlem and white New York, in-between dangerous and comfortable, in-between seedy and venerable.

My second-floor walk-up apartment was small and boxy: a living room and bedroom with a tiny kitchen squeezed in between. Its only attractive quality was three tall windows looking at Central Park. HB made no judgment on the apartment, but it must have seemed cramped to him as a man who'd lived in a spacious house in Ohio. I spent most of my youthful summers in that house; my parents thought a taste of Middle Western childhood was a better solution for me than staying in our New York apartment.

To my surprise HB loved television, loved switching channels with the remote, loved the fact that you could watch sports and movies on TV. We came across an old Ronald Reagan movie he remembered seeing (*Knute Rockne, All American*). When I told him that Reagan was still alive and expected to run for president, I thought he would be amazed but he said, "Makes sense in a way. All presidents are actors."

We watched the CBS evening news with Walter Cronkite and HB was impressed. "People can find out what's going on, much more than they used to when there were only a few radio reports and skimpy afternoon newspapers and *TIME* magazine. Where is Mr. Cronkite when he does this report?"

"In a CBS studio on West Fifty-Seventh. Just a couple miles south of here."

"That close? You ever met him?"

"No, actually. I work for a different TV network and my show is on in the morning. Our paths don't cross."

He studied my bookshelf of family photos, gazing with special interest at a picture of me with my parents and Sportie on the day of his funeral.

"I'm glad to see that you're a reader," he said, scanning my messily crowded bookshelves and pulling out books he evidently intended to read. I had a few Dickens novels, which he added to his to-read stack. He said he'd owned a complete leatherbound collection of Dickens and had read all of them.

"I remember writing a letter to Sportie when I was nearing the end," he said. "She was reading *The Pickwick Papers* as a distraction from tending to me and I put the letter in an envelope and stuck it into the book about twenty pages from where her bookmark was, so she'd come upon it when I was gone. I kind of hoped she'd find it *before* I was gone but my train left the station sooner than expected. Very personal stuff, deathbed stuff, not easy to say when you're eye-to-eye and the hourglass of your forty years together is down to its last grains. It's hard to do verbal justice to your emotions at a time like that. I was never much good at that kind of conversation."

"Few people are," I said.

"I'd give a lot to know if she found the letter. I guess I relied on it to do something I lacked the courage to do right, meaning face-to-face."

"Your heart was in the right place," I said.

"She was a great woman. I wasn't in her league."

He seemed to struggle for a moment, then asked, "Tell me how it went for Sportie after I was gone."

"Let me pour a drink." I needed the boost alcohol would give me. I also needed a minute to get my answer together. I poured us both scotches on the rocks. He held the glass like he was about to drink, but never took a sip.

"Sportie outlived you by about twenty years. She insisted on staying in 614, even when it got to be too much for her. She developed dementia, although I didn't realize it for too long. I sent her money every month and sent little letters and cards and I went out to McGill a few times, until she stopped recognizing me. I got her into an old folks home.

"I was very caught up in my career in those days. I had a few newspaper jobs and finally got hired by the *New York Times* as a junior cityside reporter. Later the *Times* put me on sports, mainly baseball. The jocks loved me because I was a tall young blonde with a sense of humor. I had a much livelier sense of humor in those days.

"Anyway I was so wrapped up in my career and social life that I slowly forgot about Sportie. Not *forgot*, but *neglected*. I felt guilty but I didn't do enough. What did she die of? I think it was old age and loneliness. I was responsible for her. She had no one else. And I didn't do enough. I hate myself for this."

I couldn't go on. I was on the verge of a massive landslide of emotion, but I fought it back. We were still for a long and painful minute. I couldn't bear eye contact and sat with my head down, like a little girl. I heard the ice melting in my drink.

"Lake," he said, and I looked up.

"Everybody has things they regret."

"I'm so sorry, HB."

"Sportie wouldn't want you to let this torture you."

I realized I was having one of the most serious conversations of my life with a man I knew to be dead. And yet to some degree I felt pardoned, forgiven, relieved of guilt, almost refreshed.

I downed the scotch.

He asked, "What about your mom and dad?"

"Neither made it to their sixties. Cancer. Too many drinks and cigarettes."

He said, "Why don't we take a walk? Show me the neighborhood."

* * *

There wasn't much to show and night had fallen but I needed cash for the week so we walked a few blocks to my bank where I demonstrated the ATM machine. He had been a financial guy in his working years and he was impressed but remembered his favorite bank teller from McGill, Karen Darby. "This ATM thing would make tellers like her obsolete, wouldn't it?"

"Not quite," I said. "Banks still have tellers. Not that I've talked to one in years."

"I used to make sure to get on Karen's line when I came in to deposit my paycheck and we'd chat. She always had a good story or two. But she had a tough life. Her husband was a terrible drunkard and she supported the family. It was unfair, what was asked of her."

Then he added, "She had beautiful red hair and a wonderful smile."

The thought crossed my mind: hanky-panky with Karen Darby?

I withdrew $300 and gave him $100 for getting-around money.

"That's a lot of cash."

"It's 1979 dollars, not 1948."

"I'm sure it's enough. I'll be out of your hair in a short time."

"When it's over, how do you get back to the afterlife? Bus? Train? Rocket ship?"

"When it's over, it's over. *Poof.* There's no transportation involved."

As we walked along, I asked why he'd chosen to come back as a fifty-five-year-old. "I would have thought you'd come back younger, like twenty-five, in your prime."

"I understand that but for me, the mid-fifties was a perfect age. You're not old and declining and you're not young and reckless. You're still vigorous physically and you're at the height of your powers in terms of wisdom, achievement, maturity, and your general place in the universe. You've probably reached as much of your potential as you're ever going to reach. You're the full person. You're still contributing. The cookie hasn't begun to crumble."

I said, "I'm not even forty but I feel like my cookie's already crumbling. If I had to make a choice like you did, I'd pick thirty-one or two, when I had Douglas. I never got to that full-person prime."

"Things do go wrong," he said. "For me it started with your mom's sister, Aunt Margaret. She was leading a splendid life in Michigan. Her husband was a vice president at General Motors. They had fantasies of him going to the top of the heap. Margaret threw herself into it. She became a social climber. She loved entertaining GM bigwigs. She gave lavish parties. She tried to look like Elizabeth Taylor. Makeup, hair, plunging necklines, and so on. Sportie and I went to one of the parties at their Grosse Point house. Drunken, rich, full-of-themselves bastards in every direction. I hated seeing what my beautiful daughter had become.

"But then her son-of-a-bitch husband started playing around with a woman who must have looked more like Elizabeth Taylor than Margaret. To make it worse, this woman was already carrying on with another GM big shot who was the son of a bitch's main rival. I guess the woman figured that one or the other was going to win the pot of gold and she wanted to have bets on both. Somehow it all came out. Big scandal. The son of a bitch lost his job, lost his mistress, and lost Margaret, and Margaret lost everything she cared about. She came back to 614 and lived with us for a while before getting an apartment in Columbus where she could drink without us nagging her."

"And then what?"

"It took a few years before it happened but one night when she was staying at 614, she went out to the garage with a bottle of gin and her car keys. Pulled down the door. Turned on the gas."

"They told me she died of a heart attack," I said.

"Kids are never told the truth about such things. But it's not so wrong to say her heart was attacked."

"Was her death a turning point for you?" (I had a terrible feeling that I was *interviewing* him just like I did at work, pre-interviewing guests to write questions for their TV appearances the next morning.)

"I suppose. Not long after that my innards started betraying me in the form of gastro-intestinal mayhem. As time went by, I was spending a vast amount of time on the toilet. I couldn't go to work. Had to retire. We had to stop entertaining company. Do you remember my being on the pot all the time? I'm sure you do. That kind of thing plants an image in kids' minds."

Of course I remembered it. For several summers I dreaded the end-of-summer moment when I'd be told to go up to the bathroom and say goodbye to HB and he'd be on the toilet, pants at his ankles, his bare legs so thin and bloodlessly white, crisscrossed by purple veins. But he kept his dignity. He gave me the speech about working hard at school and so on. He didn't kiss me goodbye, sensing that I didn't want to get close to a near-naked old man on a toilet. It was awkward and I banished it from memory but now it floated back. I regret that one of these extremely uncomfortable bathroom scenes was the last time I saw him alive.

CHAPTER 6

We walked past a pizza place and it occurred to me that HB shouldn't be allowed to venture deeper into the hereafter without some knowledge of pizza.

I ordered a pepperoni slice. He contemplated it with amazement. His jaw dropped when I picked it up and folded it over.

"Everybody loves pizza," I said. "It started in the East and was just arriving in California when I went there for college. They'd heard about 'pizza pies,' and the slices were as thick as pie slices and barely tasted like pizza. But California caught up. I can't imagine college without pizza."

"I don't recall what I ate in college," he said with a teasing smile. "Food had just been invented then but I don't remember what it was."

"I never visualized you as a college student. Were you the first in your family? What college did you go to?"

"Berea College in Berea, Kentucky. It was founded by an abolitionist and had Negro and female students as well as whites. Ahead of its time. My father got an accounting degree there and I did the same thing, just as the century turned. So your mother and Margaret were both *third-*generation college graduates, which used to amaze people."

"Were you born in Kentucky?"

"Yes, but after college I moved to Cleveland for a job with U.S. Steel and later the phone company, in Cleveland and Toledo. And later we moved down to the Columbus area and settled in McGill."

I said, "I remember my summers there as something out of Tom Sawyer and Huckleberry Finn. Tomboy stuff. Playing ball, fishing the Olentangy River, riding my bike around town, minor mischief, and pranks. Lots of practical jokes. I remember the boys talking me into standing under a tree and Barry Bronson was up in the branches with his pants down, trying to bomb me with his turds, which he failed to do. I heard him giggling and jumped out of the way."

HB was not amused. "My lord, that is distasteful."

"I think it was my first encounter with the raunchy stuff that boys think is hilarious and girls never understand. The lesson served me well when I was a sportswriter hanging out with jocks."

HB said, "The Bronsons lived down at the far end of Cambridge Street. Barry's dad, Chester, was a water tower inspector. An odd character. I never felt the water tower was in the best hands."

Back at my apartment, I said, "I have to work tomorrow and need to hit the sack but I've got a treat for you now, HB. I'm going to introduce you to *The Tonight Show* and a fellow named Johnny Carson. He's your kind of guy, a well-dressed Middle Westerner with a sense of humor."

I sat him down on the couch, tuned the TV to NBC, and went to bed. As I fell asleep, I heard him laughing.

* * *

In the morning, I woke up still half-dreaming. As I lay on my back, I saw a dream version of myself standing at the foot of my bed, hands on hips in a stern pose, giving me a no-nonsense talking-to.

"Girl, you are looking like you're starting to *believe* this man. You gotta shake that off, honey. Dead men don't come back. Sorry about that."

"I don't believe him," I protested. But as the image of me faded away, I thought, well, maybe doubt is creeping in. Maybe I'm accepting a small part of the *possibility* that HB was not a hoax, even if I had no idea what he was if he *wasn't* a hoax.

And I realized that whatever he was, I felt close to him. I had no family and here was a chance to have a grandfather and I wanted this chance. Maybe that made me a biased juror when it came to judging his authenticity. It was a vulnerability to keep in mind. But even as I warmed to him my suspicion hadn't wavered; I'd watched vigilantly for clues that his story was flawed. But there were no such clues. He'd known things the best-prepared impostor couldn't know. And he was not just accurate on the facts, he was pitch-perfect emotionally. I didn't believe him, but he seemed so authentic that I forgot to disbelieve him.

Forgot to disbelieve him? How did he get me to do that? By telling the truth or by masterful deception? I had to test him more, at least once, before I slipped another notch toward swallowing his story.

What came back to me was my story about Barry Bronson. HB had immediately volunteered that Barry's father, Chester, was a water tower inspector. Which of course made HB sound like he knew things that only a real resident of McGill in those years would know. But could it have been something else?—an overconfident con man adding one embellishment too many, an unnecessary false detail that left an exposable flaw, perhaps unraveling the whole con?

Frankly I didn't think so. Instinct said HB was not a guy who made things up. But as a former journalist I was well acquainted with the classic investigative scenario: a small detail snagging the curiosity of the reporter who then digs deeper and finally hits the pay dirt of a big story.

It was a tiny fact but if Chester Bronson had indeed been a water tower inspector, HB's credibility would be enhanced. If not, it could be the first crack in his credibility.

Then I came to my senses: I was playing Woodward and Bernstein with myself cast in both title roles. But while their investigation led to the fall of a president, mine would lead *at best* to proving that HB had made an error about an absolutely trivial fact.

So I flushed this investigation of Barry Bronson's father down the toilet of bad ideas and headed to the office. But later in the day, during a rare quiet moment, I closed my office door and put on my journalist's hat.

Journalists pride themselves on being able to find things out by working the phone. So I picked up the phone and called the McGill mayor's office which referred me to someone in public works who referred me to other departments related to water and/or towers. I got to talk to a number of pleasant bureaucrats, but I learned nothing.

I called the town newspaper and library hoping to find some old editor or librarian who'd been around forever and served as the town's memory keeper and oral historian. Everyone I talked to sounded like a twenty-year-old.

I called the Episcopal Church, the grocery store, the drug store, and a nursing home, trying to find long-time McGill residents. I found a few but all were blank on the Bronsons. The police and fire departments seemed wary of my questions and gave me a brush-off.

But a call to the high school led me to a retired principal who remembered Barry, recalling a hyperactive kid, a likable screw-up who played the saxophone in the school's marching band. That was all he remembered but he told me, by the way, that while the Bronson family had left McGill long ago, a woman neighbor of theirs named Myra Littlefield was still on Cambridge Street and might be reachable.

She was. Myra Littlefield was a retired nurse who sounded bored and eager to gab. Barry was her senior by ten years so she'd hardly known him, but she knew he'd gone into the service after high school and, because he could play the saxophone, spent his time in uniform in the Marine Corps Band. He never left Washington, DC, playing "Hail to the Chief" at presidential events. But that's where the Barry story dried up.

Then we got to what I really wanted to know about. Chester.

"I almost never saw him," said Myra. "I guess he was always on the road for work. But then he retired and went a little wackadoodle, shall we say. He acquired an electric guitar and started dressing like Elvis. You could hear him practicing Elvis songs at all hours, sitting on the steps of his house and belting out 'Heartbreak Hotel.' Of course he never got anywhere, other than performing at some local events, probably for free."

"Myra, do you know what Chester did for a living, before his Elvis period?"

"No. Sorry."

"Could he have been a water tower inspector?"

"I wish I could help but I just don't recall."

So that was it. Dead end. I felt ridiculous investigating a not-very-good Elvis impersonator.

I thanked Myra and hung up. Luckily I had given her my phone number. An hour later she called back. "I started going through a box of old papers and came across something, a program from a Rotary Club dinner in 1967. My late husband Milton was an avid Rotarian. Here's the agenda: opening prayer, pledge of allegiance, cocktails, dinner, remarks by Mayor Norm Christiansen, and then musical entertainment. Can you guess who was the musical entertainment? 'Chet and The Jets.'"

She chuckled at that. "Chet wasn't singing Elvis songs that night but you're going to like the title of Chet's 'legendary ballad about traveling the countryside in search of his lost love.'"

"What is it, Myra?"

"'I Got the Water Tower Blues.'"

CHAPTER 7

We were on the subway rumbling through the Bronx, heading up to Yankee Stadium. When I say "we" I mean me, HB, *and his date*.

Let me back up a bit.

The baseball idea came to me after we'd watched my show until nine a.m. and then left the apartment together, boarding the #10 downtown bus, me heading to work and HB setting out on a random tour of the city. People on the bus were reading tabloid sports pages and buzzing about tonight's Yankees vs. Boston Red Sox game.

It was the hottest ticket in town, impossible to get, but I still had sportswriting and Yankee Stadium connections which I could use to arrange for us to be passed through the gates without tickets. Inside the Stadium, friendly ushers would guide us to empty seats. If the real ticket holders showed up, the ushers would guide us to other empty seats.

I figured that taking in this New York scene would be a highlight of HB's visit. We would ride the #4 subway crushed in among boisterous fans, watch the game, and probably witness some pugilistic activity in the stands as Yankee and Red Sox fans traded obscenities and came to blows, as they regularly did. At any given moment during a Yankees-Sox game you could glance around the stands and see security guys sprinting to the next fight. This was a spectacle to be seen.

As we rode the morning bus we agreed to meet later at a subway station for the ride to the Bronx. But then HB surprised me. Something caught his eye and with only a cursory wave he jumped up and got off the bus.

Here's the story he recounted later:

It turns out that there are a lot of dead people who've returned for last looks. They're everywhere and they spot each other easily, as if they were wearing illuminated name tags. HB had recognized a dead woman who stood looking rather forlornly out the picture window of a second-floor apartment on Central Park West as we rode by. When HB left the bus, he hurried back to her building.

She was no longer in the window, but HB described her to the doorman.

"Oh, yeah, we call her Mrs. Green Eyes," said the doorman. "She just called down and told me to expect you. Take the elevator to the second floor."

The woman, wearing an elegant white blouse and black slacks, was standing in the open door of her apartment when HB emerged from the elevator.

"I'm Martha Huddleston Dell of Birmingham, Alabama."

"HB Taylor of McGill, Ohio."

"Please come in."

Her green eyes were striking, especially on the face of a light-skinned, fine-featured black woman. She was aristocratic in bearing, tall and slender, somewhat aloof, and mildly pissed off.

They sat down on a couch in an opulent living room and studied each other for a moment. "I'd offer coffee or tea or something stronger, but I know you can't drink it."

"This experience is definitely flawed in that regard, isn't it?" said HB. "You'd think a trip back to life would be a sensual holiday where you could enjoy the full menu of life's pleasures."

"Enjoyment is obviously not the purpose."

"I'm not tremendously clear on what the purpose is. Are you?"

"I sense that you're new at this, HB. Just getting started?"

"Today's my third day."

"My seventh, and that's seven too many. This can't end soon enough. My decision to return was foolish. I want to move on to whatever comes next."

"You know, it never occurred to me that it might not go well."

"Well, maybe you didn't arrive to find your husband, one, remarried, and two, too busy to spend time with you because he has to go to the opera one night and a ballet the next and a fundraiser the next and so on, and three, he's a stuck-up dickhead. I chose to come back at age forty-five because that was when he and I were best together. But he looked at me and didn't show the slightest attraction. Let me ask a blunt question: you're a man, am I attractive to you?"

"Well, I'd say the sight of you standing in the window was magnetic. Unforgettable. Like a painting in a museum."

"I'm pleased to hear that. Perhaps a Vermeer painting?"

"I'm not acquainted with Mr. Vermeer."

"I was an art student. I studied at Yale and for two years in Paris."

"I studied accounting at Berea. Worked mainly in Cleveland and Columbus. Those eyes of yours must stop people in their tracks."

"From my standpoint it's usually tedious. Look, why don't they tell you what you're getting into when you come back? You have to make a decision based on nothing. You assume you'll be *welcome*, at least. It should not be done this way."

"I'll put a note to that effect in the cosmic suggestion box when I get back."

"Are you putting me down or just being wry?" she asked. "Not that I care. I'm thick-skinned. I may be a snob now, but I was also a black girl growing up in Alabama and that thickens the skin."

"You seem to have survived nicely. Judging by your digs, I'm guessing you did well for yourself."

"I married rich. My husband is Carpathian Dell, who was known as the smartest young black lawyer in the South. A good person until he sniffed the perfume of wealth and status. White law firms fought to hire him. He was a huge and immediate success, even in Birmingham. He moved to New York after my death. I died in a skiing accident in Aspen. I skied off a trail to avoid an intoxicated teenage jackass on a snowboard. I hit a tree. With my forehead. BAM! The world suddenly had one less ambitious green-eyed black girl. My husband then drowned his sorrow by acquiring a rich wife, white of course, and becoming a partner in a hedge fund. Do you know what a hedge fund is?"

"Nope. I know what a hedge is but I'm guessing you're talking about something different."

"You don't put on airs, do you, HB?"

"What would I put on airs about?"

"What did you do, professionally?"

"Accountant. Businessman. I was a state tax commissioner and did some town government work. Probably not interesting to you."

"How did you die?"

"My stomach turned against me. Ultimately it kind of exploded."

"Oh, my. Spare me the gory details."

They both laughed.

"Who are you visiting?"

"My granddaughter. Lake Whistler."

"Can you swim in it?"

"No, Lake is her name. I'm sure she hears jokes about it about six times a day."

"Of course. An obvious joke and I'm ashamed of myself for making it. I've lost my touch with humor."

"Lake said the same thing about her own sense of humor. She's a fine young woman but she's wounded somehow and doesn't explain. The awkward situation of talking to a dead person probably doesn't help."

"Yes, it hangs over every conversation."

"I sense that some people over-believe or get it all wrong while others under-believe, which is unpleasant because who wants to be under-believed?"

"That's exactly right," she said. "I want to slap them for resisting my story or for being so stupid they *don't* resist it."

"Well, what would you have said when you were alive if someone told you he or she was dead?"

"I would have said, can you run out to the kitchen and fetch me a bottle of whatever you're drinking?"

She laughed uproariously.

"HB, this is the first time since I got here that I've had a bit of fun talking to someone. Think how good it would be with martinis."

"Is there anything on your dance card for today, Martha? I'm planning to take a long walk and look at New York and I'd be pleased if you could join me."

"I've already done the long walking. Besides, my husband gave me a matinee ticket to a play."

"So you're busy. Sorry to hear that."

"No, I'm thinking you could join me. I'm sure we could acquire another ticket. This is the kind of problem I like, a problem money can solve."

"Do they have special seats for the dead?"

"Any decent theater would. We'll ask, won't we? The play is called *Evita*, a musical about the wife of the president of Argentina. Carpathian said it would be perfect for me."

"I'd be happy to go with you, Martha. I've never seen a Broadway show. But in return I hope you'll join me and Lake at tonight's Yankees-Red Sox game."

"Baseball? It's a thousand years since I've seen baseball. Let's do both, shall we? This will be my best day back. I'm so glad I posed in the window and lured you in. Isn't that what the whores do in Amsterdam?"

* * *

I was waiting at the subway station and saw them coming, arm in arm. Both were radiant.

I thought, but didn't say, "HB, you are a rascal. I leave you alone for a few hours and you come back with a sensational-looking woman on your arm." Then HB introduced her ("This is Martha, the dead woman I met when I got off the bus.") and I realized my thinking had to be adjusted to the non-sensual reality these people shared. Sportie, wherever she is, didn't have to worry.

They'd loved *Evita*. They even loved the subway ride, packed into a rowdy standing-room-only crowd of excited fans. Some were already drunk but all were good-natured. At the Stadium gate I was greeted by Yankees employees who admitted us without a hitch.

We were early and it was still daylight when we arrived, passing through the underside of the Stadium infrastructure where you could smell every cigar and beer consumed here since the Stadium opened in the early 1920s. And then came the moment every fan remembers when we emerged from a ramp and beheld the vast gloriously green field.

The Yankee players were taking batting practice in a batting cage set up behind home plate. Rather than looking for seats, I led HB and Martha to the field level, where a cop recognized me and swung open a gate. A moment later we were standing behind the batting cage watching players joking with each other and taking strong, fluid swings at easy practice pitches, enjoying the sharp crack of their bats and the soaring arc of the balls as they flew deep into the outfield and beyond. Team officials and reporters milled around. Red Sox players started to populate their dugout. Big-game fever was in the air.

I advised HB and Martha to avoid conversations with players, figuring that their death stories would inevitably come out and cause a God-knows-what kind of stir. I noticed that many players, especially black ones and especially the famous slugger Reggie Jackson, were looking Martha up and down. Reggie paused between pitches and gave her an extended and appreciative appraisal.

Martha basked in it. "He's a very powerful-looking man," she said as he turned away to brutalize an easy pitch. "Is he a star?"

"Can't you tell by his swagger?" I said.

"I like the way the white and Negro players get along so easily," said HB. "That wasn't so true back when Jackie Robinson came along."

"We don't say 'Negro' anymore," I told HB. "Black or African American."

He nodded. "Negro used to be the *good* thing you could say. And black was one of the bad things you couldn't say." Martha was amused.

I recognized the Yankees players but most were new since my time covering the team and I didn't know them personally. Only one Yankee recognized me, the legendary manager Billy Martin, who came by for a cheek-kiss with me.

"Still coloring your hair?" he said with a big smile.

He was charming with HB and Martha. Billy was known for his hot temper, but he had always been sweet to me, even when he was hitting on me (he hit on every woman) and I was (gently) rebuffing him.

"I heard about what happened to you, Lake. It's the shits. I'm really sorry," he said before hurrying off.

Martha showed no curiosity about Billy's last words. HB looked at me but said nothing.

It was time to find seats. Non-payers can't be choosers, so we ended up about as far away from home plate as possible, high in the upper deck in right field, almost a different climate zone, with an unnervingly steep downward view of the field below. Yet it was a fine perch to admire the spectacle of a magnificent sunset with long, graceful streaks of purple and scarlet rising in what Martha described as "an artwork in the sky."

"Sunset and sunrise are when the cosmos shows its hand," said HB, and Martha nodded.

"That's rather cryptic," I said. "What does it mean?"

He said, "It's a peek at eternity."

"With all respect," I said, "that sounds like bullshit."

They both laughed.

Martha said, "It doesn't translate into words, but you'll find out. Not too soon, I hope."

I was tempted to push in aggressively for a better answer but it didn't seem to be the time or place for that and they weren't volunteering anything so I backed off.

Still focused on the sunset, HB said, "There's a nice quotation I used to recite around the time of the cocktail hour. It's from Will Rogers: 'One must wait until evening to see how splendid the day has been.'"

"And that applies to this splendid day," said Martha, squeezing his arm and then squeezing mine in a mellow gesture. "I'm lucky to have run into you two," she said. "Your grandfather is a real gentleman, Lake, and not bad to look at. Be proud of him."

It hadn't occurred to me to be proud of him. But okay, I could do that.

HB signaled a vendor and bought me a beer.

Martha continued, "And you are a lovely young woman. People would kill for that hair."

A moment went by and I said, "That's all too true."

She gave me a quizzical look.

A few innings into the game a Red Sox player hit a home run and when he crossed home plate he glanced upward pointing with both forefingers to the sky.

HB asked, "What's that gesture about, Lake?"

"He's pointing to heaven, thanking God for his home run. It's fairly common among religious players."

"He thanked God for a home run?" asked HB. He and Martha looked at each other with smiles. HB said, "I wonder if the Yankees pitcher asked God to *prevent* a home run, but God said no."

Martha said to him, "Easy for us to snicker, HB. Didn't you ever thank God for anything?"

"Maybe you're right, I probably did," he said. "When you really need something, divine intervention becomes a very powerful idea. But I don't know about dragging God into your need for a home run. Hit the homer on your own."

Martha said, "Remember that old line about how there are no atheists in foxholes?"

"That's probably true. But I always thought, if God was so interested in preserving my life, why did He put me in a foxhole in the first place?"

A woman sitting behind us, listening in on this conversation and disliking its irreverence, delivered a hard kick to the back of HB's seat.

HB didn't turn around, but we sat there trying not to smile. I thought, this is like being teenagers at a movie theater with an usher scolding you and your friends for giggling. It was fun to be with these two, enjoying their vitality and snappy chemistry.

I was out on the town having a delightful time with two very lively dead people.

CHAPTER 8

From my ex-sportswriter perspective, the game was a dud. The Yankees won but the action was slow and acrimony with the Red Sox never erupted into the entertaining brawling most fans expected. But HB and Martha were attentive, full of questions, and they even got into friendly non-death chatter with fans sitting around us, not including the woman who kicked HB's seat.

Then things got interesting.

During a late inning I asked HB when he'd seen his last baseball game. His answer came quickly. "September of 1910, with free tickets given to me by Napoleon Lajoie."

"You mentioned Lajoie in Amanituck. You said he was the only famous person you'd met other than Theodore Roosevelt."

"Not just met him. I'm proud to have called him a friend."

As a fairly knowledgeable baseball fan, I was intrigued by the notion of HB having been a witness to a period of baseball's star-studded ancient history. Nap Lajoie (his name was pronounced LaJoy by fans but his own pronunciation was Lazh-a-way; he was called "the Frenchman" in the press, although he wasn't French, but his friends called him Larry) was a Hall of Fame legend from the early years of the twentieth century. He was what sportswriters called an "immortal," although, as we've learned, immortality doesn't last forever.

"Never heard of him," said Martha.

Her ignorance about Lajoie perturbed HB, as did her lack of reverence. It was the first time I'd seen him depart from his unflaggingly genial composure. "Maybe that's because the writers didn't blow him up as a *character* like the other big names of his day, but on the playing field he was their equal and more so. Batted over .400 one year, won a triple crown, set all kinds of records. When I knew him, he'd managed the Cleveland team as well as playing for it and he was such a big star the team was later named in his honor: the Cleveland *Naps*. Which later became the Cleveland Indians."

"Was he like Babe Ruth?"

"No. Except in greatness. He came before Ruth, whose prime was in the 1920s. And by the way, Martha, if you look down into right field just below us where your admirer Reggie Jackson is standing at this moment, that's precisely the ground where Babe Ruth stood when he roamed the Yankee outfield. Right down there, that very patch of grass," he said, pointing.

I hadn't seen this side of HB. He was animated, even fervent to be talking about a man who was clearly a hero. Something about Lajoie touched an emotion; something about HB was being revealed. And it was being revealed to a wider audience than Martha and me. As his voice rose, I could sense that fans around us were tuning in, eavesdropping.

"Larry Lajoie didn't have a larger-than-life existence, like Ruth or Ty Cobb did. Ruth was a lovable hero. Cobb was a villain. Lajoie was just a great ballplayer. That's what I liked about him."

"The lack of bs?"

"Yes, he was a model of no bs. Could have taught it at Yale or Princeton."

We all took a breath. But then Martha gave the story its needed push.

She said, "And you knew him?"

"I did. For a short time."

A man sitting in front of us sneaked an over-the-shoulder glance at HB, then whispered something to his wife.

"The reason I knew him was that for a year or so Larry and his wife Myrtle were the other couple in a rickety old two-family house where my wife, Sportie, and I lived during our Cleveland years, before moving to the Columbus area. The Lajoies rented the upstairs apartment, we had the downstairs. I would hear him going down the stairs the mornings before games, often wearing his uniform and spikes to the ballpark. He didn't have the thudding footstep you'd expect for a big man. He was graceful, light on his feet."

HB smiled at that detail.

"At first we just nodded hellos in passing. Then Sportie got friendly with Myrtle. They went to the store together, things like that. And then I was having longer exchanges with Larry. First about the weather, then baseball. We never talked about anything of substance but somehow a nice friendship built up. He was always affable, except when he was having trouble with his junky car, which annoyed the hell out of him.

"Larry was a plain man. Rough-hewn. He didn't have much education but he was bright. The funny thing was that because I went to college and knew my way around numbers, he looked up to me as if I was the star and he was just a dumb athlete. But he didn't know or care about anything but baseball. Everything else meant nothing to him because he was a genius at baseball."

Martha interrupted. "Some great artists are like that too. Oblivious to everything but art."

"Yes, Larry was like an artist. It was the honor of a lifetime to know him."

By now HB had the attention of fans behind, below, and beside us. And you could see they were spellbound and bewildered.

"Here's my Larry story. Early in the 1910 season the president of Chalmers Motor Car offered to award a luxurious new car—the Chalmers Model 30 touring car—to the player with the best batting average in the Major Leagues. It came down to a ferocious race between Larry and Cobb. It was the talk of baseball. Larry really wanted that car. He promised that if he won it, he would take Sportie and me for a victory ride and a steak dinner."

"Did he win?" asked Martha.

"There was a confusing ending to the season. Cobb seemed to have won but there was some unsportsmanlike shenanigans on both sides. Cobb tried to win by not playing the last few games to preserve his high batting average. Meanwhile, an opposing team that hated Cobb tried to help Larry with easy pitches he could bunt for singles. There was a big uproar that Mr. Chalmers solved with statesman-like brilliance. He gave cars to *both* players."

"Did you get the victory ride?" I asked.

"We sure did. Sportie and I and Larry and Myrtle donned our Sunday finest and climbed into that beautiful vehicle and rode around downtown Cleveland honking the horn and waving. Everyone cheered us. Kids ran after us."

HB was loving it, transported by this ecstatic memory.

"We went to a snazzy restaurant for dinner, Don Brant's Cleveland Steak House. We got a standing ovation walking in. Larry waved and signed menus for everybody. Mr. Brant had to post two big bozos to stand near our table to hold back the autograph-seekers and glad-handers because otherwise Larry wouldn't have had time to lift a fork.

"We had succulent chops and washed them down with great whiskey. I noticed that Larry's hands were so big that his whiskey glass disappeared in his hand and he seemed to be drinking out of his thumb. We all got drunk as skunks. Myrtle, who was normally quiet as a mouse, couldn't stop giggling and Sportie was having a grand time. Larry was in superlative spirits. Here was a man who never showed a spark of comedy but suddenly he was telling side-splitting anecdotes about his childhood in Rhode Island.

"It was the best goddamn night out I ever had. Mr. Brant made a show of ripping up the check. 'Larry and his friends eat on the arm at Brant's!' he proclaimed. That means free of charge, Martha. I don't know how the hell we got home alive because Larry was three sheets to the wind and I was afraid he'd crack up the new car, but somehow we made it.

"After that night we went separate ways. The baseball season was over and the Lajoies drove back East and then Sportie and I made the move down to McGill, and that was it. We exchanged Christmas cards for a few years."

"That is a lovely story, HB," said Martha.

HB said, "It was worth coming back from the dead to tell that story again and relive that night, especially in this great house of baseball."

The man in front of us turned around and said, "Can I ask you a question? I mean, are you a hundred fucking years old or are you just the biggest bullshitter the world has ever seen?"

There must have been a half dozen other eavesdroppers with the same question. The woman behind us gave HB's seat another kick. I saw a bottomless pit of trouble ahead if I let HB and Martha reply. Especially sharp-tongued Martha.

"Gotta go," I declared, jumping to my feet. We made a fast exit.

As we headed for the subway HB said, "I keep being surprised that people get so vexed over some of my stories."

"They just don't understand," said Martha. "It makes them mad."

"I spotted a few dead people in the stands," HB said. "We should have sat with them."

CHAPTER 9

Back at my apartment, HB and Martha got into a stud poker game that lasted for hours. I went to bed but barely slept. I heard them talking and laughing and I envied the fun they were having. I woke when I heard the apartment door open and close. I jumped out of bed and ran to the door and found them halfway down the stairs.

"I'm walking Martha home," said HB.

"I could stay here and play cards all night, but I owe it to my ex-husband to come home," Martha said.

"We had a good time tonight," I said.

"Here's to Nap Lajoie," she said, tipping an imaginary champagne glass to her lips.

She came back up the stairs and gave me a hug but said no more.

"Hope to see you tomorrow," I said.

Her face said maybe not.

I'll never forget those green eyes.

* * *

HB and I were watching my show in the morning when I got a call from Minnie Horch. HB didn't remember her. I whispered, "She rode back with us from Amanituck."

He nodded. "Oh, yes, the one who wants to meet Goethe."

I put Minnie on speaker.

"Lake, I know it's way too early to be calling but I have a question for HB. Hi, HB. I have an Uncle Ronald who is pretty close to the end from cancer and he has a question, if you don't mind."

"Go ahead, Minnie."

"The question is, when you die, how do you know you're dead? I mean, you could be dreaming or knocked unconscious or your brain goes blank but you're still alive. I've read about people who've died and been resuscitated saying they remembered speeding through a bright white tunnel. Is that when you know you're dead? What happens when you come out of the tunnel?"

HB said, "I think these people weren't thoroughly dead or they couldn't have been brought back. Tell Uncle Ron that dying can be any degree of painful but once you cross the line the pain is gone and so is your life. You just know it. I don't remember a white tunnel."

"Could you hear anything, like voices of people in the room? Doctors or your wife? Did you kind of have a vision of the room like a camera zooming upward as your spirit ascended from your body?"

"Nothing like that. It's not a movie, Minnie," said HB.

"Maybe the heart stops before the brain so you have a moment of consciousness before death catches up with the brain. So if it *was* a movie you could hear the murderer revealed and then be resuscitated and point a finger at the killer."

HB was about to respond but suddenly stopped. He had the strangest look on his face.

I stepped into the silence. "Minnie, do you really have an Uncle Ronald?"

"Not really. Well, I did, but he died a million years ago."

"What made you call this morning?"

"I woke up really scared."

"Of what? What are you scared of?"

"I think I have leukemia."

"Oh, shit. I'm so sorry about that, Minnie."

"I don't know for sure."

"You don't know? What did your doctor tell you?"

"Actually I haven't seen him yet but I'm going to make an appointment. But since I met HB, I can't stop thinking about dying. Who could answer my questions better than HB?"

"Sure. I understand. We'll talk, okay?"

"Can I get in one more question? HB, does achievement matter? Is it all forgotten when you die or do you get credit for hard work and accomplishing things and doing good deeds? Because I could make a much better effort."

"It doesn't matter," said HB. "All that morality about the virtue of hard work—it doesn't get you anything when you're gone. But I'd encourage it while you're alive."

"Okay. Goodbye. Hey, thanks, HB."

She hung up.

I said, "I guess meeting you had more effect on her than I thought. She's kind of child-like, isn't she?"

"We're all children when we think about death."

He seemed distant.

"HB?" I said. "Earth to HB?"

HB said, "Martha's gone."

"Oh, fuck."

"I felt it a moment ago. I could feel it in the air."

"Are you sure she's gone? We could telephone." I looked up Carpathian Dell's phone number and dialed it. A man answered on the first ring.

"Dell," he said, in kind of a choked voice.

I asked for Martha.

"You're calling Martha? Who is this?"

"My name is Lake Whistler. My grandfather HB Taylor and I are friends of Martha's. We took her to a ball game last night."

"A ball game? How can you be friends of Martha? What kind of shit is this?"

"Can we speak to her?"

"No. She's not here," he said. I thought he was about to hang up but then he continued.

"She was here thirty seconds ago. She was looking out the front window. She said she was watching to see the #10 bus go by. And then she was gone. I checked all the rooms in the apartment. She's nowhere."

"I guess her time just ran out. Her visa expired."

"Her visa? What the hell are you talking about?"

"I'm sorry. I didn't mean to make light—"

He hung up on me.

"I wonder if this guy understood anything," I said. "He had a golden opportunity. His deceased wife came back and he treated it like a pain in the butt. He blew it. I don't think he understands what he had or what he blew."

"Maybe this is the moment we all have when people die, when it's too late and we realize we blew it in one way or another. We didn't say or do enough."

"You didn't blow it with Martha. You were great with her."

He shrugged. "We knew this was coming," he said. "Part of the deal."

"How many days was she here?"

"Seven. Seven and a fraction."

"Seven would be one day longer than my marriage."

"What do you mean by that? You had a six-day marriage?"

I couldn't bear to explain, so I switched it back to Martha.

"How do you feel? About her being gone."

"Well, it's a kick in the gut, isn't it? I feel the loss people feel when someone dies but I don't feel that terrible awe of death because it's no mystery to me."

"It's like she died twice."

"When we were just getting to know each other, I worried that I was being unfaithful to Sportie. Not that Martha and I were horsing around but it felt like I was kind of romancing another woman. I didn't want to spoil my perfect record of fidelity to Sportie, which goes back to 1905 or maybe 1900. But now I think meeting Martha made me feel closer than ever to Sportie. It made me miss her pretty badly. When you're dead you're spared that feeling of missing people, but I guess I'm back to life enough to be feeling it now. That's probably why these visits only last a week. Any longer and you'd start feeling like a living person again."

"It took you a long time to walk her home. There wasn't any hanky-panky, was there?"

I was attempting a teasing remark but it was thoughtless. To my relief he took it with a smile. "No, no. At first it was grim talk. She wanted to tell me about her son, Ryan, who died of some drug thing in his first year of college. So that was pretty sad but then she insisted on a mood change and we walked the rest of the way singing."

"Singing? What song?"

"'Row, row, row your boat, gently down the stream.'"

"'Life is but a dream.'"

"Yes. And then we sang, 'Buffalo Gals, won't you come out tonight.'"

"You just walked along singing?"

"Yes. Pretty damn loud."

"So it was a good last night for her. Yankees, poker, some good laughs, walking down Central Park West singing at the top of her lungs."

"I hope so."

"HB, it's pretty sad talking about Martha being gone, but I'm going to make it even worse. It's time to let you in on what happened to me."

* * *

"There was a guy named Douglas Grigatis, a physical therapist by day and a professional banjo player by night. Extremely talented at both. Very dedicated and idealistic.

"We met when my sportswriting career was winding down and he was doing PT work with the Yankees, helping injured players. I covered a game one day when I'd come to work after a really bad back spasm. I could hardly stand up straight. When I tried, I'd get a pain in my back that felt like a butcher knife going in.

"He spotted me hobbling around the clubhouse, looking pathetic. Put me on the table and did lots of work. Massage. Exercises. Electricity. He was also very funny, great to talk to. I'd had back spasms before that took a week or more to get better. This time it was about three days. Even after it was better I kept coming around saying I needed more therapy. He knew I didn't need it, but he gave it to me. I was always hoping he'd go beyond the professional boundaries of therapy but he played it straight."

HB chuckled.

"Then one day he asked me if I'd like to see him play banjo. Of course I did. He and his group had a gig at a country music bar downtown. I met him there. I walked in late and he was doing a solo—perfect timing. He was playing the 'Dueling Banjos' song from the movie *Deliverance*. It was a duet in the movie but he played both sides. Brought the house down.

"Everybody wanted him to play it again, so he did. Brought the house down again. But it turns out there was a really big *Deliverance* fan in the audience. His name was Vic. He was a Mafia guy. Probably the only Mafia boss who likes country music. He also likes shots of booze, a lot of them, so he was pretty drunk and when the band took a break Vic approached Doug and slipped him five hundred-dollar bills and said the money was for all the guys in the band and he'd really like to hear 'Dueling Banjos' again.

"So when the band came back they were happy to do it again, not that the band did much because it was mainly a solo. And Vic walks up to the little stage and gives each band member another hundred. So they do it again. By now the rest of the customers have had enough and you can hear them grousing but nobody wants trouble with Vic. And Vic still wants more, except now it's for even more money, and he's also shoveling cash to the owner of the club who sees that he's got a mobster on his hands and the guy is handing out hundred-dollar bills, and so what if some customers are pissed off.

"They play 'Dueling Banjos' again and again. Doug is exhausted. Finally Vic's had enough and gives Doug $1,000 and leaves, saying he'll be back tomorrow to do it again. 'So be here, and don't disappoint me,' he said. By the way, he never came back.

"Doug and the band guys were ecstatic. They'd never had such a windfall, a few thousand bucks. It was midnight already but we went out and hit every downtown club and gave back a lot of cash in the process, but it was the night of a lifetime. And it was my first night sleeping in Doug's crappy walk-up apartment and I slept there for many months thereafter."

"Well, well," said HB. "A mobster brought you together."

"You could say that. I fell into a good TV job, which led to my current job. We were both doing well. At one point Doug had a banjo gig in Charleston and I went along and we had a ball and decided we were meant for each other.

"The Charleston club signed him up for another gig but we had a week in between so we came back to New York and got married at City Hall. We did our normal jobs that week but on Saturday night we were going to a big party in our honor at the apartment of one of the band guys, who lived way downtown.

"It was in a pretty trashy neighborhood. The building was practically a tenement. We took the elevator to the fifth floor and rang the bell. You could hear the partying inside. I guess nobody heard us ring so Doug knocked loudly.

"At this point three teenagers came running down the stairs. You knew right away they were out of their minds on drugs. They saw us standing there. One of them stopped and did a double take, pointing at my hair. His two friends stopped and they stared at me. Then the first guy pushed forward coming at me and said loudly, 'I ain't never done a yellow-haired lady.'

"And Doug stepped forward toward the kid and without a word the kid pulled out this huge gun and shot Doug in the heart. In that narrow little hallway, it was the loudest sound I ever heard. Deafening. I was told later that Doug was probably dead before he hit the floor. The kids disappeared. And there I was crouched over Doug on that grimy floor when somebody from the party finally opened the door.

"So that was my marriage. Six days."

I was surprised to have gotten through the story without breaking down.

"That's the worst damn thing I ever heard, Lake," said HB. "I'm so sorry."

"How could God let a thing like that happen?"

"I've never heard a good answer to that question. But it does kind of suggest, doesn't it, that God doesn't supervise everything that goes on. Or *anything* that goes on. Maybe that's not how He sees his role."

I went on. "Anyway, the story made all the newspapers and amazingly the cops arrested the three kids. I saw them in a lineup. I couldn't identify the shooter. The light was dim in that hallway and he had a watch cap pulled down over his forehead and it happened so fast and it was so loud. They never found the gun. I don't think any of them were prosecuted."

"That's infuriating."

"I got to know the investigating detective, Melvin Aptosari. He told me the kid did it to make his bones in a gang—you had to kill a white guy to get into the gang. Aptosari said he was pretty sure which one did it and he promised to keep an eye on him and maybe nail him for his next crime. 'I know you want him punished and for now the State of New York is not going to do it for you, but life will do it. He's going to die in jail or on the street. He's seventeen going on dead.'"

We sat quietly for a while. Then HB asked, "What did you do next?"

"I tried to go back to my normal life. My life was work and grief, nothing else. I became chief writer and I could make a day's work last ten hours and then I could get up and go to the studio at four a.m. and be around during the show till nine and then maybe go home for an hour or two before coming back to work for a new day. Everybody on the staff was supportive.

"But I never recovered. I saw a shrink but she didn't help much. I let myself go. I did pills. I'd sit here at night and drink a bottle of chardonnay by myself. I fell out of love with New York. Lost interest in romance. Guys looked at me for a moment but then backed off as if they'd seen a warning sign saying, BEWARE. DAMAGED GOODS. She'll cry or scream or go hysterical on you."

"You seemed to get along with that fellow on Long Island."

"Brendan Leary? Yes, he's been good. But that's a once-a-year thing. It's never going anywhere."

"What's the reason for that?"

"Differences that would catch up to us pretty quickly. I'm middle class, he's blue collar. He's public high school, I'm elite university. He's Bronx, I'm Manhattan and suburbia. He's Catholic, I'm nothing. He's dealt with raw reality as a cop and bar owner, I just deal with bullshitty TV stuff. He's a hunky never-married Irish bachelor who's very popular with the ladies, I'm a gawky sad-sack widow who still loves her husband."

"You're not gawky and you're not a sad sack."

"Thanks, but that's how I feel sometimes."

"I got a good feeling from Brendan."

"He's a good guy."

"Thanks for telling me your story, Lake."

"You're my grandfather so you ought to know. My only living relative, although you're not really living."

"Things will get better. I don't have supernatural vision, but I see something good coming for you."

"Good? Like a fling with a tall, dark stranger?"

"Life is full of surprises. They're not all bad."

CHAPTER 10

The story now shifts to my working world so I should explain what my day on the job looks like.

The show is created in two separate locations. The day-side office looks like any office. Other than the hyper behavior and off-color language of most of the staff, there are few signs that a daily two-hour live network TV talk show is being produced here.

Meetings about tomorrow's show start the day. The booking staff works the phones lining up guests. The director's people prepare the production. The writers try to reach and pre-interview the next day's guests and write out scripts with introductions and suggested questions that shape the interview (usually about five interviews in two hours), though often interviews on live TV jump the tracks and take on a shape of their own.

At some point in the afternoon the writers brief the "talent," meaning the on-air hosts of the show, Gary Warren and Gina Harkness. He's the star, she's the sidekick. He interviews the serious or famous guests, she gets the fluff, especially the girly stuff.

The day is packed with stress. Nothing goes smoothly. Crises erupt constantly and preparations that had consumed arduous effort are ruthlessly junked as work leaps into new preparations.

The day's news has a major shaping impact on bookings, with new guests being booked and already-booked guests being unbooked. Sometimes planned-for guests cancel late and have to be replaced. Other times late bookings or myriad other complications or availabilities force a near-total overhaul of everything. The strain takes its toll: egos flare, screaming disputes break out, sooner or later everyone is either called an asshole or calls someone else an asshole. Then they knuckle down and do their jobs.

My job as chief writer is to guide the writing, sit-in on talent briefings, and hammer the typewriter until a script of seventy-plus pages is finished. Getting to the final script is a long journey. On a good day I get to the office at ten a.m. and go home around eight p.m.

Around four a.m. a surprisingly large production crew assembles in the basement of a network building a few blocks away. I have no idea what half of these people do, other than creating population density in very tight spaces. The studio set, which looks like a living room, is rebuilt (it's taken apart every day so the studio can be used for other shows), dressed, and brightly lit. Technical details are ironed out under the barked commands of the director in his darkened and cramped control room. There is no studio audience.

Guests arrive and are escorted to the "green room" where they await their fate before the cameras, drinking coffee or stronger liquids and often mingling with other guests. Celebrities bring their PR people, agents, or assistants. Makeup is applied. It is a tense environment. The anxiety level rises with every clock tick toward airtime.

The on-air talent arrives and usually avoids contact with guests—we don't want their best interaction taking place off-camera before the show even starts. The show's producers and the executive producer attempt to keep the anarchy under control while coping with changes. Occasionally network executives arrive, sometimes with VIP guests, and crowd into valuable space in the control room. They have to be continually shushed so the director and his people can hear what's going on.

If breaking news requires it, everything is thrown out at the last minute and redone on the fly at frenzied speed. There is an exhilarating, high-adrenaline pleasure to throwing away meticulous preparation and just winging it. The off-camera bedlam that precedes the show can be a better show than the show itself. The trick is to keep the craziness from showing on the air.

My presence is usually not required in the morning part of the process, though sometimes there is an issue with a difficult guest or production matter that requires in-person care. I try to avoid being there because sixteen-hour days are not sustainable. However, I have been awakened by early calls at home and heard my boss holler a single sentence, "Get your ass in here," and I jump out of bed, brush my teeth, and charge out into the night like a marine hearing enemy fire.

The studio is about thirty blocks from my apartment. Taxis are scarce at that hour; I have been known to run all or most of the way and arrive in hyperventilating condition.

The day I left HB home (he is a speed-reader and knocked off *A Tale of Two Cities* that day before taking a walk in Central Park) began normally, except two of my six writers called in sick at the last minute so in addition to my regular duties I had to handle their assignments as well. One was fairly simple: setting up a debate on whether jury trials should be televised. The other, in a celebrity slot, was with a well-known singer plugging her new album of children's songs. She and our host, Gary Warren, who started his career as a singer and never misses a chance to display his vocal skills, would sing a few songs together. It would be cute and uncomplicated to write. I briefed Gary and typed it up. He loved it. By midday I was patting myself on the back for neatly handling everything and I was looking forward to wrapping the script up early and hurrying home to HB.

That's when the show's producer, Tom Selby, appeared in my office door with a broad grin, waving a booking sheet. "BINGO!" he roared.

I felt my easy-day plan dissolving as a big-name booking replaced my nice little duet with Gary and the singer.

"It was a titanic battle to get him, but we got him," gloated Tom.

"Who?" I asked, trying to look enthusiastic.

"*Burt Reynolds!* He's plugging a movie. He chose us because he loves Gary from some Hollywood hijinks back in the day."

Tom slapped the booking sheet down on my desk. It contained little information: just a scrawled "Burt R" and the phone number of Burt's hotel. "He'll be waiting for your call at four p.m. Promptissimo!"

Tom whirled and vanished but a moment later Jean Maxey, one of my writers and my best friend on the staff, took her place in my doorway. "I could take that Burt Reynolds interview off your hands," she said. "He is the stud of all studs."

"In that case, I'll assign it to myself, Jean. You get back to the snake guy." Her assignment was an interview with a herpetologist who'd written a book saying snakes could be good pets (but first you have to stop being afraid of them).

Jean waved her forefinger at me in a mock warning.

"I'm going to be really pissed if you fuck him," she said.

"Oh, okay," I said. "I won't fuck him. Just for you."

* * *

I've done many phone interviews with stars and celebrities. Some are gracious and great. Others are bitchy and bored, making it clear they think they're wasting their time talking to a writer. Sometimes they're right but more often the very short on-air interview benefits from the focus and structure the writer tries to create.

The basic understanding with celebrity guests is that you give them what they want—e.g. a chance to promote their new movie or book to a nationwide audience—but they have to give you what the show wants: a few minutes of good television with a recognizable star. They have to say something that lifts the on-air interview at least a little bit above predictably mindless celebrity chatter. The writer's task in the pre-interview is to extract a line of conversation which allows that to happen.

This isn't so easy. The writer frequently has to put up a determined struggle to get past everyday celebrity bs and find interesting angles which sometimes the guest might prefer to keep private. The writer has to gently invade that privacy while keeping the celebrity's trust that revelations won't get out of hand. Another challenge is finding out what directions to avoid, for any of a long list of reasons.

On some occasions the tension between the guest's and writer's motives simply disappears and both sides enjoy the conversation. The pre-interview is great and that virtually guarantees that the on-air interview will be great.

In this category my telephone pre-interview with Burt Reynolds was the best of the best, my all-time favorite, worthy of a niche in the Pre-Interview Hall of Fame.

For two reasons.

Reason #1: it wasn't a one-way interview. He was as interested in me as I was in him. Don't ask me why. I learned later that he had an eight p.m. dinner party to go to but nothing until then so his willingness to talk might have been about killing time. He was open about his life, a good talker, and fun-loving non-asshole with an endless supply of superlative anecdotes.

He didn't know me from Adam (or Eve) but we hit it off so why not enjoy a freewheeling yakety-yak? The specifics of what we said to each other are a blur—I stopped taking notes about three minutes in, when I already had everything I needed to write the script. The rest was a high-momentum conversational ride like I had not experienced in a long time. And not only was he good—*I* was good too. I was fast, funny, and smart. I hadn't heard this version of me in years. I charmed the hell out of Burt Reynolds.

Reason #2: instead of the usual ten or fifteen minutes, the world's number-one box-office star stayed on the line with me from four p.m. until 5:20 p.m. And when it ended, it didn't end. He said, "Hey, why don't we finish this in my hotel room?"

I could not believe my ears. After a stunned moment, I laughed.

"Wait till I tell my grandfather that America's sexiest movie star invited me to his hotel room."

"My *luxury* hotel room. Not only that, I'll ply you with alcohol. What do you drink? You sound like a vodka girl, which is my drink too. I'll order up a gallon bottle from room service."

"And what about appetizers? Or am I the appetizer?"

"No, no, nothing like that. I'll be the perfect gentleman. I know how this sounds but in anyplace other than my hotel room we'd be swamped with autograph-seekers and paparazzi. How soon can you get here?"

"Who says I'm coming at all? I can't get anywhere soon. I have a couple hours work finishing a script for two hours of live network TV tomorrow, including an interview with you."

"Hey, you can write mine up in five minutes and I'll be great and we'll both look terrific. I'm super at this. I've done a thousand TV interviews. The only times I do a really bad, embarrassing, and foul-mouthed interview are when the writer won't drink with me. And I bet you have another writer who can step in and finish the script for you."

"I do." Jean Maxey. I started to tell him what she'd said to me but thought better of it.

"I'll call you back in five minutes, Burt," I said. "If I can call you Burt."

"Call me Burt and call me soon."

✳ ✳ ✳

Feeling a first-rate tingle from the Burt conversation, I walked down the hall to Jean's office. She had snake research all over her desk and didn't look happy about it.

"You won't believe this, but Burt Reynolds just invited me to his hotel room."

"Holy shit. What did you say?"

"I said I'd get back to him in five minutes."

"This never happens to me."

"We had a fantastic conversation. Almost an hour and a half."

"That's a new indoor record. So are you going or not?"

"Come on, I can't go. Even if I desperately wanted to go, which I do. What would you do?"

"Did you see that nude centerfold of him in *Cosmopolitan* a few years ago? But what would I do? Hmm, let me overthink that for a minute."

"Seriously. Be serious, Jean."

"Okay. Seriously. I'd really want to go but in the end I'd probably wimp out. Every girl over twelve knows that if a man asks you to his hotel room, you say No. He doesn't want you there to discuss Kafka or Kierkegaard."

"He sounds like a really nice guy. Honorable intentions aren't completely impossible, are they?"

"Isn't he going with Dinah Shore? Or Sally Field?"

"I think Dinah was a long time ago. I don't know about Sally Field. Somehow that didn't come up."

"Lake, whatever you do you're going to remember it forever. And whatever you do there'll be reasons to regret it. If you don't go, you'll regret not having the balls to have the experience of a lifetime just to prove that you're a virtuous maiden. If you do go and have wild screaming animal sex, you'll regret it because you'll feel like a slut or groupie who let herself be exploited by a famous man. And if you go and just have an entirely innocent and fun conversation, you'll probably be a little disappointed and regret that it didn't come to anything more than that. By that time you'll probably be in love with him and he'll dump you."

"Jean, if I go, which shoes should I wear? I can't meet him wearing my pink sneakers."

"You've got at least a dozen pairs of shoes under your desk. I've never seen so many shoes. You're a shoe freak. Okay, I'd say show some style and wear the expensive red heels."

"With these old jeans and a blue turtleneck that's losing its shape?"

"Sure. Go in there looking like a working woman, not like you're dressed to kill."

"Will you finish the script for me? It's in pretty good shape. Gina's doing the snake guy. You can brief her by phone. Make sure she's willing to touch the snake."

"In return you'll owe me the whole story. Every detail, graphic and uncensored."

"Okay. I'm nervous but I'm going."

"So what tipped the scales on your decision?"

"My grandfather told a story last night about going to dinner with a famous baseball player. He idolized this guy. They got sloshed and rode around honking the horn of this guy's new car. My grandfather said it was one of the best memories of his life. He almost teared up talking about it. I haven't had enough great memories like that since Doug died. I think I deserve one."

"You definitely deserve one. I didn't know you even had a grandfather."

"He's in town for a quick visit."

"Your grandfather's in town? From where?"

"Far away. Very far," I said. "Gotta run. Thanks, Jean."

I called Burt and said I'd be there soon. He said, "Hurry. The vodka bottle just walked in. I won't crack it till you're here."

I called HB and told him I'd be a little late, an opportunity had come up.

"Carpe diem," he said. "Be as late as you want. I've just started *Life on the Mississippi*. About Mark Twain's youthful adventures as a steamboat pilot."

"Adventures are a good thing, right, HB?"

"Of course. You know an adventure I never had? Riding in an airplane."

"You've been to the afterlife, but you've never been up in the air."

"Make the most of it," he said.

CHAPTER 11

I decided against the red heels. Instead I jumped in a cab wearing the old pink sneakers I wear every day.

Reason #1: to thine own self be true. The real me is pink sneakers.

Reason #2: If this went badly, I didn't want to ride home with those red heels reminding me of what a loser I'd been.

I was nervous waiting for him to open his hotel room door but nearly had a stroke at my first look at him. In contrast to my scruffy outfit, he was spectacular in a gorgeous charcoal-gray suit, a bright white shirt, and a perfect necktie. And highly polished black cowboy boots with heels that lifted him to a height well over six feet.

He was the goddamn best-looking man I'd ever seen.

But I had this thought: a guy who expects to be ripping off his clothes for a quick and easy bang would greet me in shorts and a T-shirt. He wouldn't bother getting this dressed up. Unless this is how it's done in the major leagues of seduction.

"The hair is world class," he said, appraising me with a smile. "You didn't sound blonde on the phone."

I had no comeback.

"And I think you could use some Florida sunshine to chase away that New York pallor."

He had a glowing tan.

He held the door open and I entered the room. He was staying in a boutique hotel way downtown. "I always start a New York visit here. It takes the paparazzi a while to zero in so for a day or two I can come and go like an average putz."

It was wonderful, more like a beautiful apartment than a hotel suite. I had a sense of quiet wealth, but a lot of it. I thought, if I ever make a ton of money, develop really good taste, and remain unpretentious, I will live in a place like this.

He steered me to one of two luxurious easy chairs and we sat down facing each other.

He didn't tease me about my speechlessness, which I took as an act of kindness. I suspect I wasn't the first woman he'd left speechless.

He got up and went to the little bar and mixed two vodka-and-tonics. Medium strength, not seduction strength. The drink tasted fantastic and provided a rush of soothing relief. I started coming out of my stupefied state, recovering my poise.

"I'm embarrassed by my outfit," I said. "Didn't have time to slip into something fabulous."

"Hey, I dragged you out of work. I'm glad you came at all. I'd rather be in clothes like yours but I have to go to an extremely posh dinner party tonight. It's for the new movie, which opens on October 5, as I hope you mention in your lead-in to me."

"That's a month away. You're making the talk show rounds pretty early."

"It has to be. I'll be on location for a different picture and I refuse to be an a-hole and leave a production hanging while I go off on the interview circuit, and for another film no less. But Candice and Jill will take over."

Candice Bergen and Jill Clayburgh, his co-stars.

"Are they going to be at the party tonight?"

"Sure. They're magnets for primo guests."

"Is Sally Field going to be there?"

"Sally's not in the movie. And she's not in New York."

Did that mean he was sleeping alone?

I said, "Gary Warren's looking forward to interviewing you tomorrow."

"Great. We had some good times together in Hollywood back when he was a singer/dancer/actor. But he was always more serious than the rest of us. He used to take graduate courses at UCLA. I think he got an advanced degree of some sort. Will Gina be on the set tomorrow?"

"Sure, she's a live wire on the set."

"But he grabs the meaty interviews. Like me or Kissinger."

"He's star #1, she's #2."

"Which do you like more?"

"I'm too sober to answer that."

"I'll freshen your drink." Which he did. I was shocked to realize I'd downed the first drink in about two gulps.

I said, "Gary's very earnest, works hard, wants to be good at this and doesn't get the respect he deserves. A little insecure with people outside the entertainment world and maybe overly impressed by ambassadors and senators. He doesn't realize that major news figures are just as full of crap as Show Business people. He's not a natural in terms of journalistic instincts but that's why most of our staff writers have journalistic backgrounds. He's learning fast. Gina, on the other hand, just laughs her way through it. She feels she's the second banana so it's just a gig for her."

"Do you need anything else from me for tomorrow?"

"No. We're all set. It'll be terrific, like you said."

"Good. I'll be there at ten a.m."

"Make that five a.m. Six at the latest."

"Okay. Will I see you in the studio?"

"No. I show up only in exceptional circumstances."

"Which rules me out?" He smiled, a smile that made me weak. "Do you have a husband, boyfriend, kids?"

If I said no to husband and boyfriend, he'd think I was gay, not a signal I wanted to send. Wait—I had to stop thinking this way. I had to stop being ambivalent on what to do if he made a move. I had to have a clear Yes or No policy. Of course I knew that No was the right answer but, to be realistic, when sexual attraction enters the picture, No has very little chance against Yes.

"No husband. No boyfriend. I was married briefly."

"How briefly?"

"Six days."

"*Six*? What the hell happened? Some sort of drunken Vegas thing?"

I shook my head.

I *never* talk casually about Doug's death, certainly not with people I've only known for the length of one phone call and less than two vodka-and-tonics. I searched for a way to sidestep the question but my evasion skills had taken the night off.

Obviously reading the contorted emotion on my face he said, "Sorry, I withdraw the question, none of my business. Are you okay? Can I get you anything? There's usually a big basket of fruits and chocolates but it's not here this time. I did spot a little bag of Doritos in a kitchen drawer."

Maybe it was his good-guy decency that touched me. I think it was a straw-breaking-the-camel's-back kind of thing and I hate to think that the straw was the offer of an old bag of Doritos, but I lost it. Fell apart. The Doug story erupted with the rage of red-hot lava, the whole story, told at careening speed interspersed with snorfling sobs and disgusting nose-blowings into the Kleenex he kept handing me. I'd told HB the same story without coming apart like this. It was painful and so embarrassing. I fell into a rhythm of sobbing, apologizing, then resuming the story until the next spasming round of sobs.

My hysterics seemed interminable but at last they subsided. He'd been silent but now he cleared his throat and said, "Let me get this straight, because your story was a little hard to follow. One minute you were standing there about to go into a party and the next minute some punk jumped out of nowhere and murdered your new husband right before your eyes. Is that it?"

I nodded. I hid my face. I tried to describe how my life had disintegrated after Doug's death but my quavering narrative was frequently disrupted. I'd cried often before but there had never been a tsunami like this.

Could this be the big cathartic outpouring you supposedly need to purge your grief once and for all? Not quite, but maybe a step in that direction.

Most men are terrified of women's tears but he wasn't terrified. Shocked, yes. Genuinely sympathetic, very. He got up and squeezed into my chair, putting an arm around my shoulders, comforting me. This tenderness was not the kind of body contact I'd had in mind but it was welcome.

I kissed him. It was a thanks-for-enduring-this-mortifying-spectacle kiss. Just once, and then I apologized profusely.

"That is a motherfucker of a story," he said. "Have a little more medicine." He held the vodka to my lips and I took a sip.

I felt some composure returning. I couldn't have made a bigger ass of myself but barriers had been breached. Truth had been revealed and exchanged. It had made us friends.

He said, "Hey, why don't you come to this dinner party with me? You need some fun."

Nine out of ten men would have been desperately charging out the door to get away from me after my basket case performance, but amazingly he was trying to find a way to cheer me up. He was willing to drag a tear-streaked ill-clad not-young, not-charming, not-glamorous woman he didn't even know as his date to a party packed by rich and stunning glitterati and bigwigs.

I said, "I bet your hostess would be thrilled to have to seat an extra guest. Especially a scroungy writer who hasn't been near a shower all day."

"I bet if I ask nicely you'll be admitted. But hey, what's the point of being a movie star if you can't bully a hostess?"

"You're sweet to ask."

"I have a car and driver. We can drive to your building and wait outside while you run in, wash your face, throw on a little black dress, and run back to the car. And I'd suggest some blush on the cheeks because you're as white as a Number 10 envelope."

"A Number 10 envelope?"

"A business envelope. Bright white. Like my teeth." He gave a big smile and I laughed.

"I'll take the ride home but I'm gonna skip the party. But thanks."

We sat quietly for a moment. Then he said, "Can I get up?"

He got up, straightened his clothes, and sat down in the other chair. "When Johnny Carson performs in Vegas, he wears a tux and from the time he puts on that tux an hour or two before he goes on, he refuses to sit down for fear of the tiniest wrinkle."

"I'm glad you're not Johnny Carson," I said. "You don't look wrinkled. If you want, I could iron your pants. There must be an iron in the closet."

"I'd have to take my pants off."

"You're shy? You posed nude in a magazine."

"You have a point. But you'd be surprised how few women offer to iron my pants. Fortunately I'm not as strict as Johnny on this."

"I've seen you on Johnny's show. You're hilarious."

"Not many comedians let someone come on their show and be hilarious."

"I just introduced my grandfather to Johnny's show. He took to Johnny right away. They're both Midwesterners."

"Gramps is kind of behind the times if you're just now introducing him to *The Tonight Show*."

"He hasn't watched much TV. But you know, seriously, I never tell that story about my husband because it's so painful. But just last night I told the story to my grandfather. I think telling the story two nights in a row was emotional overload. Hence the display you just saw."

"This is puzzling me. Your grandfather never heard of Johnny Carson and now you're telling me he never heard about your husband being murdered until last night. I'd think he would have been let in on this story back when it happened."

"We're getting into an area you may not want to explore."

"Oh, but I'm an explorer. Or I've played one in a movie, maybe. But tell me," he said with a charming smile. "Why did Grandpa not know until yesterday? And what the hell happened yesterday to prompt this telling?"

I could have said, "It came up in the context of his dead platonic girlfriend Martha being called back to the afterlife."

But I *didn't* say it. You simply cannot say something like that. Not if you expect to retain the slightest credibility. I realized there was nothing I could say about HB that wouldn't open a conversation from which I would emerge looking anything but totally bonkers. So I warned myself: *do not* get into the HB story.

"Was he in prison? Was he in a coma?"

"No and no."

"Well?"

"You wouldn't believe me, unless you're an idiot."

"Well, I was hit in the head many times playing football. I've fallen off horses. So maybe I have some brain damage. But look, seriously, we had a long phone conversation and I invited you down here. I don't invite everyone I have nice phone conversations with to come to my room and have a drink with me. I stayed on that long call with you because I got a great vibe from you. I spotted you as someone I could like and talk to and that means someone I would respect and believe. So whatever you tell me, I'll believe the hell out of it. Is it really batshit crazy?"

"Yes, Burt. Double batshit. Triple."

* * *

My vow to not tell the HB story lasted about forty seconds. Then I had a bad thought: am I going to sound like I'm pitching Burt on a film comedy about a dead guy coming back to life? Burt would play HB. He would have a wild dinner with Larry Lajoie (Gene Hackman?) and a romance with Martha Dell (Cicely Tyson or Lena Horne). Maybe Sally Field would play me. The notion of a movie pitch hung over me as I started but as I heard myself speaking, I decided the story was too implausible to support a movie and my concern drifted away.

I told the story with some edits. I didn't mention that Brendan and I were having sex when HB arrived under that streetlamp in Amanituck. I left out the unpleasantness with Artie Southway and Minnie Horch's questions and the belligerent fan at Yankee Stadium.

I did describe HB's relationship with Martha Dell and Burt was fascinated by her, demanding information that I couldn't provide. I should have shown a lot more curiosity about her. Burt loved the image of HB walking her home singing "Row, Row, Row Your Boat" and "Buffalo Gals."

I realized that while HB had given a few answers about what death was or wasn't like, he hadn't really been seriously questioned, by me or anyone else. Perhaps people were uncomfortable with the topic or reluctant to ask too much, which would indicate that they took him seriously and were therefore gullible.

I summarized what HB had said about people being given the option to make short visits back from the afterlife when only one significant survivor remained. And when that survivor passed away, the book would be shut on the dead person's life, which would have no continuing meaning if he or she was not remembered.

"I guess if no one remembers you, that's a true definition of death," Burt said. "I always thought that 'Gone but never forgotten' are the cruelest words you could put on a tombstone because it's a promise that's sure to be broken."

We looked at each other for a moment.

"Lake, I know I promised to believe you but this is kind of hard to buy. Do you believe him?"

"I honestly don't know. I saw him dead in his casket but when I talk to him, he seems absolutely credible. I want to believe him. Sometimes I dislike the journalist in me that won't let me give in to believing him."

"That would take some courage, wouldn't it? To believe something so obviously unbelievable?"

"I hadn't thought of it in terms of courage."

"What's he like?"

"He's very likable. Old-fashioned solid American. Good heart. Good sense of humor. He's wandered around the city a bit but spends most of his outdoor time in Central Park. He reads Dickens and Twain. I don't really understand what he's trying to do here. Maybe there's no specific objective. He's concerned about me. He's like a real grandfather."

"Do you love him?"

"I don't know, but maybe. But I think he loves me."

"I gotta meet this guy," Burt said. "I want to see if I believe him or not. Can you bring him to the studio in the morning?"

"Sure. He'd love to see the show being produced. He never even saw TV until this week."

"Maybe after the show the three of us can get breakfast."

"He doesn't eat."

"I do."

"So do I. I'm starved. Could I have those Doritos?"

"Sure. Come on, my car is waiting. We'll drop you off at your place and you can chomp down the Doritos on the way."

CHAPTER 12

I recounted my Burt Reynolds experience to HB omitting my attraction to Burt and glossing over my emotional meltdown, but I had the feeling he understood that it had been, for me, an emotional encounter.

I asked if he would like to come to the studio in the morning and see my TV show produced? Yes, he said, that would be a hoot.

We got there about six a.m. and entered a nondescript door on a side street, descending an industrial-steel staircase into a maze of shadowy basement corridors bustling with voices and busy people. The high activity indoors contrasted with the predawn stillness outside.

I gave HB a tour of the studio set and the dimly lit control room—the latter a den of machismo where a fighter pilot culture prevailed, the director and his people joshing and cursing obscenely, barking orders, tapping buttons, building energy. The full script that Jean and I supervised had been typed cleanly, xeroxed on yellow copy paper, and distributed; everyone pointed out to me, with classic show biz humor, that the script was pure shit but they would try to make it work.

HB was delighted by the raucous hijinks. I introduced him to everyone and everyone was welcoming. I led him to the green room where he asked the traditional question, "Why isn't it green?" I said, "Somewhere centuries ago, maybe in Shakespeare's time, a green room was actually green and that's when it started and maybe no green room has been green since then."

When we arrived only one guest was waiting, the snake guy, an obvious weirdo. His big snake was being kept out of sight in a picnic cooler. We tried to talk to him, but he was preoccupied with notes. I didn't hold high hopes for his interview, though it was part of the show's magazine concept that a wide range of topics would be discussed, not just news and entertainment.

The senator from Illinois, who was the newsmaker guest in the first hour, arrived. Minutes later the lawyer and journalist who would debate cameras in the courtroom came in. Other people buzzed in and out but it was a subdued scene until Burt swept in, entering in a sunburst of celebrity charisma. Young women assistants, absent until this moment, rushed from every direction offering services. Burt cheek-kissed me and then went right for HB.

"I am so looking forward to talking with you," Burt said with a gleaming smile. "Is it true that you're dead?"

"Dead as a doornail," said HB. "Lake tells me you're a very big movie star and a real gentleman. Tell me, what's up with John Wayne?"

"Nothing, I'm afraid. Duke bought the farm a few months ago. Died."

"In a gun fight?" HB asked, getting a small laugh from Burt.

The senator was approaching, and the snake guy was hovering, trying to talk Everglades snakes with Burt. I blocked both of them, introducing the senator to the snake guy (neither was pleased about that), and led Burt and HB away. We walked down a long corridor past editing rooms (chilly because of the air-conditioning required by the big videotape machines) where producers and writers were working intensely in almost-dark rooms. I found a room where there was no activity and installed them there.

"You boys chat," I said, "I'll give you ten minutes." Then I backed out.

I gave them thirty.

I went to the control room and helped with script changes and gossiped a little. I asked permission from the producer Tom Selby for my grandfather to be a guest in the control room during the show. Tom said, "No problem. He's a sprightly guy for a grandfather. Are you sure he's not your sugar daddy?"

* * *

As airtime approaches, tension rises and time seems to speed up. I went and pried Burt away from HB, leading him to makeup. He whispered "Wow" to me but said nothing more, looking serious and focused. I hoped talking death with HB had not dampened his spirit. We needed him to provide high energy fun in his airtime with Gary.

In the control room the director and his three or four assistants sit up front at the tech console confronting a wall of monitors. Behind them is another row where the honchos occupy four or five stools: the show producer, Tom Selby, the executive producer, Andy Shafer, and in a rare appearance the network's president of morning and daytime television, Aaron Buehler, who often described himself as "the asshole from network." He thought this was likably self-deprecating; most of the staff considered it a statement of fact and referred to him as "the A from N."

The fourth stool belonged to the Standards & Practices executive, Wick Sorenson. His job is to assure that the live performance stays within the bounds of the network's moral, ethical, and legal standards. In other words, he is the censor, but I have never seen him actually censor anything.

The remaining stool was awarded to HB, in what I thought was a thoughtful bow to his grandfather status and perhaps a nice gesture to me as a staff member with a family visitor.

I found a place to stand, pressed against the back wall.

The show flew by. It was a rare day when everything went like clockwork. Burt's interview was everything we'd hoped for. After plugging his movie, Burt quickly dispensed with the questions I'd written and went off into a rollicking tale about a car trip to Tijuana that he and Gary and other Hollywood revelers had taken years ago. The story hinted at titillating details that were not often mentioned on puritanical morning television and would have been more suitable in Burt's normal talk-show terrain, late night. Wick Sorenson might have been nervous but old-pro Burt knew when to tap the brakes and the interview ended with laughter, the highlight of the show.

As commercials rolled, Buehler sat back and said, "Damn, Andy, you could just feel the energy level double or triple with that segment. This is the kind of thing we need a lot more of."

Andy said, "Yeah, if you could find a Burt Reynolds for every segment."

"That's no excuse. More creative booking could add a lot. Better guests, scintillating people, more pizzazz. Our ratings are stagnant,

Andy. Our audience share is flat. We need to give those numbers a giant goose in the ass."

"We're constantly trying new ideas."

You could feel the uneasiness in the room as Buehler, with his big deep voice, continued his complaining. It was aimed at Andy Shafer but loud enough for everyone to hear. Andy could have argued but he knew it was pointless. He had too much class to argue in front of the staff, and the accusation was unfair: many good ideas had been nixed by Buehler himself, who was widely considered to be the biggest obstacle to the show's growth. He was not a TV guy; he'd been a senior manager in charge of who-knows-what at the corporation that acquired the network and installed him to keep an eye on the TV smart-asses whose judgment the parent company considered unsound, meaning insufficiently Middle American.

"HB," said Buehler, "let me turn to you as the only non-TV professional in this room. I want your opinion. Who would *you* consider the guest you'd most like to see on this show? Who would you drop everything to watch?"

"I presume you're talking about someone who's still alive," said HB.

"Damn right," said Buehler with a laugh. "We don't book dead folks. So tell me, who really fascinates you? Who would you like to have a conversation with?"

HB said, "I don't know who's fascinating these days. But I guess I'd be interested in Neil Armstrong."

Andy said, "Armstrong? Not fascinating. He was as hot as it gets but he's been out of the news for ten years. I interviewed him once. Nice guy but dull as a post."

HB asked, "How could someone who's been to the moon be dull?"

"Great astronaut, not a guy who opened up conversationally."

"Who else, HB?"

"Sorry. I'm not the one to ask about television. I never laid eyes on it until this week."

"You never saw TV before this week? Where the hell do you live?"

Buehler looked at him quizzically. "You're the head writer's father?"

"No. Her grandfather."

"Grandfather? How can you be her grandfather? Unless you really robbed the cradle. You know, married a very young girl. Like five years old." Buehler gave an uneasy chuckle.

"Well, I'm from Kentucky and people there do marry young, but not that young."

There was a burst of laughter in the control room.

"Actually we started late," said HB. "My wife was twenty-five when we got married and we didn't have our first baby for a couple years."

Everyone in the room was listening in and it's a wonder someone remembered we were still doing a TV show. The commercials ended and Gary Warren led off the final half-hour, throwing to news anchor Ed Ramos in Washington.

The odd conversation with HB was forgotten as the show went on. The snake guy was surprisingly good; Gina Harkness was appropriately giddy but terrified by the large snake he wrapped around her neck to cure her of snake fear. It didn't cure her. Then came a filmed report on taming the mess in your garage. Then Gary and Gina teased the next day's show and signed off. Everyone was pleased and relieved—relieved because no one wanted screwups with the volatile bully Aaron Buehler in the control room.

Buehler was an intimidating figure, a big heavyset man of about fifty with a crewcut and weather-beaten face. Even in his expensive suit, he looked less like an executive than a farmer who'd just climbed down from his tractor. In fact he had a farming childhood in rural Connecticut and took aggressive pride in it, casting himself as more of a *real* American than the city slicker TV types who made up most of the show's staff. There was some truth to this. Andy Shafer was a prototype Brooklyn guy, irreverent, slight in build but scrappy in street-smart wit. Gary Warren was from upper crust Boston. Wick Sorenson was an aristocratic Philadelphian from a scholarly family. Wick, in his free time, gave lectures to highbrow literary groups and graduate classes at his alma mater, Columbia.

Andy looked around and found me and said, "I think Aaron needs to meet Burt."

Everyone wants to hobnob with the star. I realized that Burt's appearance this day was the likely reason for Aaron's visit to the control room.

With HB at my side, I returned to the green room where Burt was the center of a lively conversation among the show's guests plus Gary Warren and Gina Harkness. HB quickly joined in.

I pulled Burt aside and whispered to him that our boss Aaron Buehler wanted to say hello.

Burt understood his mission. HB stayed behind as Burt and I walked back to the control room. I told Burt that Aaron would want an autograph for his daughter Tammy. Burt said, "For you, Lake, I will pour on the suck-up and make Mr. Buehler and Tammy very happy."

And he did. He blasted Buehler with radiance. He found a discarded script and expertly extracted the page introducing him and autographed it with several sentences to Tammy plus a big signature and a drawing of a heart. Buehler was overjoyed.

I stood quietly on the perimeter of this all-male group.

Buehler, stressing his country boy background, asked Burt a question about a vehicle Burt had driven in one of his trucker movies but Burt, with HB still on his mind, had a different priority.

"Aaron, I'd love to discuss shitkicker vehicles with you but could I put it on hold and instead suggest a booking for your show? Because I have a sensational idea for you. Crazy but sensational. I think I can name someone who I believe could be the biggest goddamn booking in the history of television."

"Who would that be, Burt?" asked Buehler, thinking he was being set up for a joke.

"Where's Lake?" asked Burt, and I stepped in.

"I'm sure you see where I'm going, Lake. Are you okay with it?"

I didn't see this coming. I didn't know how to block it.

Burt said, "Aaron, would you want a guest who could reveal the secrets of death? The mysteries of the afterlife?"

"Really? Who would that be? I think you're pulling my leg."

"*Au contraire, mon fr*ère. Such a person is available and he is on the premises as we speak. HB Taylor. Lake's grandpa. He died a long time ago but now he's back from death for a visit. Or so he says. It's tantalizing, in fact."

If anyone else had brought this up, this conversation would not have lasted a moment longer. But Burt was a star and stars are not to be dismissed.

Buehler asked, "This is the older guy who was sitting next to me during the show? He knows the secrets of death?"

Shafer said, "Burt, what do you mean by back from death?"

Burt said, "I had a long talk with him. I'm not saying I believe him but he's pretty damn convincing. He met Theodore Roosevelt. Took a piss with him."

"Oh, no," said Andy. "Burt, is this a put-on? Tell me I'm not hearing this. This is—I don't know what this is. Lake, explain."

I said, "I saw him in his coffin thirty-one years ago and now he's here and he doesn't mind revealing a lot about the afterlife, starting with the fact that there *is* an afterlife. If he's a hoax I haven't been able to poke any holes in his act. But, seriously, you can't put him on national TV saying this. We have to walk away from this, whatever it is. Burt's right that it could get a hell of a lot of viewers, but I think we have to treat HB's story as bullshit or risk incredible repercussions."

"Like Congress coming down on us," Andy said. "We'd look like complete fools, laughingstocks. The media would murder us. The religious establishment would go berserko. Our sponsors could be boycotted. We'd lose devoted viewers. The FCC could yank our station licenses. Our careers would be over, especially yours, Aaron. So thanks, Burt, but you know what the tough guys say in Brooklyn? *Fuhgedaboudit.* Forget about it."

Buehler said, "But think of the numbers we'd pull if this guy is for real. Or anything close to it."

"What's 'close to it'?" asked Andy. "He isn't back from the dead or part way back from the dead. He can't be. Dead is dead. It always has been. Go back a million years. This can't be. Nobody who took a piss with Theodore Roosevelt is alive to talk about it."

No one knew what to say.

Shafer told me to go get HB and bring him back. I returned to the green room where HB was still gabbing with the senator. I motioned for him to come with me and as we headed for the control room, I asked how he'd feel about being a guest on the show, being interviewed about death.

"Me on TV? To talk about death? I suspect there are big pros and cons to that. Mainly cons. Would it be good for you?"

"I think it's just a crazy idea that will flame out pretty fast."

Buehler and Andy and others gathered outside the control room now looked at HB with new eyes. He was no longer a harmless old gent. He was something else.

In our brief absence Burt had filled the strained silence with details of his conversation with HB. Buehler was wide-eyed. Andy, meanwhile, was upset that booking HB could be taken seriously even for a moment.

Buehler said, "HB, now I understand what you said about never seeing television. They don't have TV in the afterlife, right? But look, we're all a little confused about this. We have to think it through."

"*Think it through?*" asked Andy, incredulous.

"As the man in charge here, HB, I have to ask, for starters, one basic question: are you standing here claiming to be dead right now? At this moment? And can you prove it?"

"How could I prove it? Do you want magic tricks. Do you want me to call down a bolt of lightning?"

Andy said, "Sure. That would work. Let's go outside and have lightning."

HB said, "Sorry, I was being sarcastic. I can't call down lightning. But I'm definitely dead. The person you're seeing isn't a real living person. It's just me briefly poured back into the costume of my body. I think of my body as something like a rented tuxedo, just something your soul wears until the dance on earth is done. I don't know where it goes when you die. Maybe there's an enormous cloakroom where all the empty bodies are hanging."

Most of the people in the room seemed to be having a jaw-dropping contest over that idea but Buehler was fixated on potential audience size. "Shit, can you imagine what the other networks would give for a booking like this? Andy, this is what I was saying about booking with *pizzazz*, a gargantuan audience-pull. Let's not be quick to dismiss this. Maybe there's a way."

"I don't want to be part of a way," said Andy.

"Well, that's easily fixed," snapped Buehler. "But look, HB, just one question for now, just as a sample. Is there a heaven and hell?"

"No."

"No? No heaven and no hell? *Neither*? Jesus F. Christ! Can you imagine the impact that fact *alone* would have?"

"The impact of a network imploding in idiocy," said Andy.

"We're talking about something with *worldwide* impact!"

"Yes, our bad judgment would have worldwide impact."

"You're so goddamn negative, Andy. It's news. Are you saying a report on the realities of death wouldn't be news?"

"Not if it's unadulterated bullshit," cried Andy.

"We don't have to vouch for it being true. We'd report both sides of the story. We could have a rebuttal segment the next day. Even the next hour."

"A *rebuttal*? Yeah, let's book the Pope to come on and rebut it. Come to your senses, Aaron."

"*You* come to your senses. Maybe you're not the right person to be executive producer of this program if you can't even begin to grasp the magnitude of this story."

This was getting loud. The control room crew and guests were listening raptly.

Burt, looking alarmed, tugged on my arm. "Lake, I think you and I and HB were planning to get breakfast, right?" Then he whispered to me, "This is going to get worse and we don't want to be part of it. Let's go."

I grabbed HB by the sleeve and we made a rush to the exit. I would have loved to hear the conversation we left behind, but Burt had us scampering, climbing the stairs to the street, emerging from the shadowy basement into the full light of day.

CHAPTER 13

It was a beautiful fall morning so instead of going for breakfast we walked into Central Park where Burt flagged down an empty hansom cab, an elegant horse-drawn carriage painted in regal purple with gold piping and fringe. It was a big one with a bench seat wide enough for the three of us to squeeze in, side by side.

I snuggled between a movie star and a dead guy. How many other women in history could say that?

"Geez, I didn't mean to start that ruckus," Burt said. "I swear it. I was just trying to toss out some happy horseshit, like some stupid thing I'd say for laughs at a party. I never thought anyone would take it seriously. But the big guy went for it like a big fat marlin taking the hook. What's his name again?"

"Aaron Buehler," I said. "I think he's just trying to prove that he's smarter than a roomful of TV people. He knows how to get the big ratings but we don't. But it'll never happen. Someone will talk him out of it, or force him out of it."

Burt said, "I'm guessing they're still standing there shouting at each other over whether to put a dead guy on their show. Not that you wouldn't be sensational, HB. So here's my question for the three of us: who's gonna laugh first?"

It was the perfect tension-releaser. I laughed first. Then we all did. The carriage driver glanced around at us trying to see what was so funny.

HB said, "I thought Buehler was going to crush the little guy but the little guy was a bulldog, wasn't he?"

"I'd love to hear Buehler explaining this to little Tammy tonight," I said. "But you know, a lot of people overheard that conversation. The story will leak out in no time and the tabloids will have a ball with it. And Buehler will have to back down, though he's a big macho farm boy who doesn't back down."

Burt said, "I don't know the man but I'm guessing he won't back down. He's got a huge erection over this and it's hard to say no to a huge erection."

"I hope Tammy doesn't notice," I said.

Burt said, "You don't get this kind of nutty stuff when you're dead, do you, HB?"

"I'll miss this, it's really fun," said HB. "And I'll miss *this*," he said, meaning the sights of autumn in Central Park.

"Who wants a hot dog?" Burt asked.

HB passed but I was starving and Burt asked the driver to stop while he jumped out at a vendor's stand and bought us hot dogs and coffee, which we gulped down listening to our horse's clippety-clop.

"I'm heading back to Florida in a few hours," Burt said. "You guys are invited to join me down there. Plenty of space, sunshine, good laughs. Why not come today?"

I said, "I don't think so. There's going to be some high drama in the office and I'd better be there, Burt, but thanks for asking."

We rode through the lower loop of the park and curved back northward. HB, who'd seemed lost in thought, came out of his silence and announced that he'd rather walk the rest of the way back to my apartment, so we stopped and let him off. Burt jumped down from the cab to give him a goodbye hug—a form of masculine affection that took HB by surprise. But he hugged back and then turned away.

Burt squeezed in next to me and we clip-clopped along. Then, to my surprise, we were holding hands. I don't know which of us initiated it.

Somewhat shyly Burt said, "Lake, you understand I'm in a relationship, right?"

I didn't know he was in a relationship but I kind of assumed it. I didn't know if Sally Field was still in the picture, or someone else, or whether he had a new relationship every week. I hadn't asked. But I was disappointed.

Burt asked the driver to stop. "I'm going to bail out on you too, Lake. Head downtown and get my bags."

Then he was out of the cab, standing alongside it, and we were suddenly at goodbye.

I knew I'd never see him again. I struggled for words, but emotions welled up and I couldn't get past a weak mumble until he put a fingertip over my lips.

"Look, you're right. There'll be a lot of *sturm* and a lot of *drang* out of this. But I've been around this business for a long time and when you have a battle between gratification and common sense, gratification kicks common sense's ass. Buehler's going to put HB on the show. Corporate will resist but then back off because nobody wants to be the one who scuttles the big idea.

"And then it'll be *your* call, Lake. Not theirs. He's your grandpa and he'll follow your advice. You have a veto. My instinct says you shouldn't let HB go on TV if it feels wrong because if it feels wrong, it'll go wrong. Because it's bad mojo. Whenever I think about doing a movie or something I stand back and make a mojo assessment. If it's bad, I get on my pony and ride. Even if it means leaving behind a good script or a load of money or friends I want to work with."

"How do you know if the mojo is good or bad?"

"You just feel it. But if you've got a smile on your face, that's a good sign. If your stomach feels like you just ate a spoiled pork chop, that's bad. Look, I don't know how HB's story would play out on TV but this afterlife stuff is not a casual issue to many people. I know religious nuts in Florida who might come up here to kill HB if they don't like what he says."

I said, "Killing HB might be redundant."

"Redundancy never stops a religious maniac. But look, as for your role in this, don't be a passive bystander. That's my advice. Use your power. These bosses of yours might not all be a-holes, but they all have different motives and none of those motives is about doing what's best for HB and you. You might have to stand up to them or resist them. This'll take courage. You might have to tell Buehler HB isn't doing it no matter how much Buehler wants it."

"I've never done anything courageous, Burt. I always take the safe way out."

"Which is what 99 percent of all people do. Lake, you don't have to be Joan of Arc but don't back down."

I jumped down from the cab and we embraced, and there was a kiss, a good sincere kiss which the driver interrupted, saying, "Hey, are you Clint Eastwood?"

Burt said, "No, I'm Scarlett O'Hara."

"No, you're Burt Reynolds," said the driver. "I always confuse you with Clint Eastwood."

"Clint will be glad to hear that," said Burt, handing the driver some cash. He gave me a little wave and some good eye contact and then turned away sharply as if hiding his face.

※ ※ ※

In just a few days two men had unexpectedly dropped into my life and seemed to have enriched it, certainly making unforgettable impacts. But now Burt was gone and HB would be gone soon. I realized I would always remember this ride in the park. I further realized it was the wrong time to be riding around feeling sorry for myself. So I got out of the cab and jogged home.

HB was there, finishing *Moby Dick*.

"How'd you do?" he asked.

"How'd I do?"

"With Burt. I figured you should have some time for a romantic ride in Central Park without your grandfather being there as chaperone."

I laughed. "You're trying to get me into a romance with Burt Reynolds?"

"I sure am. He's a great guy. And I thought I detected a little chemistry between the two of you."

"Burt Reynolds is aiming a little high for me, don't you think? A global movie star?"

"You're worthy of him. If I could leave you with Burt I'd consider my time here well spent."

"Well, thank you."

It was an awkward moment. I asked if he'd enjoyed *Moby Dick*.

He nodded.

"I read it in college," I said. "I failed to love it. HB, do you believe in destiny? Do you believe you're fated to have a certain life? To live out a script, sort of? Like Captain Ahab and that whale had to meet, right?"

"It wouldn't be much of book if they never met."

"I'm wondering if Burt and I will ever meet again. I bet no."

"There's no script. Don't count on a script to bring you together."

"You give such straightforward answers and not always what I want to hear. If you were a con man, you'd be prepared with a fabulous spiel about destiny and it would be just what I wanted."

"You still think I'm a con man?"

"No. I'm at 99 percent of believing in you but that last percentage point's a bitch. It's hard to believe something that everything and everybody would tell me just can't be true. But Burt said it could come down to me making the final judgment on your going on TV because the TV guys would have agendas which would not be based on doing what's right for you. Or me. So I couldn't rely on them being right. So I had to take responsibility."

"I don't see why you have to take responsibility for what I say. I never wanted to put you in that spot."

"But you have. And it's risky. Blocking what your boss wants is risky. Insubordination and getting fired is risky. On the other hand, going along with it and being a major figure in something that turns out to be a humiliating disaster is risky too. Being a partner in deception is risky, if that's what it came to."

"A partner in deception? Is that what you'd be?"

"Not just a junior partner but a senior partner. And I would get a lot or all of the blame and I would have a lot to lose. I busted my ass to get where I am professionally. I fought my way up in a man's world. I built a good reputation as a journalist. But that reputation's out the window if putting you on TV becomes a tremendous embarrassment."

"If putting me on TV helps you, I'm for it. If it doesn't, I'm against it. What would I have to do? Just sit in a chair and answer questions about death?"

"Yeah, that's all. Just reveal to millions of people the secrets of the afterlife."

He laughed. "It's all in a day's work."

I said, "Why don't I call the office and find out where we stand."

I called Jean Maxey. Her first words were, "I wanted to call you, but I didn't want to interrupt if you were bouncing the bedsprings with Burt."

"There was no bouncing, Jean. Two little kisses and some hand-holding."

"I heard the two of you ran off after the show and haven't been seen since."

"We took a hansom cab ride in the park."

"Romantic! Like Audrey Hepburn and Cary Grant."

"What movie was that?"

"I don't know. I just made it up. But a carriage ride is not what I would have done with Burt Reynolds," she said. "Can we get serious now?"

"Yes, get serious."

"I have a message for you: at two p.m. your presence is urgently demanded downtown at the Tower of Fear (corporate headquarters), top floor, executive conference room #1. And bring your grandfather. Is it true that Buehler wants to book him on the show to talk about death? *Huh?* There's lot of tension here but nobody knows what's going on."

I hadn't had a cigarette for ten years but yearned for one now.

"HB, how'd you like to go downtown with me and witness some big-time corporate bullshit?"

"I'd love to," he said. "But it's not like I've never seen corporate bs before. They had it in my day too, you know."

I took a fast shower, washed my hair, and jumped into an all-black Serious

Woman outfit complete with gleaming black high heels that lifted me to almost six feet tall, as impressive as I can be.

In the taxi, I said to HB, "Just promise me you're for real."

"I'm for real."

"Because putting you on TV if you're not for real would be bad for everybody and I'd veto it. It's fucking with the truth. It's bad mojo."

"What's mojo?"

"I wish you hadn't asked. It's not really part of my vocabulary. It's something about the magic of having things right. If you have things right, they tend to work out well. I'm counting on this meeting to tell us what kind of mojo we've got."

CHAPTER 14

The receptionist who met us as we exited the elevator was clad in black like me, but she wore black better. She was more stylish, taller, younger, shapelier, icier, and more sure of herself in her spike heels which hammered a get-out-of-my-way rhythm on the marble floor as she led us to conference room #1. I'm betting this woman inspired incessant behind-her-back puerile sniggering among the senior male executives on the floor.

The conference room featured a large, gleaming conference table at which all chairs were occupied, mostly by men, with female assistants hovering behind them. The meeting was clearly in full swing. I assumed they started without us intentionally to squeeze in candid discussion before they had to adjust to our presence.

Two junior people jumped to their feet, vacating chairs for us.

"Gentlemen and ladies," said Buehler, who loomed large at the head of the table, "may I introduce you to HB Taylor, the subject of this gathering. Mr. Taylor is a retired businessman from Ohio who asserts that he has been dead for thirty-one years but is somehow present here today and available as a guest on our morning broadcast.

"We are gathered here to review the merits and ramifications of this unprecedented booking idea. As you may know, Andy and I discussed it earlier in a control room conversation which the media has already found out about and distorted, sensationalizing and ridiculing it.

Andy and I have been fielding calls on this in the last few hours. There are indications that we can expect an earthquake in coverage as we go forward."

"I'm getting calls too," said Gary Warren, shaking his head. "I'm concerned about where this is going. We've got a lot of credibility at stake here."

Buehler said, "I want to say right away that we are approaching this proactively. We have already engaged the premier private investigation firm in Ohio. Our man there has been on the case only a few hours, but he's confirmed that an HB Taylor was a resident and town official of McGill, Ohio, for many years and died there in 1948 and was buried in the town graveyard."

"I could have saved you a hefty fee for that info," said HB.

Buehler hadn't introduced me, apparently forgetting who I am or not caring, but Andy Shafer jumped in to provide my name and chief writer title and, more importantly, my status as HB's granddaughter.

"His *alleged* granddaughter," said a formidable-looking man who turned out to be the corporate counsel, Raymond Delacore.

"Not *alleged*," said HB with a disarming smile. "She's it."

"As you wish," said Delacore, with a mock-deferential bow.

Buehler introduced the principal figures at the table: Andy Shafer, Delacore, the Standards & Practices Vice President Wick Sorenson (I didn't know he was a vice president), show hosts Gary Warren and cohost Gina Harkness. I was surprised to see Gina—she was normally excluded from important discussions. You could tell by her shrunken-down body language that she had no intention of saying a word.

Also at the table were Ken Barbour from the network news division, Kathy Dubrovnik from promotion, Sonya Lester from community relations, Myron Klein from Carlisle Audience Research, and Geoffrey Watkins from Owned & Operated Stations.

"Finally, we're privileged to have John Parmody, CEO of Parmody Market Consulting, with us, and two special guests, Dr. Laurel Goldman and Leonard Kinzer.

"Dr. Goldman is a widely esteemed psychologist who has flown down from Harvard to lend her expertise. Leonard Kinzer is a polygraph specialist and frequent contractor to the Federal Bureau of Investigation. HB, Dr. Goldman will now take you to another room where she will chat with you briefly to get a better sense of what you're saying. And then Mr. Kinzer will administer a polygraph examination."

"Are you fucking kidding?" erupted Andy Shafer. "We've never had a guest pre-interviewed by a shrink, let alone investigated by private dicks. We've never asked a guest to take a lie detector test. We'll never get another guest if this gets out. Nobody will submit to this. It's appalling. If I were running a network talk show in North Korea, I'd be dandy with it. But not here."

"I'm with Andy on this, Aaron," said Ken Barbour. "I spent three years reporting from Moscow and this reeks of Kremlin paranoia."

I was about to declare that I was with Andy and Ken—thus tapping into the courage I'd been storing up—but Delacore pushed in ahead of me.

"But you'll concede, Andy and Ken, that this is an extraordinary situation," he said in a patronizing tone. "We've never had a guest who claimed to be dead. If I'm wrong, please correct me. This circumstance justifies a Defcon-5 level of due diligence in terms of the network's reputation and the responsibility we should establish behind a decision to put Mr. Taylor on our air."

"You mean covering our ass while we exploit this hoax as much as possible," said Andy. "I can't believe we're even talking about this. I think we've got a good shot at looking like the stupidest fuckbrains in the history of television."

The contrast between Andy and Delacore was striking. Delacore was a caricature of a razor-cut, pin-striped, arrogant, hot-shot lawyer and pillar of the elite establishment. Andy's inclination was antiestablishment, which might have been evident from his purple Grateful Dead T-shirt and non-designer jeans.

Lawyers and journalists tend to share a mutual distaste and they are instinctively at odds but these two seemed to be of one mind against putting HB on TV. Delacore's motive was protecting the corporation; Andy's was protecting respect for broadcasting. (Mine was protecting HB and myself.)

"We have serious responsibility here," Delacore said. "The audience response to Mr. Taylor's appearance could be thermonuclear, given the sensitive material that might come up, especially on the religion front."

"Like what?" asked the community relations woman, Sonya Lester.

"Like what? Like does God exist? Is there an afterlife? He's already said there's no heaven and hell. We could have some very outraged audience pushback over subject matter like this."

(Which is just what Burt Reynolds told me.)

Myron Klein, the audience research guy, spoke up. "We have a high percentage of audience in religion-intensive states, mainly the South. Hold on, I'll give you some numbers on that."

He began madly leafing through the pages of a sloppy-looking binder four inches thick, muttering in frustration at his inability to find the numbers he wanted.

Sonya Lester couldn't restrain herself. "Aaron, this is really, really where this conversation should begin. Cardinal Rule Number One is that religion is the third rail. Step on it and you bring down shitstorms beyond all shitstorms."

Gary Warren said, "Exactly. I have to withdraw from this. I don't want to be the one who does this interview. No offense, Mr. Taylor and Lake. I'm sure you understand. It sounds like a massive career-wrecker and we've all got careers to think about. I didn't spend years building my reputation to toss it all away in a clown interview."

When the star gets nervous, nervousness becomes a fast-spreading virus. Buehler said, "Gary, calm down, we haven't decided to do it. Don't make up your mind too soon. If we need to, we could have Gina do the interview. Couldn't we, Gina?"

Gina said, "Would you want me to play it for laughs or play it straight?"

"Which is worse?" asked Andy.

"This would have to be handled with ultra seriousness," said Delacore.

"It'd be throwing Gina to the wolves," said Andy.

"With all respect," said Ken Barbour, "the challenge of an interview this explosive would be way over her head. Let's be honest about that."

The women at the table flinched at that insult. Gina was clearly wounded and Gary's face showed displeasure, not just at the put-down to Gina but at the thought of giving up the spotlight to her for an interview of "ultra" seriousness, even if the spotlight might be a career-wrecker.

Sonya Lester didn't get the point. "But giving it to Gina might be brilliant. We could pitch it as an optimistic, audience-building story in a time of fear and pessimism. She could take some of the negativity about death out of it and make it a family thing with a touch of lightheartedness, like an interview with a wacky uncle everyone loves. We could angle it that way. How to deal with eccentric relatives at Thanksgiving."

"Yeah," said Andy. "What to do when Uncle Bob shows up for Thanksgiving and claims he's been dead for thirty-one years. It happens at my house every year."

"This wacky uncle approach would turn a possible first-magnitude history-making TV opportunity into a weird fluff piece relegated to the little lady of the show," said Kathy Dubrovnik. "If you're going to do something big, go big. Don't pull punches. I can't publicize it as an innocuous piece of crap we hope viewers don't notice."

"Can't we just forget about this thing?" asked Ken Barbour, looking supremely annoyed. "It's total horseshit and we all know it. We all know it."

HB laughed.

It seemed like a pivotal point. War clouds were forming. Emotions were starting to boil.

At this moment Dr. Goldman cleared her throat and said, "I'd really like to get started with my chat with Mr. Taylor."

"Under protest," declared Andy.

"Bad precedent. Ill-advised," said Ken Barbour.

"Due diligence," growled Delacore.

HB then changed everything. "I have no problem with this. I'd be glad to chat with the young lady. Let's do it."

"You don't have to, HB," I said.

"No, let's oblige," he said, getting to his feet.

I gave him a quizzical look. He looked back at me and winked.

So that was it. HB's easygoing willingness seemed to erase the conflict. Glances were exchanged around the table, showing surprise at such a quick and peaceable solution.

We watched as the shrink and FBI guy escorted HB out of the room. I heard HB asking Kinzer if J. Edgar Hoover was still alive.

I felt the anxiety you must feel seeing your child led away for a medical procedure. And I thought: HB comes from a time when people trusted authority, and that trust might not be his friend today. On the other hand, he's a cool guy. Let's see what happens.

* * *

The discussion resumed.

Buehler turned to John Parmody. "John, you're the savant, what's your take on this so far?"

"I'm thinking somebody's been smoking primo weed, perhaps supplemented by rot-gut tequila. The really raw stuff that burns like aviation fuel."

Everyone chuckled.

I'd seen Parmody in action, He was a famous TV consultant, smooth and very pleased with himself, somewhat charismatic, imputed to possess godlike wisdom for which he received extravagant compensation. The more he was paid, the more his advice was valued and heeded, even though it seemed paltry to me because it was always wrapped in an on-the-one-hand/on-the-other-hand context that made it useless. Seek controversy but stay out of trouble. Make segments shorter but let them breathe. Book more hard news guests but emphasize lifestyle topics. Another thing I'd noticed: he always left early and was never present when decisions were made. Thus he left no fingerprints on mistakes and was clear of all blame.

Buehler said, "My very first insight, John, was to see the potential of this to be the grand slam of all grand slams, ratings-wise. *The secrets of death—on our air!* Millions and, via replay and translation, ultimately billions of viewers. *Billions.* We've been in a ratings funk but this could blast us into orbit for months or years."

"Could be, Aaron, but it's always risk versus reward, isn't it?" said Parmody. "Low risk guarantees low reward. But if you want the grand-slam rewards you have to swing for the fences, which risks falling on your butt."

"Big-time," said Andy.

"Indeed," said Parmody. "So you have to bust your tail to get to the right balance. Brainstorm. Think big but be aggressive about diluting risk. Aaron, put all the talented creative people at this table to work. Challenge them. Let's try it right now, people. Folks, give me some ideas off the top of your noggins."

Delacore said, "The obvious way is to pretape the interview with Mr. Taylor. Then edit out the objectionable parts."

Andy said, "That gives you a watered-down piece of shit that's obviously been censored. And who decides what's objectionable? If a bunch of Nervous Nellies from network do it, they'll cut everything between hello and goodbye. There won't be anything left of it."

Wick Sorenson spoke up, "I think I'm the Nervous Nellie from Network that Andy's referring to. But I agree with Andy. If you over-sanitize, you dilute the impact and if you're retreating on impact, why do this in the first place? To me, the risk is too big and the impact could kill us. I'm opposed to it."

Parmody said, "Thanks, Wick. Let's get some more input."

Sonya Lester was eager to suggest an idea. "How about instead of the usual one-on-one with Gary, we broaden it to include a priest, rabbi, and minister, and an Islamic guy to react to HB and counter his claims. Put the onus on the clergymen instead of us. The interaction would be fantastic."

Parmody: "Yeah, that's interesting, but it makes a religion piece out of this. HB gets buried in the ecclesiastical yakety-yak. Give me another."

Geoffrey Watkins: "How about using the HB story as one part of a multipart report on great frauds, swindles, and con jobs? We'd use HB's story to lead off a series during November sweeps."

Parmody: "But you'd be calling HB a fraud, devaluing your primary asset. Give me another."

Ken Barbour: "How about Gary taking HB back to his Ohio town and doing a walk- around with HB giving memories of the way things were while underplaying the thing about being in the afterlife. Sort of a nostalgia piece."

"Nostalgia's pure gold," said Parmody, "but do you want to downplay the back-from-death aspect? Isn't that the grabber?"

Parmody stood up. "You're starting to tick, guys. You're not there yet but I think I've got you on the launchpad. Aaron, this is how you kick-start the creative process. Keep your eyes on the risk/reward balance. Don't fear the big risk but first you want some solid ass-covering from the psychologist and lie detector guy. If they walk back in here and tell you the story's a crock, deep-six it like the hottest potato in world history. Then spin it to the media about how responsibly you acted in rejecting it."

Everybody smiled at that.

Parmody stood up and grabbed his coat. "And now I have to fly, literally. I'm giving a speech in Atlanta tonight."

Buehler thanked him effusively. Then he was gone in a flash. High escape velocity.

Andy said, "So now we know just what to do, right? I could put my boys through a year of college for what Parmody's going to bill for that doubletalk. Can we get back to the simple though still ridiculous question of putting HB on TV to discuss being dead?"

Buehler said, "You know what Parmody left out? He left out that when the huge rewards start rolling in, nobody remembers to give credit to the boss who seized the opportunity and took the risk when the people around him didn't have vision or cojones to support him. That's what I learned from farming and it translates right over into everything else."

That shut everyone up. We were city people and didn't know that farming entails heroic decisions.

Buehler then seemed to fall into deep reflection, but he snapped out of it and addressed Myron Klein. "Hey, audience research guy. Let's talk numbers. What've you got on audience size if we put HB on?"

Myron looked terrified. "I've got nothing. There's no way to predict that. This would be unprecedented. There's no comparables."

"Screw the comparables. Gimme a guess. How many would tune in for the answers to the secrets of death?"

"In the seven to nine a.m. slot? With people hurrying off to work, getting the kids off to school, it's a revolving audience. We usually have a core of about 3.4 million, with most viewers staying for only twenty minutes at a time before cycling out with new viewers tuning in to replace them. There'd probably be a lot fewer tuning out if a dead guy was the guest and probably a lot more coming in by word-of-mouth. We'd steal viewers from our rival networks."

"Pumping it up to what?"

"I don't know. Four and a half, maybe five million?"

"Just five goddamn million? For the secrets of death?"

"Okay, we could call it eight million. Who knows? Fifteen? Mr. Buehler, you can't hold me to these numbers."

"Stop clinging to your fat-ass blue binder and think big for a minute. Don't you people know how to think big?"

"Twenty million? How about twenty-five million?—my final offer," Myron said, laughing. Everyone laughed.

"Are you telling me we could hit a goddamn twenty-five million? And we could then do a post-show taping of a Part Two of the interview and run it the next day for another twenty-five or more. That's fifty million plus. Nobody's ever hit that number on morning TV. Am I wrong?"

Myron sat there with a silly look on his face.

Everyone else seemed to be inspecting their fingernails.

CHAPTER 15

Buehler grabbed his phone and told an assistant to prod Dr. Goldman and the lie detector guy. "I know they haven't had much time but I want them in here."

Buehler then turned to the group. "Look, I'm sitting here thinking that over the course of time lots of people have talked about what death is like. Great authors, theologians, religious scholars, philosophers, poets, novelists, movie writers, even comedy writers. They were allowed to write about death without being able to *prove* anything, because everyone knew they *couldn't* prove squat. They were just making things up."

Wick Sorenson said, "They call it poetic license or artistic license. The writer gets some leeway in the interest of a more effective story."

"But journalists do *not* get poetic license," said Andy, jumping in. "Just the opposite. We're not allowed to take liberties with reality to improve the story. Though it does happen from time to time."

Aaron came back at him. "It's all about how we position it or 'balance' it, as Parmody would say. We're not reporting that an afterlife definitely exists. We're saying we've got a credible-seeming guest who says that. HB, not us. HB is like all the other writers except for his new wrinkle: he's claiming he's actually experienced death. Which would make him closer to the truth than everybody else. It's also what makes him newsworthy, and therefore a colossal mega-get for us. What he says doesn't have to be *verified* any more than anyone else talking about death has ever been verified, because nothing about death is verifiable. So we have poetic license."

"With all respect, that's nonsense, Aaron," said Delacore. "If he says it on our air we're giving it a platform. If he's a hoax, we're aiding and abetting a hoax. If it's bullshit, we're aiding and abetting bullshit. And that's a profoundly damaging position for us. We cannot have our brand linked to bullshit. And forgive my tiresome use of the word 'bullshit.' No other word suffices. It's the precisely correct word in this context."

"*Le mot juste,*" said Wick.

Andy said, "Let's put it to a vote. HB says he's come back from the dead. Raise your hand if you think that's remotely possible."

Nobody raised a hand. I had a slight twitch in the wrist but suppressed it.

"Okay," said Andy, "we're on the record. Unanimously. I think that stops this thing in its tracks. Unless journalistic values have changed in the last two minutes."

"Hold on now," said Buehler. "All we have to do is to precede HB with the announcer saying, 'The views of HB Taylor do not represent the views of this network. The network takes *no responsibility* for the accuracy of his views.'"

"But that's obvious lawyer bullshit," said Andy, disgusted.

Delacore did a loud fake cough.

"Yes, lawyer bullshit is exactly right, let's be honest about it," said Wick Sorenson. "A disclaimer saying they're not *our* views doesn't get us off the hook morally. Our standards and practices don't accept putting blatantly untrue and offensive views on the air. HB's story might be in that category. We don't require guests to prove their stories to us before we put them on the air but we have to have reasonable confidence that their story has merit and they are who we say they are. So far we've heard nothing that gives me that confidence with HB Taylor."

None of us knew much about the fine points of standards and practices but Wick Sorenson got a lot of respect. TV people are often flaky, but he wasn't flaky. TV people are seldom intellectual, but he was intellectual. We teasingly called him a censor, but he was nothing like the Soviet say-no-to-everything and hide-the-truth version of a censor. He was the let's-find-a-better-way-to-do-it censor, the adult in the room.

I said, "Could I get a word in?"

All eyes turned to me. I could feel people thinking, "Remind me who she is. Oh, yes, the granddaughter."

As I started, I heard a slight tremble in my voice. "I've been with HB since Sunday when he arrived out of nowhere and identified himself as my long-dead grandfather, which I considered utterly impossible. But since then we've talked a lot about our lives and he has been perfect—perfect—in the accuracy of his recollections and his ability to produce facts and memories and even feelings that no impostor could have known about. If this was a deception I marvel at its proficiency. I don't think he is a fraud and I don't think he's here to deceive me, or you. But it's still a big jump to believe in coming back from death."

"I'm impressed by that," said Wick. "If Lake believes, or is close to believing, that this story *isn't* false, we have to take that seriously because as the granddaughter she's a better judge than any of us. Plus she's a credible journalist. So this is a step toward reducing my objections. And Aaron is correct that the story doesn't have to be 10 percent verifiable. Some true and important stories might be hard or impossible to verify. Provability isn't always possible and, by the way, neither is *un*provability. No viewer could prove that HB is wrong."

"There we go! That's our defense!" cried Aaron, thumping the table. "If you're accusing us of horseshit, try to prove us wrong. You can't."

"That's not exactly what I'm saying, Aaron. I'm saying we can't rely on an evidence argument, either way, to decide whether to put HB on TV."

"So where the hell does that leave us?"

"It's a leadership decision. Leaders frequently have to make decisions without full knowledge of the facts or certainty that the facts are accurate and true."

Buehler felt the responsibility land on his shoulders. He quickly tried to offload it onto someone else, picking me. "What would *you* do?"

"I just don't want him exploited or embarrassed," I said. "If he's going to look like a fake and if nobody supports him, that's what I *don't* want. So don't do it if you don't feel okay with it. And if we don't feel okay with it, I'm going to veto it."

Buehler leaped at the chance to pull rank. "Excuse me, but you don't have the authority to veto anything. That authority is mine, young lady."

The patronizing "young lady" pissed me off, me and the other women. I got a rush of balls.

"No, Mr. Buehler, I do have a veto. It's called the 'granddaughter veto.' If a granddaughter advises a grandfather not to do something, the grandfather doesn't do it. I get this authority because I'm the only one here acting solely in his interest."

"But you have your own interest to act in. If this works out well it will be a very large feather in your cap, on top of your already-bright future in this company."

"Really? What's my name?"

"Your name? Come on now."

"You're telling me about my bright future but you don't even know who I am."

"I'm sorry. It slipped my mind. It's a stressful day. But I don't think you want to throw away a bright future by getting in the way of this opportunity for the network."

"The network wouldn't have this opportunity if it wasn't for me."

"An act of disloyalty would nullify everything you've done."

"Is that a threat? Are you going to shitcan me if I keep HB off the show?"

I could see he was an inch from saying, "You're goddamn right I'll shitcan you," but Delacore saw it too. Suddenly a new element entered the picture, for everyone: *litigation*. Not just Lake Whistler suing for wrongful firing but also a wider investigation into the HB booking, if it backfired. Lawsuits, depositions, testifying in court, expensive lawyers, black marks on reputations, names in the tabloids, sudden unemployment, etc.

Delacore said, "Hey, let's gear down a bit here. Let's everybody calm down."

"I absolutely wasn't threatening you," said Buehler. But he was. Imagine getting fired because I *prevented* a man who said he's dead from going on network TV. I would spend three years in law school for a promise that I could argue this case in court.

Andy flashed me a sly thumbs-up–"I'm loving this" sign.

The door opened. Dr. Goldman, Leonard Kinzer, and HB entered the room.

***

HB, who was expressionless, sat down next to me. He raised a hand to cover his face so only I could see and winked at me, his second wink of the day. His eyes were twinkling.

Standing awkwardly chairless, Dr. Goldman said, "Aaron, I think we should start with Leonard."

Kinzer, a slightly bald and rotund middle-aged man who looked like he'd spent his life suffering from acid indigestion, stepped forward. It seemed to me he was struggling to fight off laughter.

"This is one to write home about, really," he said. "I've conducted hundreds of polygraph exams. A few of them were failures for various reasons and some were inconclusive and therefore useless. But nothing like this. This was…not possible."

That created a stir.

"The polygraph receives information from sensors measuring a person's breathing rate, pulse, blood pressure, and perspiration." Kinzer took a dramatic pause, probably the first of his life. "Mr. Taylor had none of those."

Kinzer raised his hands, palms up, in a gesture that said, "I don't have the slightest effing idea how to explain this."

"Mr. Taylor had no vital signs," Kinzer said. "None whatsoever. So nothing registered on the graph. I replaced all the sensors and did it again. Nothing. Flat line. It was as if I'd taped the sensors to the leg of your desk." A giddy grin broke out on his face. I suspect there are very few good laughs in the life of a lie detector guy. Kinzer was enjoying this.

"Mr. Taylor permitted me to check his pulse and I did, but there was no detectable pulse. He's a nice, cooperative gentleman and invited me to take his blood pressure. I did that and the result was the same. *Nothing.* The systolic was zero, the diastolic was zero. Zero over zero. The man has no blood pressure."

Ken Barbour asked, "Mr. Kinzer, what do we usually call a person with no vital signs?"

"We call that person a dead person."

"Could a person with no breathing rate, no pulse, no blood pressure, and no perspiration be considered alive? Look at Mr. Taylor. Does he seem dead?"

"No. He seems alive and perfectly healthy. I don't get it. This is above my pay grade."

Buehler said, "Dr. Goldman, what've you got?"

"I'm as baffled as Mr. Kinzer. Of course my time with him was far too brief to draw even tentative observations let alone to slap on a diagnostic label but my initial impression is that he is stable and I would even use the word normal. He tells an incredible story of coming back from death to visit his beloved granddaughter. But I've interviewed many delusional people and, other than the content of his story, he gives no clue of being delusional. I can't explain that without a lot more time with him. He shows no signs of thought impairment or character disorder or mental illness. He's suffered no apparent trauma. His memory is good. We did a few puzzles and word games and his scores were above average. As Mr. Kinzer said, he was cooperative and good-humored. I wish all patients were like him."

Buehler thanked Goldman and Kinzer and they left.

Buehler said, "He's got no vital signs so he's dead. He's got no delusions so he's normal or normal enough. What more can we ask of him?"

Delacore was still probing. "Mr. Taylor, I'm obliged to ask whether you have received any payments or financial gifts from Ms. Whistler?"

"Yes," said HB. "She gave me $100 from her bank machine for getting-around cash. I took a few taxis and bought Lake a beer at Yankee Stadium and took a ferry to see the Statue of Liberty, which is very inspiring. Has everyone here done that? I still have about $70. Should I give it back to her?"

"She gave you nothing other than the original $100?"

"Nope."

"Has anyone else given you money, gifts, property, promises of financial gain, or anything else to induce you to tell your story?"

"Nope."

* * *

HB gave the table a tap.

"I know what's bothering you. The proof issue. You've hired detectives, I've talked to a psychologist, I took a lie detector, and none of these things give a hint I'm not telling the truth. But there's one thing you haven't thought of. Something that will prove my story is for real."

"And just what is that, Mr. Taylor?" asked Delacore.

"My imminent demise. I'm going to cease to exist sometime in the next few days. My stay here only lasts a week or so. I don't know how many days exactly but I got here Sunday and this is Thursday so I've used up five of my days and sometime over the weekend I'll be up in a puff of smoke. So if you can hang on till Monday, my case will be proven."

"That's not proof. A disappearance is easy to fake," said Delacore.

"Maybe so," said HB, "but not as perfectly as it's going to happen for real."

Andy said, "He's saying that he'll vanish on Saturday or Sunday so if we're going to do this, we have to do it live on *tomorrow's* show."

That was a powerhouse jolt to a bunch of TV people. TV people thrive on the adrenaline that comes with racing the clock to an on-air deadline. You could just hear the clatter of brains figuring out how to produce the TV event of all-time in a matter of hours. It was 3:40 p.m. Friday morning's airtime was seven a.m.

Delacore: "You're saying vanishing would prove your story, but we'd have to put you on the air *before* you prove it by vanishing."

"Well, that's the best I can do," said HB. "I didn't make the rules. At least you'd have proof on Monday."

"Tomorrow morning is just not optimal," said Buehler. "I was thinking we hold it till the November ratings sweeps. Build up to a stupendous audience. We can't get the maximum audience doing it on a crash basis for tomorrow. We need a promo plan, a media plan, a huge publicity effort. So much stuff. Politics. Interviews. Ballyhoo. Who knows what complications we'll run into. Tomorrow is not acceptable, dammit. We've got to get an extension."

"You'll have to pull some pretty large strings to get an extension," said HB, smiling.

"We've got the clout. I'll tell you that, my friend. We can do it."

"Aaron, you're not understanding this," said Delacore. "We have no clout. Nobody has this kind of clout. It's got to be tomorrow."

"Okay. So we'll tape it and run it later with perfect buildup."

"No," said Andy. "You can't sit on a thing like this any more than you could tape a major assassination or volcano eruption and hold it for two months. The pressure would be beyond belief. The story's already coming out. It's got to be tomorrow, live."

But Delacore brought everything to a standstill with an out-of-left-field distraction. "Before we rush off, I'm wondering if HB's whole angle is not about a money scam at all but about a conspiracy to get airtime on national television, possibly as a first step in promoting some insidious purpose or conspiracy. This would explain why a target like Lake Whistler was chosen. She has the TV connection and sooner or later someone who'd be taken seriously would suggest making HB a guest on her show and the network would fall for it because of its lust for the big audience."

"And I'm the one with the lust for the big audience?" asked Buehler, indignant. "The whole HB scam was aimed at manipulating *me*, is that what you're suggesting?"

Andy spoke up. "Wasn't this thing preposterous enough without dragging in conspiracy theories? Aaron, we need a call on this. Now."

Ken Barbour sat forward and cleared his throat for attention. "Before you rule on this, Aaron, I want to say that I'm advising the news division to withdraw participation in this because we do not recognize it as a legitimate news story and it would tarnish our respect as a news organization. So Ed Ramos will not sit in on the interview."

"So Gary's out, Gina's out, and Ramos is out," said Andy. "Who's in? How about the weather woman? Or how about the elevator man in my building? Fernando."

Then Gina Harkness surprised everybody.

She raised her hand timidly and while no one recognized her desire to speak, she spoke anyway.

"I've been sitting here thinking back to when we started this show. Do you remember how idealistic and excited we were? It wasn't going to be just blab-and-gab, something to gaze at between headlines and weather reports. We thought it could be a great opportunity to inform and inspire thought. There'd be a whole range of news and entertainment and new ideas. Sure, there'd be lightweight stuff—and I knew that would be my role, not interviewing the Secretary of State. But there'd also be serious stuff. Great stuff. Bright people with fresh ideas. We'd put stuff out there, and let viewers make up their own minds. We'd be brave. We'd take risks. Maybe we forgot about that but now we have a chance to be brave and take a risk. And Gary, *you* have to do it. This is your show. You da man. If you won't do the interview, screw it. Nobody does it. I may be over my head but that's what I think."

I did a brave thing: I applauded. Just me.

Gina nodded at me, appreciatively.

Andy said, "I still think it's a horrible idea but I agree with Gina that if we're gonna do it, it has to be Gary. Not anybody else. We can't take a huge gamble and not have our main man out there taking responsibility for it, putting his credibility behind it."

It was a moment when Buehler should have stepped in with substantial leadership. But he didn't. He seemed to have tuned out.

Gary said, "Okay."

He took a breath and went on. "Look, Gina is right. On everything. Gina, thanks for reminding us what we wanted this show to be. So I'll do it. It's crazy but I'll do it. With appropriate disclaimers, of course.

"And also with two provisions. First, I'm not going to be my usual Mr. Nice Guy. I'm not going to toss softballs or sit there nodding like I'm buying everything HB says. If I need to be adversarial, I'll do that. If it makes people uncomfortable seeing me get aggressive with a nice gentleman like HB, so be it. Do you understand that, HB?"

"Fine with me. I enjoy a good joust," said HB.

"Second, instead of me asking the questions, I want the questions to come from viewers. I'll just be the middleman, reading chosen called-in questions off index cards, with me jumping in with follow-ups as necessary. Someone will have to screen the questions to keep out wacko stuff and redundancy and make good choices. You're a Yale man, Wick—"

"Columbia," corrected Wick.

"Okay, you're a Columbia man, so could you screen the questions? I think it's better that Lake and our writing staff have nothing to do with the questions so it doesn't look rigged."

I started to object in defense of my department but on second thought, I was relieved. A blame orgy was a strong possibility if this thing bombed and I didn't want my writers or me being blamed. Plus there was the hugely suspicious-looking matter of HB just happening to be my grandfather.

The urge to get started with preparations immediately galvanized the room.

Andy said, "Aaron, say the word. Are we doing it?"

Aaron looked dazed. "Doing it?"

"Putting HB on the show tomorrow morning?"

At this point momentum rushed in and seized command. People were on their feet moving away from the table, anxious to get going. When the door opened, I glimpsed a dozen subordinates waiting in the hallway. Delacore and Barbour raced out and others followed. Kathy Dubrovnik asked HB if he would come downstairs to a studio floor and tape some promos, which would be used in a massive onslaught of publicity throughout the evening and overnight hours. Following her, HB turned and asked me if we could go for a drink when he was done taping. "Not that I can drink but I like the atmosphere. I'm having a ball. Never thought it would be like this."

Sonya Lester, who was already out of the room, turned around and stopped Gary Warren as he exited. Smiling broadly, she said to him, "This is such a win-win, Gary. America gets to hear a fascinating interview and we kick the butts of our competition."

Gary said, "Lose-lose is also possible," and brushed past her.

Aaron Buehler sat silently as the room emptied. Andy lingered, asking him, "Are you okay, boss? Is this what you want? You didn't exactly blow the bugle to start the charge."

Buehler mumbled something and then, more clearly, said, "Make hay when the sun shines, bubba."

Andy glanced at me and mouthed the word "bubba." I returned his glance and we rolled our eyes. We both realized there'd been almost no discussion or evaluation of HB's actual story. It wasn't even certain that a decision had been made.

It didn't matter. The debate was over.

*　*　*

However, after an emergency conference call that ended at eleven p.m., the company's board of directors canceled HB's appearance.

The board had been unable to contact its chairman and CEO, Richard Creighton, who was on a plane from Tokyo. In the absence of Creighton's extremely forceful leadership, the board took the cowardly way out, nixing HB's interview on grounds of "the extraordinarily limited time to properly evaluate its concerns regarding potentially turbulent consequences," meaning repercussions from enraged viewers and religious groups, infuriated sponsors facing customer backlashes, and opportunistic senators and congressmen who would take joy in stirring up much-dreaded intervention by the Federal Communications Commission.

But by the time the board reached its decision, the network's unprecedented publicity barrage had created a national clamor to see the HB interview. Going ahead with it was more acceptable than canceling it and looking stupid or fearful, so the board quietly pulled back its earlier decision. The cancellation decision was never announced. It was replaced with no decision.

HB and I missed all this. We were in a bar on West 79th Street, sitting with a bunch of carousing croquet players who were drinking heavily after a tournament victory in Central Park.

"So HB, tell me about the winks," I said.

"The winks? They gave me a lie detector test and it proved I'm dead. They gave me a psychological exam and it proved I'm normal. Both conclusions are true. The results couldn't have been anything else. Hence the winks."

"I went into that meeting ready to use my veto," I said. "I was waiting for my gut to tell me the thing was all wrong. I never got that message."

"The mojo was good?"

"I had my eyes glued to the mojo meter but never got a bad reading. Gina was great and Gary came through but most of what people said was useless. If there was anyone in that room to have serious doubts about, it was Aaron Buehler, not you. I watched you in action and I think you're a cool guy, rock-solid. I think you're gonna be fine on TV. I can't wait to see it. I'm not worried that we're up to something bad. I don't think we're fucking with the truth. I'm nervous as hell but I think it'll be an amazing experience."

"If I could drink to that, I would," he said.

We arrived at the studio around five thirty a.m. Hundreds of people were standing around outside, shouting to HB, waving homemade placards for and against him ("DEAD MAN TALKING" was my favorite). A squad of security guys cleared a path for us.

We entered the building and descended into the production space.

CHAPTER 16

Andy Shafer lit up when he saw us. His first words were, "Guess how many called-in questions we've got already?"

He was pumped. Everyone was.

"It's over 2,000 since we opened the lines at five a.m. Kathy Dubrovnik and her people did a fantastic job getting the word out. Did you turn on your TV last night? HB was everywhere. More promos than programs."

At Andy's suggestion we bypassed the green room and spent our preshow time hiding out in the same empty editing room where HB huddled with Burt Reynolds. Assistants brought in coffee and bagels. The makeup woman came in and applied makeup. "I probably haven't had makeup on my face since my funeral," HB said. The makeup woman giggled.

I considered a glass of scotch but decided not to. Not before six a.m.

HB said, "Lake, I don't care if anyone else believes me or if anyone watching this show believes me but I want *you* to believe me. And if you don't, this week has been a waste of time."

Wick Sorenson came in and sat down with us. Wick usually wore casual clothes but today he was wearing a dark suit and looked like the dean of students. Later I realized everyone was dressed better than usual, maybe because bosses and important visitors would be around—and in fact all production spaces were jammed with unfamiliar guests. I was glad I'd worn the black dress, which would be appropriate for a postshow celebration if HB did well or a firing squad if it was disastrous.

Wick said, "Your segment is set for ten minutes and we'll probably extend for a second segment if the first goes well, but we've got enough viewer questions to last until Christmas. I'm putting together a good mix."

"Got any advice for me?" asked HB.

"Advice? Well, succinct is better than verbose. Concrete is better than abstract. Don't try to be funny because it often comes out wrong. Don't use off-color vocabulary. Mainly we just want good answers. We're hoping for positive answers. In the morning show environment people want to start their day on an upbeat note."

"Is death upbeat?"

"Do your best," Wick said. "HB and Lake, you might have heard that I lecture sometimes at Columbia and other schools. European literature. Last night I went looking for a passage from Dante that was buzzing around in my mind. Let me read it."

He took a piece of notepaper from his jacket pocket and read aloud:

In that heaven which receives most of God's light
Have I been,
and have seen things that no one
descending from up there
has the knowledge or power to tell.

Wick said, "The reason this passage stuck in my mind is that when I read it, I realized Dante came up against the challenge of describing the mystery and magnitude of heaven and knew he couldn't pull it off, in that sentence anyway. So he backed away. He faked it. He said no one could do it. No one had the knowledge or power to tell what you see in heaven."

"I guess that was pretty clever," said HB.

"All writers do it when they come up against their limits. They evade what they can't handle. They write around it. But Dante made it work, didn't he? He made indescribability an attribute of death. He said death was too fantastic to imagine."

"But you want me to go on TV and describe what Dante couldn't."

"You've got a big advantage over Dante. You've been there."

"But he had a big advantage over me. Genius."

"You have real observation going for you. You've seen it. You're like an explorer who comes to the top of a peak and looks down and sees a whole new civilization. All you have to do is tell us what you saw, in plain language. You don't have to be a master of description. You don't have to know everything about it. Just tell what it's like, and that will be breathtaking. Look, Dante talks about knowledge and power. You have that knowledge and we're giving you power by putting you on TV."

HB said, "I'm wondering if I can rise to the occasion. You've got me worried that I'm supposed to deliver something bigger than what I've got in me. I sling the bull pretty well after a few scotches, but I am not up to the challenge of defining death. And for another thing, I don't know that much about death. I'm relatively new at it. When did Dante write that?"

"The early 1300s," Wick said.

"So he's been dead, what, 600-plus years. He's had the full experience by now. Imagine how great he'd be on your show. I wish he was doing it instead of me."

Wick said, "We tried to book him but his English is atrocious."

"We'd have to use subtitles," I said.

The humor broke the tension, but HB was still nervous. He said, "I'm afraid I'm going to be a disappointment."

Wick said, "No. Nobody will be disappointed."

(It occurred to me that Wick's reward for trying to encourage HB with the Dante quote was that he'd put himself in a dangerous position: if HB walked out because Wick unnerved him, Wick would get the blame for a major network embarrassment. I also realized that Wick, whose job was keeping the show within the network's responsible boundaries, was now helping to produce a segment many viewers would consider a historic breach of responsible boundaries. Wick had a lot on the line. And so, I realized, did I. Whatever happened, I would be forever labeled as the dead guy's granddaughter.)

"Okay, I'll do it," said HB, to our relief. "But I have a condition."

"Name it."

"I want Lake out there sitting with me."

"Fine," said Wick.

"Not a chance!" I yelped. "Forget it. Absolutely not. I have violent stage fright. I'll puke. I've never been on TV."

"Lake," Wick said, "I'm sorry, but duty calls. You've got to do this. You won't have to say a word."

"Just to hold my hand," said HB. "Once I start jabbering, I'll settle down."

"I like it," said Wick. "It's better than HB sitting there solo. It humanizes him to be with his granddaughter."

Wick stood. "I'll go fix it with Andy."

He was halfway out the door when I called him back. "Wick, what's *your* opinion on all of this? Your honest opinion?"

He paused for a moment. "Common sense says this is insane and inadvisable. But I was inspired by what Gina said about letting viewers decide, and that's our defense if this thing blows up on us. Gary was inspired too. Wasn't that an amazing turnaround? He's actually enthusiastic about this."

He left. The makeup woman came back and powdered my face.

"My hands are shaking," I said.

"Happens all the time, dear," she said. "Just keep your hands in your lap, out of sight."

When she was gone, HB said, "Lake, thanks for going out there with me."

I didn't reply. Didn't trust my voice.

Andy stuck his head in the door.

"Ready for your TV debut, Lake?"

"I'm terrified,' I said.

"We're up to more than 5,000 questions. Buehler is over the moon about how big this is going to be. He's had about twelve orgasms."

"What's an orgasm?" HB asked.

Andy laughed. "I guess they didn't use the term in your day, HB. Lake, explain it to him. You're on in three."

A minute later a young woman came and led us to the studio set, which looked like the living room of well-decorated and highly WASPy suburban home. We were seated on an orange couch. The only people in the room, besides us, were the camera operators and a few crew guys.

Gary hurried in and we all shook hands.

Gary said to me, "Burt Reynolds called me about you, Lake. Said you're a great gal."

"He's a great guy," I said.

"The best," Gary said. He pressed a finger to his ear where he had an earpiece. "I never wear this thing but today's a little different. I have a message to HB from the control room. Wick says, 'Fake it like Dante.'"

HB chuckled. "Tell him thanks but I'm not a faker."

"I believe that," said Gary. "I don't know what you are, but I don't think you're a faker."

The floor manager was using his fingers doing the countdown to air, 5-4-3-2-1.

The camera's red light blinked on, and Gary took over.

STEVE ZOUSMER

CHAPTER 17

TRANSCRIPT OF 9/7/79 BROADCAST—Part 1

GARY WARREN

Let me introduce one of the most remarkable guests in the history of this program.

His name is HB Taylor.

Mr. Taylor will tell you that he has COME BACK FROM DEATH.

The PURPOSE of his visit is to spend time—about a week—with his granddaughter, Lake Whistler.

We must tell you—full disclosure—that Lake Whistler has been a writer and chief writer OF THIS PROGRAM for almost four years. She is joining her grandfather this morning. [2-shot of Lake beside HB.]

The only facts we know FOR SURE are that a man named HB Taylor was born in 1876, died in 1948, and lived for about 35 years in McGill, Ohio.

NOTHING ELSE of what he'll say this morning has been VERIFIED, despite our efforts—which include private investigators, a psychological examination, and a lie detector test.

We take NO RESPONSIBILITY for what he says.

We urge you to think SERIOUSLY AND SKEPTICALLY before accepting anything he says as truth.

HOWEVER...we're taking a chance with him because we think you'll agree that he tells a fascinating story. If it's true, you'll hear things that have <u>NEVER BEEN REVEALED</u> about what happens when you die.

You MIGHT OR MIGHT NOT like what he says, but we think you DESERVE to hear his answers and DECIDE FOR YOURSELVES.

The questions I'll be asking <u>are not MY questions</u>. They're <u>YOUR</u> questions, submitted by viewers.

We've received THOUSANDS of them. We apologize if <u>YOUR</u> question is not addressed.

Good morning, Mr. Taylor. You certainly don't LOOK dead, but you say you ARE dead.

HB TAYLOR

Yes, I'm dead. I usually don't look like this. The body and clothes are supplied just for my visit. I've said it's like renting a tuxedo. And like a rented tuxedo, you have to return it in a week. With no soup stains.

GARY WARREN

I guess death hasn't dampened your sense of humor. But let's get started. Here's the central question: is there an afterlife?

HB TAYLOR

Yes.

GARY WARREN

Just "yes"?

HB TAYLOR

I'm trying to be succinct.

GARY WARREN

Whether there's SOMETHING OR NOTHING AFTER LIFE is one of the greatest of all mysteries. And you've just given us an answer in a single syllable.

HB TAYLOR

Lake said the same thing, like the answer's too simple, let alone hard to believe. Frankly, if I turn back the clock thirty-one years, I wouldn't have believed it myself. I would have bet on death as the Big Nothing, lights out, total blackness forever. But I was wrong. And now I bet you're going to ask, "HB, what is the afterlife like?"

GARY WARREN

Is that funny? Why are you smiling?

HB TAYLOR

Because you have no idea how impossible it is to describe death. A few adjectives won't cut it, believe me. Could you even describe life? If I asked you to describe life, could you do it? Go ahead. Try it.

GARY WARREN

You're evading the question.

HB TAYLOR

Damn right. Because how can I describe death to someone who's only known life? It's like trying to describe day to someone who's only known night. Just ask Dante. Dante made indescribability an attribute of death. Which didn't stop him from trying to describe it.

GARY WARREN

I didn't expect to be talking about Dante but unless I'm mistaken, Dante was alive when he wrote about death. So what he wrote came from his imagination, not direct experience. But you say you've had that direct experience. Which means you're not making it up. You're telling it like it is. So tell us about it. What surprised you about death?

HB TAYLOR

What surprised me? The first thing is that the living think of death in terms of finality, which is a brutally powerful idea of course, but death isn't final because here you are in the afterlife. You realize there's a natural flow from life to death, a natural continuation. The second thing is that there's very little magical stuff about it. It's kind of no-nonsense. So when you get there you have a feeling that, while it's very different, it isn't that surprising in terms of what should come next. It kind of makes sense as the next step.

GARY WARREN

How so?

HB TAYLOR

Now *you're* smiling.

GARY WARREN

Because I can't believe we're having this crazy conversation.

HB TAYLOR

Look, I'll try to explain, even though it's impossible. When you realize you're arriving in the afterlife you think, wow, I'm about to be ushered into an unimaginable show, a spectacular adventure with astonishing otherworldly goings-on. But it's not that way at all. It's a low-keyed transition. It's simple, like all really big things. One thing it definitely *isn't* is a cartoon fantasy of paradise. You don't have angels and a heavenly choir or an omniscient guy on a throne. Or a devil. There's no devil.

GARY WARREN

You're telling me what it's *not* like. But what *is* it like?

HB TAYLOR

I said it's unsurprising but that doesn't mean it's *like* something. There is nothing to compare it to. You don't really know yourself what it's like, because nothing's revealed, at least not right away. There's no welcoming committee to show you around. There's no map. You feel a lot of energy and you hear a kind of a rumbling, throbbing hum—I don't know what causes it. You understand there is a lot of discovery ahead for you and it's nice to find out there's a lot going on after life and your trip is far from over. And maybe will *never* be over.

GARY WARREN

We'll come back to what death is like. But what was dying like?

HB TAYLOR

I'd been very sick for a long time. Life stopped being good. I was ready to check out. But at the last minute, my thinking changed. I desperately didn't want to go. I would have done anything to stay alive.

GARY WARREN

They say your whole life flashes before you in the last seconds before you die. Is that what happened?

HB TAYLOR

Well, it wasn't like some sort of high-speed movie of my life. What I remember is wanting to *reexperience* things, another breakfast with Sportie, time with my two girls. I remembered the giggles and squeals coming out of their bedroom when they played together. I'd have given anything for another hour of that, another day of it. But when the moment comes, you can't beg or bargain. And then I felt life drain out of me. In a quick cold stream, like I'd sprung a leak.

GARY WARREN

Some people who've been resuscitated have said that when you're starting to die it feels like you're speeding through a tunnel and everything is dazzlingly white.

HB TAYLOR

People ask about that white light. I don't remember it. I remember the opposite, absolute sudden darkness. Deep darkness. You know that old line about it being so dark you can't find your butt with both hands? It was like that. I recall thinking, "Well, this darkness is just what I expected, isn't it?" And then I realized, "What I expected? What am I doing *expecting* things if I'm totally dead? What am I doing being aware? Being *conscious*." That was a big surprise. And gradually there was a glow, like a fabulous dawn. But I knew I was dead and gone. It wasn't a dream.

GARY WARREN

Were you in heaven? Is there a heaven and hell? I can't believe I'm seriously asking that.

HB TAYLOR

There's no heaven and hell. You die in your own individual way but once you're dead it's the same for everybody.

GARY WARREN

Are you saying there are no rewards and punishments? That's a central concern in people's lives. Many viewers asked whether God is watching and judging everything they do.

HB TAYLOR

I grew up believing that. I believed God keeps a close eye on every deed and thought of every single person on earth and assigns something like a score that determines whether they go north or south when they kick the bucket. I was a future accountant so the record-keeping difficulty of that fascinated me. But there's no score keeping. There's no scrutiny from above. There's no moral judging process that results in rewards or punishments. If you led a decent life and had love in your life and did some good, that's your heaven. If you had your chance and botched it by being a rotten son of a bitch, that's your hell. If you were guilty of something really bad, you have to stew in that guilt for eternity.

GARY WARREN

So if you aren't in heaven or hell, where are you?

HB TAYLOR

Where? Well, first, you have to remember that when you die you shed your body. So you're not in your body anymore. And you're not in a casket six feet under. All that's left is what I call a particle, a tiny dot of a thing that escapes from your body on your last breath. Your whole being is compressed into that dot. And that's where you are. In that dot.

GARY WARREN

A microdot?

HB TAYLOR

I'm not familiar with that term. I just call it a dot because that's the way I see it in my mind. It's like a period at the end of a sentence, only smaller.

GARY WARREN

And where does this dot, uh, reside?

HB TAYLOR

Minneapolis.

GARY WARREN

What? [audible laughter among studio crew]

HB TAYLOR

Just joking. Sometimes this death talk gets so grim you need to make a joke. But let me try to answer your question. I really don't know where the dot resides. No place you can find on a map. But it doesn't matter because your physical existence is down to almost nothing. You have no anatomy. No outer shell, so to speak. You're weightless and shapeless. Imagine being the smallest particle of air or a drop of water in the ocean. You coast along with the wind or the current, whatever it is, but you're not up in the sky and you're not wet. Gary, I'm sorry but that's probably the best I can do on what the afterlife is like.

GARY WARREN

So what do you *do* in the afterlife? Does floating along with the current get boring?

HB TAYLOR

That's like asking if a drop of ocean water gets bored.

GARY WARREN

You mean it's a stupid question? Okay. But I have to say it: It sounds a little disappointing. Boring.

HB TAYLOR

[Laughs] Well, death isn't there to entertain you. It's not an amusement park. But it's not disappointing or boring. The depth, the light, the flow, the enormous energy and magnitude of it—you take it seriously and it's constantly fascinating. And it gives you a feeling of being a natural part of the fabric. You're minuscule but you're part of it.

GARY WARREN

Does anything ever *happen*?

HB TAYLOR

There's a sense of something very big that never stops happening. Infinity. Death is your ticket to infinity. It's exciting to be rolling along ad infinitum. And when you're surrounded by infinity there's no sense of time. You're free from time. There's no clocks. No deadlines. No birthdays. No years flying by. No getting old. I had to ask Lake how long I'd been dead. I had no idea.

GARY WARREN

Are you with other dead people or are you alone?

HB TAYLOR

Both. You're alone but not lonely. You feel the closeness of everyone who's ever died. They're all there with you. Like neighbors you don't have to talk to.

GARY WARREN

You don't interact with them?

HB TAYLOR

No. There's no socializing. It's like being fellow passengers but never talking. You don't make new friends. You don't meet fifth-century Mongolian tribesmen or encounter famous dead people, like running into Napoleon. This week I talked to a woman who wants to meet Goethe. I'm afraid she's out of luck on that one.

GARY WARREN

Okay. Let's get to what might be the biggest question, asked by many viewers, and again, I caution viewers to listen skeptically. HB, is there a god?

HB TAYLOR

Everybody asks that. Even dead people.

GARY WARREN

What's the answer?

HB TAYLOR

Well, the best way to put it—

GARY WARREN

Excuse me, HB, I have to ask you to hold that thought. The control room is telling me we can extend this interview for another segment and we'll pick it up where we left off, but first we have to take a commercial break. Really? Andy, for real? HB, I apologize for this. Lake, I apologize. We'll be right back.

COMMERCIAL BREAK (2:55)

✱ ✱ ✱

So HB and I were sitting there with Gary and we could see that the mask of professional coolness he wore on the air had dropped off to reveal tremendous agitation over having to interrupt the interview just as he asked the biggest question he'd ever asked on television.

HB, of course, was unaware about the value system of TV production so I explained that it is the height of bad taste to disrupt an important mood or moment by jamming in commercials, which are invariably the *worst* commercials, involving the most-crass products or attention-shattering antics. It happens fairly often but it's a gross breach of professionalism. And with a large and critical audience watching, it's even worse.

Looking into the camera but speaking to the control room, Gary said, "I'm saying we'll tell them whether God exists but first they have to watch a message on cleaning their gutters?"

"Sorry, Gary," came the director's amplified voice.

"*Sorry?*" asked Gary, fuming. He jumped up and stormed off the set in the direction of the control room.

I decided I had to witness the control room scene. I told HB to stay on the couch and chased after Gary.

Unlike many TV stars, Gary is not a temperamental screamer. He is from an old New England family with a strong sense of decorum. So he did not go by the usual prima donna playbook of charging into the control room spewing profanity. But his barely contained rage got everyone's attention.

By the time I'd caught up with him he had the massive Buehler and the diminutive Andy Shafer pinned against the wall in the narrow corridor outside the control room. I kept my distance as Gary vented at Buehler and Andy: You embarrassed me and our show. You interrupted a question about the existence of God. The critics will *obliterate* us for this. They won't hear anything HB says, just that I cut him off on the verge of a disclosure affecting billions of people so we could sell glue or whatever we're selling."

Not a word was said about the content of the interview. The nature of death took a back seat to concern about media reaction.

When the star explodes, there is only one thing to do: say whatever it takes to pacify him. Promise what must be promised. Even Buehler got into it. Technically he was Gary's boss but as a business-side executive he had scant experience soothing performer egos and hit an instant wrong note by stressing the sponsors' ecstatic pleasure at seeing their commercials dropped into the interview at a "high-attention" moment.

The commercials-are-good argument inflamed Gary even more, but Andy scored quickly with a good-soldier confession that the decision to run the commercial was not only wrong but his. He accepted the blame and offered himself as a human sacrifice.

Buehler then got wise to the commercials-are-bad tactic but probably tipped too far, promising Gary all the time he wanted and no commercials for the rest of the way. "This moment in TV history will pay revenue and reputational dividends for years to come and I don't want it sullied by dog chow commercials."

The commercial break was nearly over. We began a hurried procession back to the set with me trailing as the two bosses flanked Gary and heaped on praise about how well it was going. The phone lines were overwhelmed, even with extra operators laid on for the expected crush of viewer questions. The audience was expanding, not trailing off. A crowd was gathering outside the building and news crews were arriving to cover the story of HB's interview. There would be a press conference later this morning.

The Associated Press reported that President Jimmy Carter had walked out of a security briefing to watch the interview with Mrs. Carter and his office staff.

Gary was mollified. The bosses dropped back as he and I rushed to resume our places on the set. In a whisper Gary asked me if he was being adequately tough on HB.

I told him he was doing great beyond belief.

* * *

Gary's calm and purposeful expression vanished the moment he inserted the earplugs linking him to Andy in the control room. Frowning, Gary said, "Stop whispering, Andy, I can't hear you."

"Five seconds," said the floor manager, beginning a countdown.

Gary dropped his hand from his ear to his lapel mic and covered it so he could speak to me and HB without being heard by the control room.

"King Richard just walked in."

In my world, these words struck fear.

"Where is he?"

"In the control room, with Delacore and a flock of lackeys. Everyone's scared shitless."

King Richard was Richard Creighton, the CEO of our company. He was a dreaded figure. Once, at a network cocktail party, I'd heard an inebriated senior executive saying, "The definition of a good day is when you have no contact with Creighton. The definition of a horrible-beyond-belief day is when you *do* have contact with him."

Then we were back on the air.

CHAPTER 18

Gary opened HB's second segment with a solemn apology for the "inexcusable and inappropriate" commercial interruption that cut off HB's answer about the existence of God.

HB, in a likable attempt to ease Gary's discomfort, then went off on an amusing comment on commercials, saying there were no commercials in the afterlife. Further, he said, there were no products to buy or sell. There was no money and therefore no quarreling about money, no greed, no worrying, and no crime involving money. People weren't measured by their money or lack of it. In these respects, he noted with a smile, the afterlife looked pretty good compared to earthly life.

HB's comment was delivered so cheerfully that it was tempting to chuckle in agreement but, as I later learned, King Richard took vehement offense and seized this moment to clarify the single acceptable reaction, raising his voice to bellow a famous quotation attributed to Queen Victoria, "*We are not amused.*"

The reason he was not amused was that, as the man in charge of making money for the company, he considered HB's remarks an affront to capitalism.

"Who is this middle-aged flower child?" he roared. "Who is this man who has us *apologizing* for commercials. Commercials are our lifeblood. We run them to make money. We run them so our sponsors can sell their products and build a strong and prosperous American economy. And I should mention, we run them to pay our salaries. We should thank God for commercials. And if anyone's sensitivity is offended by the crassness of this perspective, drop to your knees and brace for the blade of the guillotine that hovers over your fucking neck."

The control room's crew fell into frozen silence. Aaron Buehler went into lap-dog mode, jumping down from his stool and offering it to Creighton. But the King did not sit. He stood ramrod straight, a posture he'd perfected as a three-star general in the army where his fiery reputation attracted national attention.

A few years earlier, when he retired from the army at age sixty, the network plunked down a staggering package of powers and compensation to win the competition for his services. It was hoped that he would lead a reign of terror that would whip the company out of its doldrums. So far he had delivered on the terror but failed to vanquish the doldrums.

It was fitting that he was known as the King. He savored nicknames but, except for his own, favored demeaning ones. His nickname for Buehler was "Haystack." Andy was "Shrimpboat," because shrimp are small. Wick Sorenson was "Monsieur Élite," because Wick was Ivy League-educated and probably spoke French.

The King wore his nickname proudly. He was an imperial presence, a silver-haired six-footer with a snow-white mustache whose pencil-thinness seemed to assert patrician lineage, though it turned out he was the son of a Wyoming podiatrist. Despite his debonair good looks, he radiated thuggish intimidation and a field of force that made you hop back instinctively as he approached. I had encountered him only once, in an elevator we shared—just the two of us—in the Tower of Fear. I'd mumbled a tremulous hello and he glared at me as if the 127 pounds of Lake Whistler were intolerably impeding the upward speed of *his* elevator. I was so rattled that I stabbed a button lower than my desired floor just to escape the elevator as fast as possible.

It occurred to me as I sat on the orange couch listening to HB's riff on money that there were now two audiences passing judgment on this interview. One was the millions of viewers watching across America. The other was King Richard, standing rigidly in the control room, breathing fire.

GARY WARREN

HB, let's get back to the big question—and I'll remind viewers to take HB's answer with skepticism. Does God exist?

HB TAYLOR

Well, God didn't come around and introduce himself to me, if that's what you're asking. I didn't see him or hear him. Never have. Which doesn't prove anything either way, of course. I have an opinion on God, but it's not based on anything I've encountered as a dead person.

GARY WARREN

We'll get to your opinion but first let me ask you about a quotation from Michelangelo that was called in by a viewer. QUOTE "If we have been pleased with life then we should not be displeased with death, since it comes from the same hand of the same master." UNQUOTE. Your reaction?

HB TAYLOR

That's a fine quote. It catches the fact that life and death are connected, like a progression of the same vision by the same master. I take it that by "master" he means God. Which makes sense to me. Life and death have to come from *some* hand, don't they? I see what a vast and complex masterpiece the universe is and what a miracle life is and I think, *something* caused this. Maybe not God as Michelangelo saw him—the guy he painted on the ceiling of the Sistine Chapel. But of course Michelangelo needed an image, didn't he? He wouldn't have gotten away with painting a big question mark in the middle of the chapel ceiling. I'm betting that God is not in man's image, maybe surprisingly far from it, maybe no image at all, just a process. But *something*. Nobody knows. All I can tell you for sure is that just dying doesn't get you the answer. You don't meet your maker. Which doesn't mean you have no maker.

GARY WARREN

That will certainly upset a lot of people. But I take it that you do believe in God?

HB TAYLOR

What I believe is that there's a whole lot more to things than I ever grasped, and we have to be humble about that. We don't know more than a tiny fraction of what it's all about so I'm leery of anyone who tells us what's right or wrong to believe. I'll leave it at that.

GARY WARREN

Let's move on to our most-asked viewer question: When I'm dead will I be reunited with my deceased loved ones? Some people even told us they'll welcome death because they think they'll be together again with someone they miss very deeply.

HB TAYLOR

I'd bet that almost everybody who's lost someone close to them has hoped or believed they'll meet again "on the other side." Well, it's hard to face never being together again but I'm afraid that's how the turkey trots. We're separate in death. It's not a social place. It's not a family place. You don't have the kind of relationships you get in life.

GARY WARREN

There's no communication? Nothing?

HB TAYLOR

None. At least nothing direct. You do kind of know things but without being told directly. But there's no communicating between the dead and the living or between the dead and other dead. Your deceased loved ones are not waiting for you to show up and begin a new life in the sky. They're not looking down on you, following your life. They're not applauding or disapproving what you do or being overjoyed that you made the football team or had a baby. You have vivid memories from your life but after a while you stop dwelling on them and tuck them away. Death isn't about going back, like trying to recapture Christmas morning in 1972. It's forward-looking.

GARY WARREN

Death is *forward-looking*? Forward to what?

HB TAYLOR

To something worthy but you never get to it, as far as I can tell. Everything is forward-looking. The universe is forward-looking. Life is forward-looking, too, isn't it? We're always rushing forward to the next thing. What's the point? Maybe it's just to keep the ball rolling.

GARY WARREN

That's a frustrating answer.

HB TAYLOR

You don't get answers. Ever. In death or in life. I understand that people want answers, sometimes so desperately they'll accept any bs that comes along. And *cling* to those beliefs and be shaped by those beliefs and sometimes hate their neighbors or kill each other over those beliefs.

In the control room Creighton exploded. "Is he taking a giant dump on religion? Is he saying Americans with religious beliefs are desperate people clinging to bullshit? Didn't any thought go into what this charlatan was going to say? Haystack, did we *ask* him about religion? Why didn't the writers ask him in the pre-interview?"

Buehler was speechless but Andy intervened. "It's not the writers' fault. Gary wanted our writers to stay out of it so it didn't look like we were controlling it."

"We fucking *should* have controlled it," barked Creighton. "That's what they're for. I'll fire the lot of them. How many are there, Haystack?"

"I don't know," said Buehler.

"Six plus Lake," said Andy. "And they're in the union so firing them—especially because they did nothing, at Gary's request—will be a battle and we'll probably get our ass kicked."

"You fucked the dog, Haystack," thundered the King. "And so did you, Monsieur Élite. Your job is to protect our standards. Why didn't you put a stop to this? And you, Shrimpboat, get on that IFB right now and tell Gary to get away from this before it gets worse."

Everyone heard Andy order Gary, "Change direction. No religion talk."

Gary flinched at the volume and urgency of Andy's voice coming through his earpiece.

At a momentary loss, he searched through his list of phoned-in questions for a suitable change of topic. He found one: How about reincarnation?

HB TAYLOR

Reincarnation? It's fun to wonder if the guy driving your bus was Leonardo da Vinci in a previous life. Or if in your next life you might come back as a giraffe or wombat. But I doubt it. There's no need for that. It's comical and—you haven't asked me about this—there's no comedy in death. Not a single laugh. There's also no food or booze in death. You can't get a cold beer or a fresh tomato. There are no great literary works by Dickens or George Bernard Shaw, no beautiful grandchildren, no rollicking Friday nights with your friends, no rainbows, and no sexual stuff, no orgasms.

"No *what*?" shouted Creighton. "Did he say *orgasms*?"

Andy ordered Gary, "Apologize for saying orgasms. We can't say orgasms."

The King said, "Delacore, front and center. You got a pad? I'm gonna dictate a crawl. Take it down." Delacore had no pad and looked panicky but one of his assistants, a woman, stepped forward with a steno pad and ballpoint and took down what Creighton said.

GARY WARREN

We sincerely apologize if HB's word selection has caused any offense. But let me quickly get on to another question: Many people ask, is there music or color in the afterlife?

HB TAYLOR

Color, yes. The best sunset you ever saw, a real humdinger with colors you never imagined, and it never ends. Music? No. It's surprising. You'd think there'd be great music by Mozart or other geniuses. But not everyone loves Mozart. Do Arabs or Africans love Mozart? Do Chinese love Sinatra or the Andrews Sisters singing about the "Boogie Woogie Bugle Boy" of Company B?

GARY WARREN

HB, we're almost out of time. Talk about how people reacted to you this week?

HB TAYLOR

A mix. Some took me seriously and others didn't. Some got their backs up pretty severely. What I care about is how my granddaughter feels about me. I hope Lake believes me because otherwise she'll go forward unsure if everything we've said to each other and learned from each other this week was false or under false pretenses.

GARY WARREN

So, Lake, I have to ask, do you believe him?

LAKE WHISTLER

We agreed that I would just sit here and say nothing. Silent as a sphinx.

GARY WARREN

So you won't say if you believe him or not?

LAKE WHISTLER

I'm a sphinx.

GARY WARREN

I know you and you're no sphinx. But okay. HB, your visit here is almost over. Are you sad to go?

HB TAYLOR

Sure, but I've had a helluva time. I got to see the Atlantic Ocean and a beautiful beach. I saw New York. I met a lovely dead woman and went to a Broadway musical and a Yankees game with her. Being with her brought back the love I'd felt for Sportie, my wife. I also got to meet a real movie star, Burt Reynolds. I thought a lot about the life I led and I feel good about it. I reread some great books. Most of all, I spent time with my granddaughter. And now I'm on national television. Not many dead visitors put together a week like I've had.

GARY WARREN

A lot of people will be extremely displeased with some of the answers you've given this morning because they conflict with their beliefs. What do you say to them?

HB TAYLOR

I'm not trying to monkey around with anyone's beliefs. I'm sorry if people are unhappy or if my answers haven't been good enough. Most people won't believe me anyway so I'm guessing the damage will be minimal.

LAKE WHISTLER

Can I say something, Gary? I love my grandfather.

My voice cracked as I said it. I was stunned. It just came out of me. HB took my hand.

Gary was thrown, unprepared for this sudden emotion. I think he was moved by it, maybe even choked up. He was struggling to find a response when he got a message in his earpiece. It was from Andy: "Look at the crawl."

Gary's eyes went to the studio monitor (which I'd never noticed) and HB and I turned to look. The image was the three of us but a large-type bold-face message was "crawling" across the bottom of the screen. I missed the first few words but here's how it went:

...EXTENDS ITS PROFOUND APOLOGIES FOR THIS APPALLING INTERVIEW WHICH VIOLATES THIS NETWORK'S HIGH STANDARD OF RESPONSIBLE PROGRAMMING.

A MAN WITH NO CREDIBILITY OR CLEAR MOTIVE WAS ALLOWED TO SPEW DETAILS OF LIFE AFTER DEATH THAT ARE UTTERLY UNVERIFIED, UNBELIEVABLE, AND ANTI-AMERICAN. THESE VIEWS ARE IN FLAGRANT CONFLICT WITH COMMONLY HELD BELIEFS WHICH WE RESPECT DEEPLY.

WE WILL IMMEDIATELY ENGAGE A TOP INDEPENDENT LAW FIRM TO INVESTIGATE HOW THIS DISGRACEFUL TRAVESTY WAS ALLOWED TO HAPPEN.

THREE PERSONS SHARING RESPONSIBILITY FOR THIS FAILURE OF JUDGMENT HAVE ALREADY BEEN TERMINATED. THAT NUMBER IS EXPECTED TO INCREASE SIGNIFICANTLY. WE PRAY FOR FORGIVENESS FOR AIRING THIS ABOMINATION.

CHAPTER 19

Then we were off the air, suddenly, as if a plug had been yanked out of the wall.

Bringing a live TV show to a perfect on-time close is an unappreciated skill and there'd been sloppy finishes before but never anything this jarring. One moment you saw the three of us gazing at the monitor with our mouths agape, the next moment you were watching the awkward opening moments of a different program, a local station talk show where the hosts had not quite recovered from the shocking message that had just crawled across the screen.

"What the fuck?" I said to Gary.

"What the fucking fuck," he said back to me, and that was probably two more "fucks" than I'd ever heard out of Gary Warren.

The studio monitor went black. The studio was hauntingly silent until the silence was shattered by a booming amplified voice. The King himself.

"This is Richard Creighton. *Your boss.* I am going down to the studio floor. All personnel will assemble there, pronto. Anybody who sneaks out is not invited back."

"Who do you think got terminated?" I asked Gary. "Me? You?"

Gary shook his head, flabbergasted.

HB, on the other hand, was trying to conceal a smile. I asked what he thought was so funny. He whispered, "I've been through *real* termination. This is child's play."

The King made his entrance, striding out of a dark corner of the studio into the bright lights of our warmly decorated living room set. He was surrounded by an entourage including the corporate counsel Raymond Delacore and several other lawyerly looking men who hurried behind him at ass-kissing distance. Then came the motley crew of control-room staff followed by VIP guests who tagged along uninvited to witness the unfolding spectacle. I presumed that most of them were executives of our sponsoring companies. No doubt they were in shock, wondering about how to assess the debacle that had just taken place.

Creighton grabbed a chair from the dining room section of the set and hopped up on it with surprising agility. "Gather 'round everybody. I want to tell you a story.

"It's about quitting smoking. I was about thirty, a soldier in horrendous combat in Korea. I was hooked on smoking. Three packs of Camels per day. It was killing me. I could barely breathe. Couldn't run, couldn't stop coughing. I remember the exact moment. Bullets flying, gunfire deafening, and I thought, 'Mortal combat versus quitting cigarettes—which challenges you more, soldier?' It was smoking. So I shot the smoking habit between the eyes. Cold turkey. Crumpled my last pack of Camels and ordered a fucking artillery attack. Never smoked again, not a puff. The next few weeks were torture. I found out what it was like to be an addict in withdrawal. Agonizing frustration, jangled nerves, shaking hands, homicidal rage. I thought I was about to explode.

"Do you have any goddamn idea why I'm describing this feeling to you? Guess the fuck why?"

He paused and made a gesture inviting guesses. None came.

"Because that's what I felt in the control room watching the piece-of-shit show you just put on our nation's airwaves. That same head-to-toe quivering rage. That show disgraced me. It disgraced you and our industry. And our country. It was unpatriotic because garbage like this confuses people and confused people are weak people and weak people make a weak nation. Haystack Buehler held a meeting yesterday and there was a raise-your-hands vote on who believed HB Taylor had come back from the dead. *Nobody* raised a hand. It was unanimous. But you drank the Kool-Aid. And, to make it worse, without me in the room to provide much-needed courage, our board of directors gulped the Kool-Aid, too, and gutlessly backed off a decision to kill this thing. They let it go on the air. There will be dire consequences, ladies and gentlemen. Heads have rolled and the rolling's just begun. It will be like a bowling alley around here."

There was utter, graveyard silence in the studio. No one made eye contact. I couldn't tell how people were reacting. Terror or dismay, or both?

Gary Warren, the only person in the room with the stature to interrupt Richard Creighton, said, "Dick, you're not the only one who's pissed off. I'm pissed off about that crawl. Where did it come from? Who did that? No one has ever called my work an abomination. Nobody's ever *apologized* for anything I've said or done on television. No one has ever *prayed for forgiveness* for what I said or pulled the plug on me."

"Who did it?" Creighton repeated, smiling. "*Me.* I dictated every word. If it was a blow to your fragile ego, Gary, I suggest you go somewhere and have a good weep into your hanky. As for you, Mr. Taylor—nice old HB Taylor, the All-American grandpa designed by central casting—I'm going to find out what your game is. We're hiring the nastiest law firm in New York to investigate who you are and who let this happen. I would advise you to acquire the services of a very good attorney."

"Thanks," said HB. "I've got the $70 my granddaughter gave me. Will that cover my legal expenses?"

"You're quite the homespun humorist, aren't you? Mark Fucking Twain."

"And here's a question for your investigators," said HB. "If you're so horrified by what I said on your show, why didn't *you* prevent it? I mean you, Mr. Creighton. Where were you? Can you explain to your board how this happened on your watch? Isn't that how it works in the military? The commander is accountable for everything under his command whether it was his fault or not. Punishing subordinates doesn't get him off the hook."

"I'll tell you where I was, Mr. Taylor. I was on the way back from Tokyo, where I negotiated an unprecedented Asian-American deal that could have enormous consequences for this company, unless the deal collapses because of the credibility we've flushed down the toilet with this show."

I doubt if anyone in the room cared about the Asian-American megadeal. The concern was about getting fired.

"So, Dick," said Gary. "Exactly who are you firing? Am *I* among the fired? Because I'm guilty. Yes, I was against the HB thing at first but I changed my mind and supported it after Gina made an impassioned comment reminding us why we created this show in the first place. We had some pretty high-minded ideals and I believed in them. But we've drifted away from what it was intended to be."

"I know all about Gina's great comment," Creighton said, sneering and glancing at Delacore, who had obviously given Creighton a report on the meeting. "Believe me, Gina, it won't be forgotten when your contract comes up. Or sooner."

"You're threatening Gina?" Gary said. "Are you firing her?"

"Not yet. As for you, Gary, I heard about your so-called brave decision to 'let viewers decide for themselves.' So you let an alleged dead man go on our air. You let us provide a platform for the most ludicrous baloney ever heard on nonfiction television. He said being dead is like being a drop of water. He joked about Minneapolis or Leonardo da Vinci driving a bus. He said there's no *orgasms* in the afterlife. He said *orgasms*, Gary, on network TV. That is not fucking allowed. Imagine children turning to their mother and asking, 'Mommy, what's an orgasm?' He said this in response to your questions, so I'd say you're extremely accountable. I haven't fired you yet, but I'm not averse to it. Not averse. I don't care if you're the star. Stars can be replaced."

Gina stepped forward. "Are you averse to *this*, asshole?" She gave him the finger, did an about-face, and walked out, shouting, "I quit." I could feel people in the room resisting the urge to applaud.

"How about me?" I asked.

"Yes, the granddaughter. The sphinx," said Creighton. "The jury's still out on you, Miss Whistler. You brought your so-called grandfather to us, which is bad, but I'm told you warned at one point that we shouldn't put him on the air, which is a point in your favor. As is your refusal while on the air to say you believe him. I don't know what went on between you and Burt Reynolds or how Burt Reynolds ended up booking guests on our show, but our investigators will find out."

Andy said, angrily, "Movie stars don't book guests on our show. And Lake had no responsibility for putting HB on the show."

"The investigation will decide," said Creighton, with what looked like a smile. "But the final decision was made by Aaron Buehler. *Haystack* Buehler. The executive in charge. I should say, the executive who *used to be in charge*."

Andy said, "Your investigation might find some fuzziness about Buehler making the decision. I think the decision got made without him."

"I've also terminated Monsieur Élite," said Creighton. "This Wick Sorenson. We've paid him a handsome salary to be in the studio every day with you people to guard against abuses like the one that unfolded here. It was his primary job to stop it. He didn't. So, au revoir to Monsieur Élite."

"Wick's a good guy," I said. "He was helpful. He did the right thing. The brave thing."

"Don't tell me about bravery. I'm a soldier. I've seen brave men die. And I will not permit their deaths to be mocked by Mr. Taylor's make-believe drivel about death."

HB: "I mocked the deaths of Americans in combat? I forget that part."

Gary asked, "Who was the third person you fired?"

"That would be the person I call the Win-Win Woman. She was gung-ho for the interview. Then she rode down in the elevator gushing about what a fantastic booking it was, a win-win for us and our viewers. Then she spread this win-win crap throughout the building and through our viewer communities."

"Who the hell is the Win-Win Woman?" asked Andy.

Creighton turned for help from Ray Delacore, who said, "Sonya Lester. Director of community relations."

Andy: "You fired Sonya? Someone you never even met?"

Gary: "That win-win thing had zero impact. I forgot it in a minute."

"I beg to differ about the impact, Gary," said Delacore. "I think it may have tipped the group chemistry in favor of going along with booking HB. The little extra thing that solidified the decision."

HB said, "The investigators will get a good hee-haw out of that idea."

"You can't fire Sonya," Andy protested. "She has eight kids. And she's a widow. Her husband is a prominent rabbi and leader of the Jewish community. And the Jewish community knows how to raise a stink. You have to unfire her."

The joke—Andy later compared it to a prank on a substitute teacher—was that Sonya didn't have eight kids, wasn't a rabbi's widow, and wasn't Jewish. In fact, she was black and gay, not to mention capable and well-liked.

Creighton's bullying was losing force and he sensed it, smelling subversion in the air. Andy had pranked him, HB was unafraid of him, and Gary was standing up to him.

Creighton was sputtering. There was rage in his eyes. "Henceforth," he barked, "our policy is that this show was atrocious. We deeply regret it. That is my opinion and it's also *your* opinion. That's what we'll say to the media and Congress and it's what you can and will say to your family and friends. Don't cross me on this."

There was some muttering over that, the group's first sign of resistance to Creighton's rant. He heard it and didn't like it but before he could speak, Gary Warren said, "I'd like to go on the record with two things, which your investigation can consider. One is that I like HB Taylor a lot more than I like you, and I bet most of America would agree with me. And two, Gina Harkness came up with just the right word for you. Hmm, what was it? Ah, I remember now. *Asshole.* You're an asshole, Dick. And I don't work with assholes. I quit."

"You're fired."

"Too bad. You were slow on the draw, Dick. I quit before you fired me."

That got a laugh. Creighton realized he'd lost the audience and, much more seriously, he'd also lost Gary, the star the network's morning TV was built around.

"Mark my words," he said. "*Dire consequences.*"

With that he jumped down from the chair, whirled around, and marched out of the studio, his henchmen scurrying after him.

CHAPTER 20

Creighton's departure released a wave of almost paralyzed emotion. Seeing Gina and then Gary calling Creighton an asshole had the satisfying taste of fictional scenes in which the heroes thrash the bullies.

But otherwise the events were numerous and concerning. The show's two hosts had walked out. Where did that leave the show? Could the show survive a debacle like this?

Three executives had been fired by a boss who seemed to be reliving the torment of quitting cigarettes.

The show had run an incensed crawl denouncing itself. That was without precedent. We were in unknown territory.

A discussion of death had yielded revelations about the afterlife which, coming from a seemingly trustworthy figure like HB Taylor, were disturbingly tempting to take seriously. Everyone had to face the question I'd wrestled with since HB arrived: was he for real or something else?

But for the moment there was only a deflating state of shock and a shuffle toward the exits. Everyone wanted to flee the studio and escape into sunlight and fresh air.

A member of the network's security staff pulled HB and me aside and warned us about the large and loud crowd that had gathered outside. It was unclear whether this crowd was for or against HB, angry or adoring or a volatile mix. We accepted a guard's offer to lead us out by an alternate route. We followed him down a shadowy corridor to the opposite side of the building where a freight elevator lifted us to a small lobby where we exited onto a quiet street.

HB said, "That Creighton looked like he was about to rip apart at the seams. If I was a soldier under his command, I wouldn't know whether to be more scared of the enemy or him."

We headed to my office—the only destination I could think of. I realized that this story was going to pursue us and there would be no escaping it. Where would we go? What would we do? How would this affect HB's small amount of remaining time?

Then a larger thought pushed into my mind: had Creighton's denunciation established the definitive verdict on HB? Would Creighton's impact eclipse HB's impact? Or blot it out entirely?

The city's tabloids were going to feast on this story. How would they play it?

Most of the pedestrians we passed hadn't been at home watching TV so we got little reaction from them, and the one person who stopped HB, a middle-aged woman, was oblivious to Creighton's crawl. All she cared about was an autograph and she made us wait while she rummaged in her handbag for a scrap of paper for HB to sign. She said, "Make it to Arlene, see you in heaven, love and kisses from HB Taylor."

HB obliged and wished her a good day.

Walking into the show's offices we encountered a cacophony of ringing telephones and staff members trying to squeeze in words of response to impassioned callers. We hurried to my office where there was a brief moment of sanctuary as I plopped down in my chair, at my desk, putting my feet up and exhaling deeply. HB sat down in my one visitor chair. Julie Tommaso, the writers' secretary, came in looking frazzled. "We heard about that horror show in the studio," she said, shaking her head. She was carrying a cup of coffee for me. She said, "I think there's a bottle of scotch in the conference room cabinet if you'd like something stronger."

I said no. HB said yes but added that he was only joking.

Julie handed me a handful of pink phone message slips. "There's going to be a press conference at noon, downtown. You and HB have been summoned to take part. Andy's going too. Gary and Gina are nowhere to be seen."

"Is Andy in his office?"

"No. We think he went to the gym to blow off steam beating the crap out of a punching bag."

Jean Maxey came in. She kissed HB on the cheek and told him he'd been fabulous. "But talk about the shit hitting the fan with that maniac crawl! Nobody knows what to think. Is the show in trouble? Are Gary and Gina really out? And 'Haystack' Buehler? And Wick and Sonya? But you were great, HB. You were so cool. I laughed out loud at the Minneapolis line. I can't believe you said *orgasms*. By the way, Lake, that was a really beautiful touch by you at the end, about loving HB."

I was looking through the phone slips. "Julie, who are these people?"

"Reporters, agents, writers, photographers. These calls came in *before* the crawl. Then the calls slowed down and turned negative but then they speeded up again. Some politician in Ohio wants HB to endorse him. A 'filmmaker' wants to discuss a cinéma vérité documentary about HB's week. A financial adviser wants to manage the moneymaking opportunities he says are about to come HB's way."

HB laughed at that last one.

Julie said, "No, for real. All these people are looking for ways to cash in. One guy wants to license your name for a chain of séance parlors. Another wants to put your smiling image on 'collectors' item' dishes, mugs, bras, and panties. And of course there were calls from women who want to meet you either because you 'need a woman who can cater to your every need' or because you're a 'messenger from God.' Only a few said you're a hoax but one said you're a 'Satanic blasphemer' and ought to be killed."

"*Killed*? I got a death threat?" asked HB with a big grin.

"More than one death threat. And threats against the network, producers, Gary, etc."

"Oh. That's not so funny."

"I have to get back to phone answering," said Julie. "And it's not just our phones. All of the network's phones are ringing downtown at corporate and at all the phones at the owned-and-operated stations. You can't get through to anybody."

Jean said, "My mother got through. My mother's never called me about anything I've ever done on television. But she wanted to know what HB's 'really like.' She said she wanted to believe him because he's such a good guy but it was a little too much to swallow."

Julie stuck her head in the room. "Burt Reynolds on line four."

"I'll take that one," I said.

To give me some privacy, Jean invited HB to take a tour around the offices and meet the staff. He hopped up and off they went. Julie exited, closing the door behind her.

Burt's opening words were, "I reject all responsibility for this."

"You made it happen."

"Let's keep that between ourselves, okay? My redneck buddies might not enjoy me having a role in letting this atheist communist on television."

"HB did mention you, though, didn't he?"

"Once, but nobody noticed. Lake, I didn't really think it'd happen. I was so impressed with HB but I can hardly believe they let him on the air. But somebody sure had second thoughts, given that crawl. Who did that? I've never seen anything like it. Was it Buehler changing his mind? Trying to blame someone else?"

"No. In fact Buehler got blamed. And fired. And a few other people got fired. And after the show Gary and Gina both quit. It was quite a scene."

"I wish I'd seen it. Is your job safe?"

"Probably not for long. I'll bet there'll be a big clean-out of everyone involved with this."

"By the way, I thought HB was great. And you came through big-time at the end, about loving him. I teared up."

"Where are you?"

"In Jupiter. My Florida stomping grounds. If you're ever down this way, I've got a bed for you. A big one."

"Thanks, Burt. You were a real gentleman."

"Well, unfortunately, not everyone thinks so. This is what I want to tell you: I got a call ten minutes ago from a so-called reporter for one of America's great grocery store sleazy gossip tabloids. It seems that before you were even off the air, the reporter got a call from a certain Central Park hansom cab driver who for a fee told a story of what happened after HB departed from our ride around the park. A lot of smooching between you and me which escalated into what HB would call orgasm behavior. In broad daylight."

"Jesus. I don't know what to say to that," I said.

"I told the guy I'd kick the shit out of him and sue him if he used it. But he'll use it. I just wanted to give you a heads up."

"Thanks, Burt."

"Frankly," Burt said, "I wish the story was true."

It took a moment to figure out what he meant and then I didn't know what to say. I mumbled something about how I had to go and hung up. Good girl that I am.

Ten seconds later I called him back and said, "I do too."

And then I hung up without another word.

* * *

I noticed a message from Minnie Horch. I had HB sit at my desk and call her back while I made a run to the women's room. Jean Maxey followed me in and asked, "So how did the Burt Reynolds call go?"

"He told me there's a rumor that he and I shared an erotic moment in a hansom cab."

"Oh, wow. Is it true?"

"No."

"*Quel dommage.* Maybe next time."

"Jean, do I look as messed up as I feel?"

"No, you look great. I've never seen such color in those pale Nordic cheeks. But you can be sure there's some monster bullshit ahead."

I got back to my office as HB had just finished with Minnie Horch.

"That woman is—"

"Ditzy?" I suggested.

"That's a new word to me but it sounds right. She asked me if she donates her eyes when she dies if she'd be blind in the afterlife."

"Would she?"

"Nobody has eyes in the afterlife. Vision yes, eyes no."

Then came a surprise, a call from Carpathian Dell. It took a moment to realize he was Martha Dell's husband. He said he had seen HB's interview and finally grasped what had been going on with Martha. I put him on speaker.

"I just couldn't focus on it," Dell said. "It was so crazy and caught me so off guard. I did not handle it well. I feel so guilty. HB, I heard you say there's no communication between the dead but is there any way around that? Could I somehow send a message through you to tell her how sorry I am."

HB said, "I'm sorry. It doesn't work that way."

Mr. Dell broke down. In an anguished voice he confessed to how thoughtless he'd been to Martha, how sad he was that on her last night she was at a baseball game with us and not with him. Wasn't there anything that could be done?

HB gave me a look and said, "Well, Mr. Dell, now that I think about it there is an 'exception' that allows a dead person to communicate with another dead person. You can only use it once and I've never used it but out of respect and affection for Martha, I would do this for you. I'll deliver your message to her."

When the call ended, I asked HB if the "exception" really existed.

"Of course not. But if it makes the poor man feel better, what the hell."

"I think you were only a minute away from a money offer. A bribe."

HB shrugged.

Andy's secretary came to the door and said, "He's back. Can you come over?"

HB and I walked the hall to Andy's office and sat down.

CHAPTER 21

Andy said, "The press conference has been postponed indefinitely while the King huddles with the board of directors. I'd give anything to hear that conversation."

"Didn't Creighton badmouth the board about drinking the Kool-Aid and backing out of blocking the HB booking?"

"Yep. I bet the King is squirming over that remark."

"Have you spoken to Gary or Gina?"

"Not yet. Their managers are coming in this afternoon."

"Who's going to host the show on Monday?"

"I don't know. We're booking a bunch of clergy to discuss the interview but I have no idea who the hosts will be."

"Burt Reynolds called," I said. "He told me one of the grocery tabloids has a bogus story about me having sex with Burt in Central Park."

"In the park? Couldn't he afford a hotel room?"

"We didn't have sex. We did take a hansom cab ride, but no sex."

"Sorry. I hate to tell you this, but true or false this story will stick to you for the rest of your life. Get used to it."

"So, Andy," I asked, "what's the verdict on the show?"

"That's not a simple question, is it? There's the reaction to HB and then there's the entirely different reaction to Creighton and the havoc he wreaked. The story of his reign-of-terror performance in the studio leaked in about twelve seconds and is already being reported in the media, by the way."

"I'm concerned that people accept Creighton's opinion and decide HB is just a phony and that's all there is to it."

"It's too soon to tell, but we've had an avalanche of phone calls and I assume there'll be some analysis of what they're saying. We knew the interview would provoke a lot of people. The religious establishment is up in arms, of course. Lots of viewers are saying they'll never watch us again. Politicians are waiting to see which way the wind is blowing, but I bet there'll be righteous calls for investigations and new regulations and maybe penalties from the FCC. That's what freaks out the board."

I asked, "Is it all negative?"

"No, not by a long shot. A lot of people think HB was wonderful. But—and this is interesting—many of them are selective. They accept *some* things he said but reject *other* things. For instance, he says there's no heaven and hell but they *insist* there's a heaven and hell. They think HB just got it wrong, somehow."

HB said, "Got it wrong? If there's a heaven and hell, I would have been in one or the other of them. I'd have noticed the difference."

"And they're really pissed you said they won't be reunited with deceased loved ones. They call you 'cruel' for saying that. They won't accept it. But here's another reaction: some viewers reject your version of the afterlife because it's not spectacular enough. Remember when Gary asked if death is boring? These people don't want boring. They want an extravaganza, fire and brimstone, titanic battles between God and Satan. A great show."

HB was thoughtful for a moment but then said, "Years ago I was on a business trip to Chicago. Somebody offered me a ticket to the opera. I'd never seen an opera, so I said, what the hell, how bad can it be, and I went. I liked it. I remember almost nothing about it except at one moment near the end, the whole cast was on stage singing, really booming. And then this solo soprano voice rose up over everybody. It just rose up. The purity and power of it were overwhelming. It didn't seem like any human voice I'd ever heard. I remember thinking it was a voice from heaven. Maybe that's what people want. They want opera."

Andy said, "But they won't get it."

"Not in my experience," said HB.

I said, "I think it's depressing that when mankind finally gets some answers to the big questions they say, 'Nah, not the answers I wanted. Not good enough. Give me something else.'"

HB asked Andy, "Did Mr. Buehler at least get the big audience he wanted?"

"We won't get final ratings numbers for a while. I'm betting it was a big audience but not as astronomical as Buehler dreamed of. Here's an interesting thing about the crawl. Lots of people just don't read words rushing by on a screen. They think it's crap they don't need to know."

"But the powers-that-be will pay attention," I said. "So my question is, does the King's disclaimer and prayer for forgiveness get the network off the hook?"

"I doubt it. I don't see any way to shake the blame, no matter how much Creighton apologizes or fires people. Which I hope does not include me because I have two boys to put through college."

Andy's secretary came in carrying the early edition of one of New York's tabloids.

She didn't speak. She just held up the paper so we could read its screaming front page:

MAYHEM IN THE MORNING
NETWORK PRAYS FOR FORGIVENESS
Review by Carolyn Cavalney

Cavalney was the paper's TV critic. She hated morning TV and blasted us at every opportunity, but there'd never been an opportunity this juicy.

* * *

Andy opened the newspaper and read silently for a moment.

"It's predictable. Her opening line is, 'It was a day like no other in broadcast history.'

> First: an absurd interview purportedly revealing secrets of the afterlife.
> Second: a thunderous eruption of executive spleen in the form of an on-screen crawl blasting everything said in the interview and everyone who'd made it happen.
> Third, a bloodbath. The program's stars, host Gary Warren and cohost Gina Harkness both walked off their jobs during a vituperative post-show staff session featuring unprintable exchanges with network boss Richard Creighton.
> Next, the network's president of morning and daytime TV, Aaron Buehler, was fired in a face-to-face shouting match with Creighton.
> Standards & Practices Vice President Wick Sorenson also got the boot, though less noisily.

A peripheral figure, community relations chief Sonya Lester was axed for 'excessive enthusiasm' for running the interview.

Then, in a once-in-a-lifetime TV event, the network's own board of directors came in for a savage knock from Creighton who accused the board of 'gutlessly' retreating from a decision to kill the interview.

Creighton proudly admitted dictating the over-the-top crawl which included a prayer that the network be forgiven.

The crawl crossed the screen without warning and left Warren, his interview subject HB Taylor, and Taylor's granddaughter, Lake Whistler, speechlessly gaping at a monitor.

The show ended without a sign-off. The screen went black and when the picture returned, local programming was underway, though stumblingly.

Creighton assembled the staff on the program's studio set and began a diatribe described as 'deranged' with a bizarre opening anecdote about quitting cigarettes during a Korean War battle.

He promised a full-scale investigation, legal action, and more firings in what shaped up as a housecleaning to absolve the network for a 'disgraceful and abominable interview, an all-time low in the history of television.'

I said, "She's barely mentioned HB so far. This is all about Creighton."

"I'm an afterthought," said HB, laughing. "An afterthought on the afterlife."

"I'm afraid not," said Andy. "She finally gets around to the interview. She calls it 'twenty-three minutes of made-up malarky.' She says, 'Gary Warren lobbed superficial Sunday School-level questions at Mr. Taylor, letting Mr. Taylor depict a benign afterlife where the dead spend eternity floating placidly along like drops of ocean water.'"

HB said, "Sunday School questions are not superficial. They're the best questions—simple and basic and obvious. They come from children and we're all children in the face of death."

"'Mr. Taylor described a "humdinger" of an endless afterlife sunset. He snickered at reincarnation. He said there's no heaven and hell. He said deceased people are compressed into microdots. Asked where these microdots are located, he replied, 'Minneapolis.' He later said this was a joke, though he said there are no jokes in the afterlife and no sex, using a synonym for sexual climax that had probably never been uttered on TV.'"

Andy paused, a pained look on his face.

"'An unforgivable lapse of professionalism took place when Gary Warren announced a commercial interruption just as Mr. Taylor began an answer about the existence of

God.'"

I asked Andy if he'd told the truth when he took the blame for the commercial break.

"I asked Buehler if he wanted to kill or delay the commercials. He said no, run them now. The sponsors will be delighted. So we ran them."

Andy read on. "Now Cavalney gets around to you, Lake. Want to hear it?"

"Fire away."

"'Ms. Whistler, who appeared to be in advanced rigor mortis as she sat in near silence next to Mr. Taylor (even refusing to reply when asked if she believed him), is rumored to have brokered Mr. Taylor's TV appearance using the influence of the movie star Burt Reynolds, with whom she has been romantically linked. Ms. Whistler is the widow of the musician Douglas Grigatis who was murdered in a gangland assassination.'"

"Makes it sound like Doug was a mobster, doesn't it?"

Andy seemed weary. "Cavalney goes on for a half dozen paragraphs. She predicts a major show of remorse by the network, a flock of sacrificial lambs, politicians milking the story, writers pontificating about it."

Andy gave us a dejected look. "We shouldn't have done it. We all knew it was crazy, but it happened anyway."

※ ※ ※

HB and I trudged back to my office, feeling down. It's no big deal for me to feel down but I hated to see his usual high spirit deflated.

I took a call from a *60 Minutes* producer I'd had a few lame dates with. He said Mike Wallace wanted to interview HB. "This is what you dearly need to redeem yourself, a rigorous pro-quality interview, not a softball event like you had with Gary Warren. If your guy can stand up to Mike, he'll get the respect he's not getting now. If not, he'll be exposed as the fraud he probably is. And by the way, how long are you going to stick with that candy-ass show you work for?"

Was he dangling a job possibility? I didn't know or care. I said I'd call him back. I had no intention of doing so.

"Not how we wanted to end this thing, eh?" said HB.

I wondered how much more precious time he had left with me. A day? Two at most? What would life be like without him? He was my family. My friend. The only person I could truly depend on. I loved him.

I picked up my ringing phone.

"Hey, Lake. It's Brendan."

CHAPTER 22

"Hi, Brendan. Did you see it?"

"Of course. First time I ever saw a woman I'd carnal knowledge of on television."

"Really? I bet it happens all the time."

"How are you?"

"Not sure. This thing seems to be exploding. I've covered hot stories where the media and protesters *descend* on whoever's at the center of it, but I never thought about what it's like to be that *descendee*. HB's got only a day or two left and I don't know what to do with him because if we go out on the street we'll be mobbed."

"That sounds awful. Why don't you come out and hide in Amanituck? Where it all started, where you felt the ripple in the air."

"It seems like twenty years ago, doesn't it?"

"I'm in New York now but driving out there today. Leaving in a few minutes, actually. I could swing by and pick you two up."

"But maybe our fame has spread to Amanituck. They have TV there, don't they? When they find out we're at your house you'll be under siege too."

"We can avoid everybody. There's nobody in the house. We could eat at home and walk on the beach tonight. Then when he, uh, goes, you'd be with me instead of alone."

"I'll ask him," I said. "HB, Brendan Leary's on the line. He's inviting us to Amanituck, right now. Okay, Brendan, HB's giving it a thumbs-up. He asks if you've acquired any scotch since Sunday. He can't drink it but he'd like to look at it."

"No problem. Where should I meet you?"

I told him how to find the delivery dock on the ground floor of my office building.

"We'll hide behind something. Honk twice and we'll run out."

***

"We've got a plan," I said to HB. "But is this good enough for your last day or days on earth? Amanituck's hardly a special place in your heart."

"Special? The only special place to me would be 614."

"Except it's 500 miles away."

The last thing I wanted on this long day was a trip to Ohio.

"Lake, I think I told you that I left a letter, an intimate letter, for Sportie. I stuck it into a Dickens book she was reading, *The Pickwick Papers*. I don't know if she found it. I would love to know that."

"So you want to travel 500 miles on your last day on earth to see if a book she was reading thirty-one years ago is still there and if that letter's still in it?"

"Or not in it. Leaving that letter instead of talking to her directly is the biggest regret of my life, but I'd feel a lot better knowing she got it."

"That book could be anywhere. Most likely it was thrown in someone's trash. Or it could be in an old bookstore 100 miles away."

He'd asked nothing of me until now. This is what he wanted.

I dialed Brendan's number and caught him walking out the door.

"Change of plan," I said.

"Okay, I'll drive you. Where to?"

"Ohio."

"Ohio? That's a long drive. But okay, I'm in."

"We don't have time to drive. Can you drop us at the airport on your way to

Amanituck?"

"I've got a better idea. I'll come with you. I'm a New York boy, I've never been to Ohio."

I was kind of glad Brendan would join us. An Ohio trip with HB, including his disappearance, would be a challenge. Having Brendan along might help.

"What time's our flight?"

"Whenever the next plane leaves."

"So we're totally winging it, right? I love it. Are you okay with me horning in?"

"You've always been a horny guy."

* * *

We had to fly to Columbus via Chicago, with a long wait at O'Hare. I told the stewardess we were famous and needed security at O'Hare and she fixed it: we got off the plane first and were driven in golf carts to a VIP lounge where we sat until the Columbus flight was ready.

We shared this accommodation with an unknown-to-me rock group and their roadies, all of whom managed to stay deliriously stoned during the wait. They didn't recognize HB so there was no death talk. Even HB was bored, though when airborne, he was fascinated by flying. His nose was pressed to the window all the way.

We reached McGill in our rental car as darkness was falling. We checked in to the first motel we saw on the town's outskirts. HB said that other than a few coffee shops and a soda shop he couldn't recall a restaurant in town. In thirty-five years, he had never dined out.

But things had changed. There was a bar-restaurant, Jimmy's Tavern, across the street from the motel. We sat down at the bar. Brendan and I wolfed down beer and hamburgers as we planned our tour of McGill. We decided we'd scout out the town and get a nighttime impression of it including a drive-by of the old house at 614 Cambridge Street.

I hadn't been in McGill since the late 1960s when I came back for a few short visits to the rapidly declining Sportie. The town had changed a lot since HB's time, and it changed even more since my 1960s visits. The old American small-town look was gone, along with the old charm. The storefronts were modern, neat, uniformly designed, and sterile looking. The old barbershop—my parents took me to a *boys'* barbershop—was gone. The jewelry store, to which we'd raced to see the shattered windows after periodic break-ins, was gone too. The old grocery store was now a CVS. The town seemed rebuilt to the point of unrecognizability.

The Episcopal church, which looked as ancient as Notre Dame, was still there, as was the graveyard.

"That's where I'm buried," HB said dryly from the back seat as we drove past.

Then we turned onto Cambridge Street. It was simple to find 614 but the 614 we remembered had been dramatically renovated. Its big square shape remained but everything else was different. There were lots of large windows, some with lights on brightly as we slowed to a halt outside. There was a new garage replacing the old decrepit shack, a blacktopped driveway replacing what used to be unpaved tire tracks over grass, and a broad open lawn shorn of the majestic elms that used to throw shadows over the house to the point of concealment.

"Lots of changes," said HB.

"We'll come back in the morning and get a better look in daylight," I said, sensing a plunge in spirits. "Let's go back to Jimmy's Tavern and have a nightcap."

We went back but barely finished one round of beers. We were tired; it had been a long day.

The young bartender stopped in front of us. "You're HB Taylor," he said. "I heard you were back. Mrs. Graham over at the motel spread the word. Everyone's talking about you. A reporter was in here today asking for memories of you. Anecdotes and such. Nobody remembers anything. Too long ago."

HB said, "What's your name?"

"Jimmy Cully. This is my place."

"Jimmy, might I have known your parents?"

"No way. We're fairly new in town. What was it like being on TV and answering all those questions about death? Are you on the level? And you," he said, looking at me, "you're the granddaughter who's like the sphinx. Never speaks, right? Cat got your tongue?"

Brendan didn't like his wiseass tone. In his cop voice he said, "Be careful now, Jimmy."

"No offense," said Cully. Apparently trying to regain lost favor, he pressed the flattery button. "Tell you what, HB, I didn't see you on the tube but I heard what you said and I totally bought into it. It seemed a lot more realistic than the religious corned beef hash they feed you as a kid. Satan and so forth. The old-timers who come in here say you were a great guy."

HB said, "You said you didn't hear what I said on TV, but you agree with it. Then you said nobody had any memories of me, but they thought I was a great guy."

"A bartender hears all sorts of things. Contradictory."

"A lot of bullshit," said HB. Brendan and I perked up at the flash of irritation in HB's voice.

"Yeah, that's what bar talk is about: bullshit," Cully said. "People come in here and say whatever comes into their head whether it's right or wrong. And then they go home and forget every single word of it."

HB was a serious man and couldn't help bridling at Jimmy Cully's appraisal of human discourse as nothing but blather. I think what HB was hearing was something he hadn't thought of and didn't like: that *his* story would be regarded as blather, fodder for ignorant bullshitters who would muddle and misconstrue everything he'd said until it was valueless, worthy of nothing but derision and dismissal. HB was okay with being disbelieved, even rudely, but the notion that the Jimmy Cullys of the world would shape his future place in people's thoughts did not go down well.

"Check, please," I said.

We walked back to the motel, where I'd rented a room for HB and a room for Brendan and me. Brendan, who usually came to life in bars, was uncomfortably subdued. So was HB.

Approaching the motel we noticed a guy sitting, waiting, on a flimsy metal folding chair outside the doors to our rooms. He stood, slightly ominously, as we approached.

"Hey, HB."

He was a big guy, sixtyish, bald, and sloppy looking in jeans and a T-shirt. I noticed a parked motorcycle, probably his.

"You knew my dad," he said.

"Your name is what?"

"Earl Bridgewater."

Earl Bridgewater. Strong memories of him at HB's funeral rushed to my brain. Waving his fist. Giving us the finger. His face inflamed with racist rage.

He said, "Mrs. Graham told me you checked in. I do odd jobs and repairs here at the motel. I also do part-time security at the university branch and pick up odd jobs by day."

"I recall your dad, Earl. I believe he had a roofing business."

"Yeah. I took it over when he died but I didn't know how to run a business, except how to run it into the ground. Plus I was buzzed half the time. Had to sell out. But let me tell you this, my dad and me were on Main Street one day a long time ago and you walked by and said hello and even tipped your hat to us. Which not many people did due to our lowly place in the social order. And my dad said you was an exceptional person and important guy and I should try to be like you instead of him. Which I didn't do but I always remembered him saying that. So I admired you from afar and that's why I went to your funeral."

"And yet, Lake tells me, you behaved in a reprehensible manner."

"That was the old me," he said, smiling.

"Do you want to explain yourself?"

"Yes, sir, I do. That's why I'm here. Your coming back from the dead is an opportunity for me as well as you."

"Let's hear it."

"I want to say I'm really sorry for being a dick at your funeral. I saw all these black people in our part of town and it seemed to go against the normal way of things and seemed wrong to me. And then once I started being a dick I couldn't stop. But afterward my mom came down on me, chewing me out about it on a daily basis. She said dad and her didn't raise me to be the town shithead but I was doing a helluva job achieving that role on my own.

"So I went over to 614 and apologized. Mrs. Taylor sat me down in the sunroom and brought out a plate of chocolate chip cookies. I got a helluva scolding but she forgave me. She ordered me to get racial stupidity out of my system. I didn't even know it was in my system, but I promised I would. And I did, pretty much. I saw the light. I had a—what's the word for seeing the light?"

"Epiphany?" I suggested.

"That's it. A big one. I even went to some school integration rallies in the 1950s. Later on, when I was driving a taxi, I drove Mrs. Taylor to her doctors and later to the sanitarium or whatever it was. I never took a fare from her. She was a good woman. Had a tart tongue on her but nice. Tried to get me to put my life together but that was beyond her ability. I got too many of my dad's fuckup genes."

"I accept your apology, Earl."

"Thank you. That means a lot to me after all these years. Do you plan on going by 614?"

"We drove by tonight. We'll get a better look tomorrow."

"It's a lot different from the old place. They changed everything. Put on an addition in back with a hot tub. I got some work carting away construction debris. Wanna see inside it?"

I remembered HB saying a lot of dead people chose not to return for last visits because there'd been too many changes. The landmarks of their lives had been obliterated. They didn't want to see the new versions. So it might have been wise to skip going inside the house, but HB's mind was on his letter to Sportie.

HB said, "Earl, I would very much like to see inside the house. Can you arrange it? Do you know the residents?"

"Yeah. Dr. Vijay Kumar and his wife, Celia, and four kids. He's a cock doc."

"A what?"

I figured it out. "A urologist?"

"Yeah. Personally I've never had a need for his medical services. Why don't you meet me outside 614 tomorrow morning and we'll knock on the door. I bet they'll be proud to show you around. Is eleven a.m. okay?"

"Yes, fine. Earl, what happened to Robert Deems?"

"Mr. Deems? He passed and his son moved to Michigan but his grandson Mike's still here and doing fine. He's kind of a leading citizen in town. He's the assistant principal of the high school."

"The assistant principal!" exclaimed HB. "Robert drove the school bus and now his grandson is assistant principal of the high school? I like that story quite a bit."

"Yep. Mike Deems. He was a basketball star at Ohio State. Six-foot-five. He runs a pickup basketball game for dads on weekend afternoons at the school. You could go over there if you want to meet him."

"I'd love to. Earl, do you remember Karen Darby? A teller at the bank?"

"Karen Darby—could I forget her? With that red hair and fantastic figure, like Rhonda Fleming in *Gunfight at the O.K. Corral*. She was some sight in a summer dress."

"She's not around anymore, is she? What became of her?"

"She stayed true to her douchebag husband until he blew his brains out, what little brains he had. She went away after that. They say she met a pilot from Wright-Patterson Air Force Base and they went off together. But then she passed."

"Karen passed?"

"Yeah. They had an In Memoriam picture of her in the bank for a while."

"That's terrible," said HB. "See you in the morning, Earl."

CHAPTER 23

HB clearly felt saddened by the death of Karen Darby. I didn't want to send him to his room in low spirits and I worried his time would expire with no warning, as it had with Martha. We invited him to our room and watched a little junk TV and HB left, saying, "I'm going to walk around outside. Breathe some McGill air."

"If I let you go on this walk, you're not going to expire on me, are you?"

"No, no. I'll be here in the morning. Don't worry."

When he was gone, I said, "I can't come to grips with how I'm going to handle this."

"You're convinced he's going to disappear?"

"Oh, for sure," I said, surprised to realize that I hadn't doubted this final step in HB's story.

"It's such a peculiar situation. It's not like he's dying, but it is," said Brendan. "He takes it in stride. What else can you do?"

"I wish he could stay. You know, in the beginning he made a little speech about how he wasn't a guardian angel who was going to impart wisdom, but it kind of worked out that way."

"What was the wisdom he imparted?"

"I don't know. Part of it is just a simple reminder that I come from somebody. That's important. I lost that when my husband died and I felt so alone. I forgot I had a family history behind me, a good family. HB brought family back to me. I sort of feel like I'm on more solid footing going forward."

"Okay, that's part of it. What else?"

"It's hard to describe. It's not an explicit lesson. It's more like an appreciation of the vastness of the whole shebang, as he calls it. We're just ants, Brendan. We go through our lives with hardly any awareness of the magnitude of things. I think being more aware, even just a little, is a good thing and I got that from HB."

He smiled. "I've found that when people die and you think about it you get a tiny peek at that bigness but it only lasts a moment. If you try to look harder, you can't do it. It's like looking at the sun. You have to turn away, and you're kind of relieved to be back in your little world. One minute you're peering into the cosmos and a minute later you're trying to remember where you parked your car in the funeral home parking lot."

"I thought HB made a good effort in his interview, but didn't it sound like he barely got off the ground trying to describe death?"

"Can we move on to another topic? I'm kind of interested in this Karen Darby. He asked first about Mr. Deems, but then he jumped over all the local friends he might have asked about and went right to his favorite bank teller."

"He mentioned her once before. Said he enjoyed exchanging small talk with her at the bank. As I think back, I recall picking up a vibe that something might have gone on."

"HB playing around on your grandmother?"

"I'd be shocked if it went that far. He told me he was faithful and I believe him."

"Maybe Karen Darby was someone he fell for, but nothing happened, and all this time he's had a secret soft spot for her. Imagine him going to the bank every two weeks, straightening his tie and so on, eagerly waiting in line for some moments with the beautiful and friendly teller he had a crush on. Then walking away with an all-day glow."

"Could be. I'd call it a *slight* flaw in his fidelity. But I can relate to it more than I can relate to perfection."

"They say nothing gets a better hold on the heartstrings than a romance-that-might-have-been. A romance that stays innocent and never gets into the biff-bam-boom stage."

"I was about to accuse you of being sensitive but you blew it at the last minute."

He persisted. "Don't you think most people have little near-romances like this? Haven't you had anything like this?"

I could have said, "I had one *this week*, with a movie star, no less," but I kept silent.

He said, "It's a classic sweetener in life, isn't it? Also kind of a cliché."

"It's a cliché when it happens to someone else but not when it happens to you."

"Are you going to ask him about her?"

"No way. If this is his cherished secret, I shouldn't intrude on it."

"Speaking of intruding, how about some intrusive behavior between you and me?"

"It'd break our once-a-year rule."

"That rule doesn't apply in Ohio. Or in motels."

* * *

Earl was waiting in the street outside 614, happily waving his arms as we pulled up.

"I already fixed it for you," Earl said, pleased with himself, maybe pleased to be making up for his wrong of many years ago. "I told them you'd been on TV and whatnot and used to live here. They knew about you. Dr. Kumar's glad to have you come in and look around."

At that moment Dr. Kumar, a small man in tennis whites, came jogging across the lawn.

"HB Taylor! Home at last!" he cried.

After vigorous handshakes he led us (Earl stayed outside) into the house. We entered by a side door that opened into the sunroom, which had once been a cozy haven but was now what Dr. Kumar called a media room. It was cluttered with electronic gear and the biggest TV screen I ever saw, which stood in the same position as the imposing 1940s Magnavox console we used to gather around to listen to the radio. The TV was on, though no one was watching. Cartoons were playing.

"Let me find Celia, my bride," Dr. Kumar said, hurrying off.

I whispered to HB, "You were laid out here in your casket the night before your funeral."

"It slips my mind," he said with a smile.

Celia, like her husband small and tennis-clad, swept in and wrapped us in huge embraces. "We saw you on TV," she said, nodding toward the TV. "You were so great. Such a down-to-earth talk. Some of our friends thought you were full of you-know-what but we loved it. So you're the granddaughter and you—"

Brendan said, "I'm the security escort. Some folks, believe it or not, are a mite hostile to Mr. Taylor for what he said about death."

"There's always a few," said Celia. "Come on, let me give you the quick grand tour. I'd offer coffee but Vijay is impatient to get going on our big tennis day. Of course we didn't realize when you were on TV that you'd lived in our house. *This* house. We've been here five years. Another family lived here after your wife and they left it a mess. But we wanted a fixer-upper so we could make every detail a reflection of ourselves. My advice: don't start anything like this without being ready to spend, spend, spend."

"Could we start with the living room?" HB asked.

I'd always been intimidated by the living room. I remembered it as a shadowy chamber that everyone avoided, preferring the bright sunroom or the dining room with its large round table that HB called "headquarters." The one memorable feature of the living room was a wall lined with floor-to-ceiling glass-doored bookcases crammed with books that were immaculately aligned on their shelves.

The bookcases were gone.

"What happened to the books?" HB asked.

"We junked 'em, the bookcases too. Elegant in their day, I'm sure, but decrepit and past their prime and not a fit for our concept," said Celia.

I wondered what their concept was. Maybe it was buying a lot of expensive and somewhat garish furniture and jamming it in at random.

Celia went on, "Most of those books were so old the pages crumbled in your hands. And we're not a family that reads the Greeks and Romans like you did or even the old American stuff like Dickens."

I quickly checked HB's reaction to the *American* Dickens: he was poker-faced.

I didn't see a single book, anywhere.

"That Dickens collection was the pride of my library," said HB. "Printed in London. Leatherbound. Cost me a pretty penny but I read every word, more than once. I'm sad they're gone."

"Well, then, this is your lucky day! They're not gone. We held on to the Dickens books. They were the only books we kept because they were a complete set and so handsome and we figured we could make a good buck peddling them in the antiquarian book market but I never got around to it and probably never will, so why don't you just help yourselves to them on your way out. They're packed up in a couple cartons out in the garage."

HB's face lit up. "That's miraculous. And a very kind offer."

I could see that HB was ready to bolt, to rush to the garage, but Celia's tour was just beginning. We had to stick it out for a while longer.

The next stop was the kitchen but, on the way, we passed through the dining room where to our dismay the great round table was gone, replaced by what looked like a corporate conference room table.

"We entertain a lot, mostly senior doctors, administrators, and pharma reps.

We have very stimulating conversations as I'm sure you did too."

"We sure did," said HB. "Lots of booze tickled the tonsils in this room, enough to float a battleship. On a big night, Lake here used to sit at the table in a high chair and we'd let her sip half a shot glass of beer. She loved being part of the party. Her first words were, 'More beer.'"

"Family legend," I said. "Not true." But I had a pang of nostalgia for that table, its dark surface nicked and scratched and scarred by cigarette burns.

"We don't believe in alcohol," said Celia.

HB's pro-booze statement seemed to sour Celia, who lost some of her verve and accelerated the tour.

The kitchen was stuffed with every large and small appliance ever invented. The hot tub was beyond the kitchen but we skipped it because the rush was on.

I remembered the stairway. I always ran up it in secret fear because it was dimly lit and so narrow I was claustrophobic. Now the lights were bright and the wall was lined with framed photos of the family posing in front of the Taj Mahal.

The second floor didn't seem much changed. Perhaps the first floor consumed their renovation budget. There was a master bedroom and a guest bedroom where I stayed during the summers with my mom and dad, the same room my mother and Aunt Margaret had shared as girls. It now held two bunk beds for the four Kumar girls who were squabbling while preparing for tennis. They barely noticed us, except when Celia told them we'd been on TV.

We heard Dr. Kumar downstairs shouting, "Wheels up! Let's skedaddle! Winner plays John McEnroe."

Down the hall, with its door partly opened, was the bathroom where HB spent so much time in gastric misery. Next to the bathroom, with its door closed, was a small bedroom I recalled as Sportie's sewing room.

HB hung back from that room.

"I died in there," he said quietly. "It was the middle of the night. I rang the bell, but Sportie was sleeping in the master bed and didn't hear it, so I was alone at checkout time. At least I was in bed and not in the john."

Moments later we were outside, the Kumars loading into one of their two Volvos. Earl was puffing on a cigarette, which drew disapproving glances from Dr. Kumar.

"Did you love the house?" Celia cried. "Just go into the garage and help yourself to Dickens." They shot off as we waved and shouted our thank-yous.

* * *

We followed HB as he made a beeline for the garage where a high shelf held two book cartons labeled "C. Dickens." Brendan and Earl lifted them down. They were unsealed.

"Unpack 'em, would you?" HB asked.

"What are we looking for?" asked Brendan.

"*The Pickwick Papers*. Dickens's first novel. I left a letter for my wife folded into it. I need to know if she found it."

There were about ten books in each carton. They were handsomely bound volumes and seemed in good condition. I could see why Celia thought she could make money on them.

Earl found *The Pickwick Papers* and handed it to HB.

He opened it with tender care. He riffed the pages several times. Nothing fell out. He did it again. Still nothing.

"Hey, that's too bad," Earl said.

"No, it's good," said HB. "It's damn good. If the letter's not here that could mean she found it, and if she found it, she read it. Of course it could have fallen out and been found by someone else or just thrown away. But this is good enough for me to believe Sportie found it. Thanks for getting me here, Lake."

"What'd you write in the letter?" asked Earl.

"That's between me and her, Earl," said HB. "Husband-and-wife things."

"Hold on," said Brendan. He was holding *Great Expectations*. The corner of an envelope was sticking out of it.

Brendan handed the book to HB, who removed the envelope. It was light blue, of quality stationery, its flap open. "This is the envelope I used. Look, this is my handwriting."

To Sportie—April 2, 1948.

"About three days before I died. I remember sitting in bed writing it."

"How'd the envelope get from one book to the other?" asked Earl.

"I'm guessing she finished *The Pickwick Papers* and then used the envelope as a placemark while she read *Great Expectations*."

He stuck his forefinger into the envelope to confirm there was nothing in it. But there was something.

"Well, well, look at this," he said, reaching in and pulling out an old and wrinkled black-and-white photograph about two inches square.

HB held out the photo, displaying it to Brendan and Earl and me. It showed HB and Sportie looking so young I was slow to recognize them, posing with another couple in a paneled room. The two men—the other one tall and broad-shouldered, towering over HB—wore dark suits and held cigars. The women were in long dresses."

"They look about to bust with joy," said Earl.

"Who's the other couple?" I asked. But I knew.

"That is the great ballplayer Napoleon Lajoie," said HB. "Larry Lajoie and his wife, Myrtle. We had the damnedest time that night. The restaurant-owner took this photo. Sportie treasured it."

Earl asked, "You think she left it for you?"

HB thought for a moment. "You mean in case I returned from death thirty-one years later and was looking for a good book to read and chose *Great Expectations*? No, I don't think that, Earl. I think she just chose to save the photo in that envelope, maybe because it was my envelope with my handwriting on it." He then turned and walked away, a hand covering his eyes.

But he turned around quickly, smiling. "I thought I was about to shed tears," he said, "but dead men don't cry."

I asked Brendan and Earl to repack the books and put them back in the garage, except for *The Pickwick Papers* which I took as a souvenir.

Later HB gave me the photo. "I wish I could take it with me," he said. "Take good care of it."

CHAPTER 24

As Earl roared off on his motorcycle, HB and Brendan and I began a stroll around the 614 neighborhood. HB rattled off the names of the 1940s residents—the Browns, the Deweys, the Hopes, the MacFarlanes—and pointed out the little white house at the far end of Cambridge Street where my mother was born in the year before HB bought 614.

We made two brief stops to visit Cambridge Street residents: Myra Littlefield, who'd helped in my investigation of the water tower guy, Chester Bronson; and Len Savitch, who'd been my lawyer during Sportie's decline and later for the sale of 614 after her death. Both seemed to have expected our visits. The word was out that HB was back.

The sky had clouded over. A light sprinkle was beginning.

"Do we think it'll rain out Mike Deems's basketball game?" Brendan asked.

"Let's try it," I said.

HB took a last look at 614 as we pulled away. "I never thought this before, but it was a pretty ordinary house, wasn't it? Raised two girls here, lived through two wars and the 1918 pandemic, which nearly cooked my goose, and of course the Depression, which was well-named, believe me. We never gave a thought to fancying up the place."

"Nobody's house was fancy in those days," I said. "Nobody had fancying-up money. But it was a great home."

With Brendan at the wheel, we drove to the high school and circled around back to the basketball courts where a tall black man in a hooded red rain jacket was by himself, shooting baskets.

He smiled and waved as we approached.

"Mike Deems?" HB asked.

"HB Taylor? Lake Whistler? Brendan?"

"Brendan Leary," said Brendan, shaking hands.

"Earl Bridgewater told me you'd be dropping by for some hoops."

"Looks like no one else dropped by," said Brendan.

"Scared away by a little rain. It's just as well. We're a bunch of out-of-shape dads in our forties. On a slippery court like this, Achilles tendon ruptures are only one bad step away."

Brendan said, "I'm out of shape in my forties. How about some one-on-one?"

"Sure. First to ten points? HB, we've got a lot of catching up to do but first I have to kick some New York ass."

"I'm not losing to a high school principal," said Brendan. "Oh, sorry, *assistant* principal."

The two men wheeled around and went at it, fiercely competitive but good humored. Mike Deems was three or four inches taller and silky-smooth with spins and moves that would excite a crowd. Brendan had no frills. He was way overmatched athletically but tenacious. He played an energetic game and managed some respectable shots.

HB and I sat down on a bench and watched.

After a while HB said, "Lake, I don't want to be the old coot handing out cheap advice. But I like this fellow. Brendan."

"You've mentioned that. Yes, he's a pretty cool guy. Oops."

Mike made a high-flying dunk and the cool guy ended up sprawled on his backside. Mike took a quick 6-3 lead.

HB continued, "You've had some pretty harsh setbacks. You lost your husband. And I think you just had a disappointment with Burt. By the way, I think Brendan's as good as Burt Reynolds."

"Minus the looks, wealth, and fame, of course," I said, getting a smile from HB.

"He's a good man. And available, it seems. And he likes you."

"Understood."

"The best advice I can give you is to keep going without getting down on yourself and when luck comes along, jump on it. Starting with Brendan. That's my dime-store advice."

"I don't think they have dime stores any more, but I appreciate it. I'm going to miss you, Grandpa."

Mike had the ball and a 9-5 lead. Instead of finishing Brendan with a drive to the hoop, he dribbled several steps backward and put up a long jump shot. It was a sporting gesture, giving Brendan a chance by taking the hard shot instead of an easy one. But it went in.

They came off the court high-fiving and wet from sweat and rain.

"He had home court advantage," said Brendan.

Mike said, "This rain's getting worse. Follow me over to my house."

* * *

Mike lived in the black part of town on what in HB's day was called "the other side of the tracks," though I discovered there were no tracks. The homes were small but tidy and well cared-for. Mike lived in the house his father and grandfather had owned.

HB said, "I sat in this kitchen many times but this is my first visit in daylight."

"Yeah, we had to sneak you over in the dark of night, didn't we? That went on for years, as I understand it. I always wondered how it got started."

"I remember it well," said HB. "Theotis Ames came over to Village Hall one day to take care of some paperwork for one of the projects he was always working on. My Caucasian colleagues gave him the full bureaucratic runaround. They told him he'd have to go to Columbus to get what he needed.

"'Do white men have to go to Columbus for it or just Negroes?' Theotis asked, and that earned him an extra helping of obstruction.

"He'd stalked out in frustration and was standing on the steps outside the building when I came out. He was muttering and smoking, working up the fighting spirit to go back inside for another round. We didn't know each other but we got to talking and I offered to escort him back inside and assert some authority on his behalf. Twenty minutes later he had what he needed and we were friends for life. He said, 'I don't know how to thank you but I can offer the best supper you ever had if you'd do me and my wife the honor of being my guest this evening.' And he just about turned white when I accepted, after getting Sportie invited too."

"You never had a car. How'd you get over here?"

"Theotis had a friend named Ollie, a mechanic—"

"Yes, I remember him. We called him Ollie Oldsmobile."

"Ollie drove his Olds over to 614 and picked us up and we made a fine night of it. And later Theotis asked if I'd come back and sit down with some of his friends and offer some business counsel. All this on the QT, of course. That's how it got started. Regular Tuesday nights. Your grandfather was part of the group."

"I have some good news for you," Mike said. "Theotis is alive and kicking and looking forward to seeing you today. In fact, I'm gonna phone now and tell him you're here."

"That's goddamn great. Did he know I was coming?"

"Yes. When Earl Bridgewater called me I called Theotis and some of the other old boys."

"Earl is doing one good deed after another."

"He's making up for his churlish youth. He's come a long way."

"Who else is still alive, besides Theotis?"

"Herb Witherspoon is fine. You'll see him later. Demetrius Williams. Marlon Jenkins."

"They must all be in their eighties," HB said. "What about the Barnes brothers? And Hobart James?"

Mike shook his head.

"And when did your granddad pass, Mike?"

"About a year after you, HB. But my dad is still going strong. He just retired from teaching high school math in Grand Rapids. He'll regret missing you."

We sat in Mike's living room, nibbling cookies and chatting with his wife, Claire, while Mike phoned Theotis Ames. He ducked back into the room and said, "HB, Theotis wonders whether you've seen your grave yet and if you'd like to, because he wants to be there when you see it. We could meet over there."

HB turned to me and Brendan. "Sounds like a fun place to meet, eh? Let's meet at my grave."

"That's a sentence few people have spoken," said Mike.

* * *

We drove to the cemetery as Mike and Claire and their two kids led the way in their car. Brendan said, "I think I'd be a little weirded out to visit my own grave. How's it feel to you, HB?"

"I'm curious to see it," said HB. "But as I've told you, death is an unsentimental place. Emotions are low-key, close to nil. Maybe that's part of my reactions this week. Things I would have expected to hit me hard are hitting me light."

I said, "Maybe that's to protect you from being emotionally overwhelmed every single minute. Spending your whole visit sobbing."

I asked, "What's the most memorable experience of the week for you?"

"That's easy: my first minutes in Amanituck, seeing you tiptoeing over the grass in your bare feet at five a.m. And me thinking, 'Goddamn, there she is. That's Lake grown up.' But let me turn the question around. What was most memorable moment for *you*?"

"I'd have to think about that. It might been watching you having so much fun telling the Nap Lajoie story to Martha Dell. Or the hansom cab ride with Burt. Or the wink you gave me after you totally blew the minds of the shrink and the lie detector guy."

We passed the church, then got to the cemetery.

The Deems car parked and unloaded. So did we.

Suddenly Earl Bridgewater was there. "Follow me," he said.

We followed him up a grassy slope through rows of gravestones large and small, some new and some weather-beaten. The rain had tailed off but the ground was still slick.

"I was here when we buried Sportie," said Earl.

"Thanks for that, Earl," said HB.

And then we were standing at his modest gravestone.

HB TAYLOR
GOOD CITIZEN
March 10, 1876-April 5, 1948

Sportie's was next to it.

MARY LOUISE TAYLOR
STALWART WIFE
May 23, 1883-October 6, 1969

"Well, well, well," said HB. And we stood silently. And then came a big deep voice bellowing, "HB Taylor, you old son of a gun!"

Theotis Ames, a grizzly bear of a man, swept up HB in an embrace, lifting him off the ground, kissing his forehead.

"God damn, if anybody could come back from the dead it'd be you," roared Theotis. "You look great. Young. Like when I first met you."

"This is how I looked at fifty-five. I was older than you then."

Then Theotis came at me, seizing me in a rib-crushing embrace and swinging me around. "Lake Whistler, what a beauty you turned out to be." He put me down and gave a big handshake to Brendan.

Theotis said, "How about that headstone, HB? 'Good Citizen' was my idea. If ever this town had a good citizen, it was you. 'Stalwart Wife' was my idea too. How you been, HB?"

"How've I been? I've been dead, Theo. How about yourself?"

"HB, I'm doing great. I got eight vacuum cleaner stores and two car washes. I made a bundle with a Pontiac dealership, which I sold for a fortune. I got four grown children, all college grads. I got eleven grandchildren, all doing great. And all my success goes back to your guidance and the confidence you gave us all that we had a chance."

"Thank you, Theo. You were too smart and ambitious to be kept down. You would have found a way without my help."

"Maybe I had the brains and skills and so forth, but there's always just a little bit of belief in yourself you need to do big things. And you provided that. You gave that to me, and us, HB, and that's why we love you and won't never forget you. Sitting with you made all the difference. But look, we could stand here complimenting each other till the sun goes down but right now, we gotta get back in the cars because we got a surprise for you."

CHAPTER 25

We drove for a minute and pulled into the church parking lot. It was late afternoon and I wondered why the parking lot was so full, but as we walked toward the church, people started appearing from all directions.

Mostly black people at first, but then a scattering of whites and then more than a scattering. We recognized a delegation from Cambridge Street: Vijay and Celia Kumar and their daughters, Myra Littlefield, Len Savitch, and others. Earl. The bartender Jimmy Cully. Lots of spouses and kids. HB's geriatric cronies from the old days took turns embracing him and there was a lot of strong affection passing back and forth.

Mike Deems took a position on the church steps and called for attention.

"We're here for a celebration! We're going to celebrate the return of HB Taylor! Give him a hand!"

There were whoops and cheers. HB smiled and waved. Brendan and I looked at each other quizzically, not sure what to make of the celebration concept. But on second thought: HB's good citizen standing was evidently close to legendary and he'd appeared on network TV, giving McGill a moment of national media attention.

Of course his back-from-death story was problematic but here he was being embraced by Theotis Ames and others who knew him in his pre-death years and would vouch for him now without a moment's reservation. He was not counterfeit to them. That made a good-enough case for his authenticity, at least enough to permit setting doubt aside for one afternoon.

Mike said, "I'm going to say a few words so everybody get comfortable. HB, maybe you and Lake would like to take seats on the Carruthers bench."

We did as he told us, sitting down on the handsome stone bench located on a patch of grass just off from the church doors. HB knew this bench. It dated to 1927 and was dedicated to his predecessor as village clerk, Paul Carruthers. "Old Paul was a stickler for accuracy," HB said admiringly. Then he whispered to me, "And a helluva crafty poker player. I had to dull his wits with whiskey to give the rest of us a chance."

Mike continued. "I think you all know the story of what happened here at HB's funeral. It's become part of our folklore. The black community came over to pay respects, which was an amazingly courageous thing to do and a shocker to the white folks. There was a very tense stand-off that could have ended in a real bad way, ripping our community apart."

Theotis piped up. "I was here. Mike's right, it was tense. There was a minute or two of teetering on the brink of getting real ugly. The kind of trouble that came later in the civil rights movement: violence, cops busting heads, the papers writing it up, everybody upset. But it didn't happen. Because of HB. Because people said to themselves, this is HB Taylor's funeral and we're not gonna let it turn into a race riot. We respected him too much to let that happen. So we kept our tempers under control."

Mike said, "Thank you, Theo. I think it was a day when the goodness of our community was tested. And we passed the test, but just barely. Now, when we found out yesterday that HB was back in town, we wanted to do something special, but we didn't have much time to prepare. We had the idea of a reenactment of that scene here at the church, mainly to illustrate what happened as a history lesson for our young people. But as we got into it, we realized it was a tricky idea that might leave a bad taste. Nerves are still kind of raw from that day and we didn't want to stir up old bad feelings or offend anybody."

Earl Bridgewater spoke up. "I'm glad of that decision, Mike, because I would have had to play me in a reenactment and I didn't want to be that person again, even pretending."

Earl stepped up on a church step and turned to address the crowd.

"I want to grab the opportunity of HB's return to apologize to everybody, only thirty years too late. I was pretty damned ignorant that day. Mrs. Taylor said I was 'beneath contempt' and that was putting it kindly. To the black folks and even the white folks I embarrassed, I want to officially say that I'm sorry. I apologized to Sportie years ago. I apologized to HB last night and he accepted my apology, I'm glad to say. So I finally got to say it: I'm sorry."

Mike said, "Good, Earl, I'm glad you got your chance to say that. But let's talk about today. After we dropped the reenactment idea, the next idea was to simply sing a song together. We liked this but what song? Religious and patriotic songs came to mind but we wanted something lighter so we asked, what's a song that makes people have fun?

"We decided to go for disco. We chose one of last year's top hits nationwide. So get ready. With permission from Reverend Harper, I'm going to introduce the stars of last year's McGill High Talent Show: Ricky Steadman, Ruthann Mikkelsen, Antoine Baker, and Vincent Huebner. Let's hear it for their prize-winning rendition of 'YMCA.'"

The four kids made an exuberant entrance from the church, taking positions on the church's top step. They wore costumes—construction worker, native American, GI, cowboy (the cowboy was played by the girl, Ruthann)—and jumped eagerly into the song with the famous arm movements spelling out YMCA: arms stretched up and out to make the Y, arms inverted and pointing down with fingertips touching to make the M, both arms to the left to form the C, arms up and fingertips touching to make the A.

There wasn't a musical instrument in sight, but they performed with verve and high volume and people joined in as though it was the most natural thing in the world. White people, black people, old and young people, singing along and laughing as they did the arm movements. Theotis Ames had his whole family on their feet dancing and then everyone was dancing.

When the song ended, some big male voice shouted 1-2-3-4-5 and they did it again.

By this time Brendan and I were into it and HB was up and dancing as he caught on to the arm movements. HB's dancing—"Dead Man Dancing," I whispered—brought a roar of applause.

That was the scene: a mixed crowd dancing to an a cappella 'YMCA' in front of the old gray McGill Episcopal Church on a late September afternoon as cars drove by, their passengers wondering what was going on at the church.

When it ended everyone lined up to embrace HB and say goodbye. I don't think anyone grasped the imminence of his departure. Theotis Ames offered to host a big morning breakfast at his home. HB hugged and thanked him but said no, he couldn't make it. "I've got an appointment I can't break," he said.

It was a sweet moment and a fine ending to the day. As the last of the huggers and handshakers moved away I couldn't help thinking it would have been a Hollywood-perfect moment for HB's disappearance. He may have thought so too. There was an expectant look on his face.

We didn't try to say goodbye, knowing that words wouldn't be good enough. We held hands and he squeezed my hand a little too hard. I figured he was entitled to some tension since he was, after all, facing his second death.

I kissed his cheek. We braced for the end.

But it didn't happen.

* * *

"I was about to slip away," he said a few moments later. "I felt the tug and a bit of a tingle. But I fought it. I don't know how this works, but I think I got a short reprieve, a bit more time *if* I do something useful with it. And I know just what I want to do."

I was surprised; he seemed surprised himself. We stood there staring at each other. He said, "Lake, thanks so much for shepherding me around this week and bringing me back to McGill. I wanted to see the town and 614 again and put my mind at ease about the Sportie letter.

But there's something else I want to do I didn't think of until last night when I was taking my midnight cruise around McGill."

"What is it, HB?"

"Well, I walked past a house where I saw a kid's bike lying on a front lawn. The kid hadn't bothered to use the kickstand and the bike fell over. I stood it up and started to resume my walk but then I thought, wouldn't it be a hoot to borrow that bike (returning it later, of course) and ride around town?

"So I did. The minute I was on that bike I felt like a twelve-year-old. My legs were inexhaustible. I pedaled all the way down High Street and back on Evening Street. Had a ball going downhill on Hyde Street, which is very steep with a big sweeping curve at the bottom. Did it twice, feeling the breaking-loose joy of speed. Howling like a cowboy on a bucking bronco. Ringing the bell a few times, just for the hell of it. The night was cool and everything was still and lit by bright moonlight."

I asked, "Okay, so what is it that you want to do? Get another bike?"

"No. I'm talking about the moonlight. I stopped to gaze up at the moon. It was a beauty, Lake, just a day or two past full, I think. And I thought of men getting up there, walking around on that thing, leaving footprints where there'd never been a footprint. Out of everything I've seen this week—everything that's happened since I died—the only thing that really knocked my socks off is the landing on the moon. I wish I could go back to death and tell everyone about it. I can't do that, of course, but they'd be astounded, knocked on their blocks. Everyone who ever lived and looked up at the moon would be astounded."

"I hope you don't want to go to the moon, HB. I got you to Ohio but, sorry, no moon."

"Of course. But I want to meet Neil Armstrong."

"This is what you want to do? Meet Neil Armstrong? Why?"

"I'm not sure. I just have the sense that he and I might something in common."

"Like what? I don't see anything you have in common."

"We both went to different worlds—though not *similar* worlds—and we came back. Don't you think we'd have something to say to each other about that?"

"I don't know. Like what?"

"Like what it was like."

"What it was like? I don't recall him ever saying what it was like."

"Neither have I, about death. I've tried. I did my best but now that my time's running out I'm regretting that I haven't done it justice. My answers to Gary Warren were just superficial description. They should have risen *above* description. Or maybe what I'm saying is they should have been *deeper* than description. What I said didn't have any more effect on people than a bag of adjectives. There hasn't been a single person I've talked to all week who seemed to grasp anything near the fullness of what I had to say. Do you get what it's like to have something big to say but no one gets it? That's what Armstrong and I have in common."

"But let's be honest, most people didn't take you seriously or thought you were a crank."

"Not everybody. Gary Warren took me seriously, or at least tried. Burt Reynolds was very intense about what I told him, whether he believed it or not. I think you took me seriously or did your best to. Maybe Wick Sorenson, somewhat. Maybe Brendan. Maybe some TV viewers. I think Armstrong would take me seriously because we've both had the experience of coming back from places that most people can't begin to imagine."

"You're saying you'd have a bond of some sort?"

"Yes, that's it. That's my hunch. Like being members of a very small fraternity of people who've been through huge kind-of-unimaginable experiences and can only talk to other people who've been through huge kind-of-unimaginable experiences. Because other people just don't get it. What we say about death or the moon just bounces off them. Like the old stories of soldiers coming home from World War II trying to describe it to their wives and being frustrated because their wives had no idea what they were talking about because they'd never experienced combat. Never *felt* combat."

"So Martha Dell was the only person you really connected with this week because she was also dead?"

"Exactly, we had that in common. The conversations I had with her were the only conversations when it didn't feel like there was an uncrossable gap between me and whoever. And I wonder if it would be like that with Armstrong."

"You're amazing me, HB. I never sensed that you cared so much about getting across to people."

"I didn't. Not at first. I wasn't here for that. Not getting across to people didn't bother me much because I was just here to be with you. Then it got complicated."

"Because I put you on television."

"I guess that's right. Suddenly I was on TV talking to millions of people and it was different."

I said, "You went from a private visit to your granddaughter to educating mankind on the reality of death. That's a pretty large upgrade to your mission statement, don't you think? So now you're disappointed that in twenty-three minutes of a morning TV show you failed to reshape humanity's conception of the afterlife. Give yourself a break."

"Remember our conversation with Wick about Dante and indescribability? Maybe there are things that just can't be described. No matter how talented you are. How about Shakespeare? I wonder if Shakespeare would have made the decision I made, to come back to life after being dead for a few decades. Imagine the soliloquy when he debates it—'To be *again* or not to be *again*, that is the question.' Or what if he did come back and couldn't resist scribbling out a play about the secrets of death?"

"And the play gets booed because the audience thinks it's bullshit."

We both laughed at that. I said, "You shouldn't fault yourself for not providing a Shakespeare-quality description. And as for disappointment, to be honest, I bet disappointment is what you'd get from Neil Armstrong. I've seen TV interviews with him. He seems like a nice person, intelligent and so forth, but kind of narrow in terms of self-expression. He's a technology guy, a terrific pilot who became an astronaut and now—last I heard of him—he teaches aeronautical engineering. Does he have any soaring insights or illuminations he hasn't revealed yet? I doubt it. I think you should drop this idea, HB."

"No. I want to do it. I feel like I should do it. Can you find him for me, Lake?"

"*Now*? Are you kidding? It's twenty after six on a Saturday night. Nobody's in their office answering phones. People are out doing things and going places. I have no bloody idea where Neil Armstrong is."

"He's from Wapakoneta. Not far from here. We could drive there in less than two hours."

"Wapakoneta's where he grew up but I don't know where he lives or where he is now. You've got so little time left and you want to spend it searching for Neil Armstrong? And even if I could get him on the phone, he'd probably beg off on meeting you. Politely, I'm sure, but he's a serious man who would probably consider it wasted time to listen to some nut who says he's dead."

"But I'm not a nut. You know that. I'm not a crazy old geezer babbling about death. I was on national television. It got plenty of attention. Even if he's been busy thinking about aeronautical engineering, he's probably heard about me. Lake, I went on your show. Let me get something out of it."

Brendan was standing a few feet away, listening but staying out of the conversation. Now he stepped forward and said, "Lake, time's a-wasting. Let's find Armstrong."

* * *

Brendan noticed Mike Deems's car about to turn out of the church driveway onto Main Street. The Deems kids were waving goodbye to us out the window. Brendan made a frantic dash toward the car, waving his arms. Mike stopped and rolled down the window so he and Brendan could talk.

HB and I stood there watching. Brendan trotted back to us.

"Mike said last he heard Armstrong teaches at the University of Cincinnati. Mike says we can come over to his house and use his phone if we need to."

We jumped in our car and sped after the Deemsmobile.

HB said, "I'm betting you find him, Lake."

As we drove, I made a mental list of calls to make. I'd call the University of Cincinnati. I'd try the Cincinnati airport—maybe Armstrong had friends there. I'd try to reach a NASA spokesman. I'd call Jean Maxey and see if she could reach any bookers who might have astronaut phone numbers in their Rolodexes. I'd call reporters who covered space for major publications. I'd call anyone I could reach in Wapakoneta—police, fire departments, restaurants, the mayor, congressional offices, the Rotary, the Elks, VFW, and Walgreens. I'd ask information for phone numbers of Ohio residents named Armstrong and call them all, hoping to reach a relative.

"I'm gonna run up a phone bill, Mike, but I'm good for it."

"No problem. I'm fascinated to see how you do this."

"It's not complicated. You just call everybody and hope to get lucky. You try to get them involved in helping you find the solution. If you get even the smallest bite or clue—somebody who sold him a car or repaired his furnace or goes to the same gym—jump all over it. You never know what's going to work."

"Can I play?" Mike asked. "I have a second phone line upstairs for school and business calls. I could try a few."

"Great. Why don't you take the Wapakoneta calls. Or anything else."

Mike's wife, Claire, led HB and Brendan into the kitchen while I got busy on the phone in the living room. It didn't take long until we crashed into the problem of Saturday night: nobody was home. Everyone was out. Why couldn't people have lonely Saturday nights at home watching television, like me?

We made dozens of calls. Nothing worked. Darkness fell. Theotis Ames came over with a mountainous delivery of fried chicken. My voice was turning hoarse. Mike came downstairs and made a "no luck" gesture. Brendan declared a beer break.

"I'm out of ideas," said Mike. "I even called my old basketball coach at Ohio State. He said he'd met Armstrong once and he was a very nice, self-effacing guy. Imagine that? The first man on the moon is self-effacing?"

"My question," said Brendan, "is what if we find him but he's far away? Say he's in Houston. What do we do then?"

"It's a thousand miles to Houston from here," said Mike. "That's, what, a twenty-hour drive? Or a couple plane connections tomorrow?"

"More time than I've got," said HB.

The phone rang. Mike picked it up, said hello, listened for a moment and said, "One moment, please." He grinned broadly.

"Guess who's calling," Mike said.

CHAPTER 26

HB nodded when I asked if we could put Armstrong on speaker but I'm not sure he knew what I meant. He looked kind of stunned.

There was an awkward silence until a voice said, "Are you there, Mr. Taylor?"

"Mr. Armstrong? Yes, I'm here. Call me HB."

"Call me Neil."

"Neil it is. Neil, I told my granddaughter that talking to you was my preferred way to conclude my time on earth. And now you're on the line so pardon me if I'm a tad flustered."

Armstrong chuckled. "You'll have to explain this concluding your time on earth idea."

HB said, "You're one of few people who's actually left earth so this ought to be in your ballpark."

"I never thought I'd left earth. I just thought I was on a very long leash and would end up pulled back to solid ground."

"Yeah, but with death the return to solid ground idea goes away. You're never going to be hauled back and there's no more solid ground. Except for a short visit if you choose."

"This is way-out stuff to me, HB. I hope I can say that without offending you. But I'm really curious about why you want to talk to me, of all people. And I understand you've made quite an effort to track me down."

"Yes. How did we find you? Or you us?"

"Through Wes Flint. Wes is the basketball coach at my alma mater, Purdue. He got a call from the Ohio State basketball coach who got a call from a former player—"

"Mike Deems," said Mike, clapping his hands with joy.

"Wes told me the dead guy from TV was anxious to talk to me."

I sat forward and spoke. "Neil, this is HB's granddaughter, Lake Whistler. Are you aware of HB's interview on TV?"

"I sure am. Everybody's talking about it. I saw the last few minutes of it. I'm not a TV watcher but I was here in Cincinnati cleaning out my office and my wife called and said I had to turn on the tube and see this gentleman from Ohio who claimed to be dead and was describing death. Who could resist that? And it caught my attention right away when you said something about there being no orgasms in death. Which didn't surprise me, by the way. But since when have they been permitting that word use on TV? Maybe I should give TV a chance."

Neil Armstrong had a sense of humor. This had never occurred to me.

"And then you were talking about the sunsets you see in the afterlife. I relate to that. I haven't been to the afterlife, but I've seen my share of spectacular color in the sky in my flying career. Where are you now, HB?"

"In McGill. Where I led most of my adult life. I've just come from seeing my grave. I died here in 1948."

"I'm not sure what you mean when you say 'died,' given that we're talking right now," said Neil. He was obviously confounded by the death story, but he didn't seem put off by it. "In 1948 I was a kid but I'd already had my flight certificate for two years so I could have flown over from Wapakoneta and gone to your funeral. I'd done practice take-offs and landings at the McGill airfield as well as other fields in Ohio. My family moved around a lot and lived all over the state, sixteen different towns. My dad was an accountant and state auditor."

"No kidding? My dad was an accountant too, Neil. And I was an accountant myself. With Ohio Bell and later for the State Tax Commission in Columbus."

"So we're both Buckeyes with accounting blood in us?"

"Yes, but that's where the commonality ends. One thing we don't have in common is flying. I never flew in my life. Until yesterday. We came out from New York."

"Your first flight was yesterday? Did you enjoy it?"

"Not as much as I'd expected. It was like riding in a crowded bus. There was no adventure to it. I looked out that little window—I was the *only* passenger looking out the window. I said to Lake, 'My lord, aren't these people even a little excited to be up in the sky?'"

"I know what you mean. I have that all the time. Did you feel cheated out of the flying experience?"

"Somewhat, I suppose. The takeoff was exciting, seeing the ground fall away. Looking down at New York was great. But then it was just about being a passenger squeezed into a seat. A guy in the row behind me snored for half the trip."

"I always felt more alive when I was flying than anything else. I loved it, even when I was being shot at."

"Shot at?'

"I was a Navy pilot in the Korean War. Seventy-eight missions."

"The Korean War? When was this?"

"1950-53."

"I missed the whole damn war," HB said. "Did we win?"

Armstrong laughed. "It's a novel experience chatting with you, HB. I wasn't going to call but Wes Flint insisted I'd get a kick out of talking to you. Said you told quite a tale on TV and created a stir with people being fired and such."

"Yes, the big boss blew a gasket, didn't he? They call him the king."

"He's the ex-king now. He got the hook."

"The hook? Creighton got fired?"

Brendan and I slapped hands gleefully at the news of Creighton's ouster.

"Apparently he said some disrespectful stuff about his board of directors. That never works out well."

Neil and HB laughed.

Brendan leaned over to me and whispered, "They're hitting it off."

Neil said, "If I had more time I'd fly over tomorrow and we could have lunch. Unfortunately I've got a big travel day ahead of me. Going to Copenhagen to give a speech and then down to Stuttgart for a big conference."

"I'm traveling too."

"Flying again?"

"No, not flying. Disappearing."

"Disappearing? Where to?"

"Eternity."

"*Eternity?*"

"Yes, and it's a one-way ticket. I've had a great week here but time is short. I might not make it till midnight."

"Are you telling me you're going to die? Tonight?"

"Not die. Did that already."

There was a lengthy pause. Sitting in Mike Deems's living room we made eye contact with each other and were tempted to laugh at Neil Armstrong's bewilderment.

"So, HB, I don't know if this is where our talk ends or where it begins. But there seems to be something you wanted to discuss with me and maybe, given your time constraints, we should jump right to it, okay?"

"Okay. I was discussing this with Lake a little earlier. Here's my question to get started: Do people ask you what it was like on the moon? And if so, what's your answer?"

I had the sense that Armstrong expected something more interesting from HB, but he tried to give a good answer.

"I get that question almost every day, and I have a standard reply. I usually talk about the magnificent views of earth from the moon. How blue and beautiful it is. And people always like to hear about hopping around in low gravity. And some people haven't realized how color-deficient the moon is, except for some meteor crystals."

"What else?"

"Well, anything they want to ask about. Did you know that Buzz Aldrin and I only had one still camera? A Hasselblad. I took most of the shots."

"And that's it?"

"Pretty much. Some people ask if I was scared."

"Were you?"

"I had major concerns about the actual touching-down on the lunar surface and I wasn't convinced we'd survive but aside from that Houston kept us too busy to be nervous. There were planned tasks every minute and hardly a moment to have any thoughts of our own. Sometimes kids ask if I saw any moon monsters. I'm always tempted to make up something crazy but of course I can't do that. So I tell them no."

"How do they react to that?"

"They shrug and walk away."

"They're disappointed?"

"Totally."

"How about the adults? Are they disappointed by what you tell them about the moon?"

"Nobody's ever complained. What are you getting at, HB?"

"Since the beginning of time people have been looking up at the moon and wondering what it's like up there, so here at long last they get an answer: great views of earth, low gravity, no color. No monsters. Thousands of years of waiting for answers and that's all they get. You could write it on a postcard."

I hoped he hadn't offended Armstrong. But in fact Armstrong seemed intrigued.

"You're saying I'm shortchanging people?"

"Not intentionally."

"What else should I say?"

"I don't know. You're the one who's been there. But I've been to death and have the same problem. All week I've been telling people about death and it hasn't sunk in. Is it because I'm not articulate enough? Or because people think I'm loony? Or because they don't have the imagination to understand or won't let themselves try? I can give descriptions, but I fall way short of the full reality. I wanted to know if it's been the same with you. If you share my frustration."

Neil said, "No. I don't give it much thought. I'm not holding anything back. As a pilot I didn't have that many thoughts that went beyond what was going to happen next. Astronauts aren't chosen for their deep-thinking skills. Certainly not for eloquence. We're uneasy with eloquence because we like hard info. I guess we assume that we're just drivers. We're specialists in getting vehicles to the moon. Specialists in what it's like or what it means will come along later."

"I understand that," HB said. "It's a good answer when you're doing it—you shouldn't be ruminating about the essence of the universe when you're about to crash into a lunar crater—but it's not good enough when you're looking back at it later and it's your job to really tell what it was like, even if you didn't grasp it at the moment. You and I have both had invaluable experience. Don't we have a *duty* to do a good job sharing it?"

"You're passionate about this, aren't you? But I agree. I'd be glad to do it better. But I don't know what to say. I'm at a loss."

"Have you ever really tried to reach deep down and put your finger on what being up there was like? Have you ever tried to describe it to your wife in the middle of the night with moonlight streaming in the bedroom window? Or to your kids, trying to pass along this precious knowledge to the people who matter most to you? Don't you want to give them great answers and not leave them staring back at you thinking, 'Come on, Dad, this is *boring*.' It can't be boring. It's the *moon*. Is there ever a moment when you're brushing your teeth or driving your car when you suddenly remember exactly *what it was like* to be up there on the surface of the moon and you remember the full inexpressible reality of it?"

I interrupted and said, "HB, maybe things just are what they are. Maybe there's nothing more to it than what Neil's saying about the moon and what you're saying about death."

"There has to be more. Neil's been to the moon. I've been to death. We've seen things others haven't seen. We know things others don't know. We know there's more to it than details about the landscape. You said you're not holding back anything but if we're not saying it well enough, we *are* holding back. We're holding back the full truth. And that *is* cheating people."

Armstrong was silent, possibly shocked. HB sat back and sighed. "Neil, maybe I'm pushing this too far. I'm beating a dead horse and I'm sorry. My hourglass is running out and it bothers me that I haven't gotten things quite right."

"Believe it or not, you're the first person who ever raised this with me, at least this strongly," said Neil. "They've probably said it behind my back but not to my face. I appreciate your being so direct. This has been an outstanding conversation."

"Talking to you has been a great honor, Neil," HB said, but we could all hear that he was unsatisfied.

There was another lengthy pause.

"HB, I got an idea," said Neil. "How about if I fly over to McGill?"

"Fly over?"

"Yes. I've got the use of a little two-seater plane, a Cessna 150. I'm talking about flying over right now, HB. I don't have much time and neither do you but I have this strong feeling we should meet."

"I have that feeling too."

"I don't get a lot of opportunities to talk about death with guys who've been there."

"I'll ask you what the moon is like and you'll ask me what death is like."

"Sure. And then we'll give each other bad answers."

They laughed.

"Neil, are you really saying you're gonna fly over tonight? Now?"

"Yeah. It's no big deal. Once I'm up it won't take much more than an hour. I'll land at the McGill airfield by, say, ten thirty. The coffee shop will still be open. It closes at eleven. Meet me there."

CHAPTER 27

The first man on the moon walked into the coffee shop and nobody recognized him but us. Maybe because instead of a space suit he was wearing a tan windbreaker jacket over a red University of Cincinnati sweatshirt, khaki chinos, and scruffy white tennis shoes. He'd packed on a few pounds and lost the Boy Scout cuteness of his moon-walking days. He looked like a supremely average forty-nine-year-old Middle Westerner.

HB, Brendan, Mike, and I were sitting at a table in a far corner and we waved to him as he entered. We stood up and introduced ourselves. He and HB did an awkward handshake that morphed into an awkward but affectionate hug. I had the surprising feeling that HB was right about a bond between them.

"It's a beautiful night for flying," said Neil as we sat down. "You know, HB, you're thinking I have no eye for aesthetics, but things are beautiful when you fly. Not just how things look but how things are."

HB asked, "How about the darkness? Is the darkness beautiful?"

"Wow, what a question," said Neil. "Sounds profound. I don't know what to say."

"Tell me about darkness when you're flying. It's right there in front of you and you fly right into it."

"I'd say darkness is something you respect. It never gave me the willies when I was flying but when I was on sea duty—I never told this to anybody—I used to go up on deck late at night sometimes and lean on a rail and look out over the water and into the darkness. At first it would be kind of serene but then all of a sudden I would get a shiver, a chill, and I'd have to break it off and get back to lighted spaces below deck. It seemed so gigantic and unknowable."

"As if you're seeing death out there," said HB.

"I never got that far into the thought. Could be. This is your field of expertise more than mine."

He looked around at the four of us, smiling, and said, "This is a heck of a way to start our talk, isn't it?"

We made non-death non-moon conversation for a while. Neil talked about learning to fly as a boy and being an astronaut. He talked about being a professor at the U. of Cincinnati where he was resigning, apparently frustrated by faculty bullshit. But it was clear he wanted to skip the chatter and get down to business with HB.

"I was thinking about this flying over, HB. I think you nudged me toward a different appreciation of what I experienced. What you said about trying to tell my wife about it in the middle of the night or boring my kids or suddenly remembering what the moon was like—yes, I've had those moments. But words always fail me. I guess we've both had that experience."

HB said, "Maybe because it's too big for words? I've wondered if the reason we're allowed to come back from death with no rules about what we reveal is that our revelations will be so inadequate that we won't be giving anything away. There's some superficial stuff you can give away, but not the big stuff."

"Yeah, you can knock yourself out saying things but nobody will understand you no matter how well you say it. Most of my fellow astronaut are more—what's the word?—*voluble* than me but I don't recall any of them saying anything that really hit the ball out of the park oratorically."

"Maybe we're just not the ones to do it," said HB. "The home run hitters will have their day. Isn't that what you said about astronauts being drivers and the people who'll find words for being on the moon will come later? You're an astronaut, I'm an accountant. We're equipped to be decent observers, but we're not poets. We do our best but we shouldn't blame ourselves for not being poets."

"I'm relieved to hear that because Mama Armstrong did not raise a poetic son. On the other hand, you got me wishing I could be better at telling people about my experience. I guess we think the fantastic experiences we've had should have awakened some poetry in us, but I guess that's not how it works."

HB said, "All week long I've been using those same words, telling people 'That's not how it works.' I guess it's time to tell it to myself."

It became clear that the coffee shop was closing up and employees were hoping we would get up and leave.

HB thought for a moment and said, "That might be as far as we can go on this."

"That's it?" Neil asked with a smile. "I thought it would take a lot more talk to solve this thing. Maybe it isn't so complicated. But doesn't it feel like we came up a little short?"

"Maybe. Two sausages short of a breakfast, as we used to say."

"But look, tomorrow I'll be in the airport and somebody will come up and ask me what it's like on the moon and I'll hate my answer because it's not good enough. You put that thought in my head and you're right. People deserve better. I'm going to work on that but, truth be told, I doubt if I'll come up with anything enlightening."

"Who knows?" said HB. "Maybe someday some kid will ask you what the moon was like and you'll stand back and it'll pour out of you, the greatest answer anyone's ever heard. Astronaut poetry."

"That would be super. Thanks to you I'm a little closer to that now than I was a few hours ago."

I couldn't resist: "It's one small step for a man, Neil. I don't know about the giant leap for mankind."

"Don't remind me," Neil said with a smile. Then he said, "This has been great. HB, I feel like I owe you."

"Don't be silly. I hope it was worth it. You flew over here on a night you're supposed to be packing for a big trip. We had a serious talk, brief but good. I'm grateful, Neil."

Neil said, "HB, you remind me of my dad. Did you play cribbage till all hours of the night?"

HB laughed. "Not more than a thousand times. Cribbage and poker and gin rummy, washed down with Haig scotch."

* * *

Neil zipped up his windbreaker and sat forward.

"Tell you what. How about if I take you up for a ride?"

"A ride?"

"In my plane. We'll fly around for a while. You'll get the flying experience you missed out on. You'll see your town from the air, lit up on a Saturday night."

"Jesus Christ, Neil. I would love that. Right now?"

"Let's go."

HB glowed like a boy on Christmas morning.

We all stood up and said goodbyes.

I said, "Neil, I don't want to bum this out but HB is extremely close to the final buzzer. You could get a surprise up there. What goes up might not come down."

Neil took a moment to process that thought, then said, "If it happens I won't land here. I'll fly on back to Cincinnati, solo. Give me your number and I'll phone you later."

I hugged HB and we shared a moment of eye contact. Then I watched as he and Neil walked out onto the airfield, the two of them yakking like old pals. We watched the tiny plane taxi and take off and pretty soon we lost the sight and sound of it.

"What a thrill," said Mike. "Getting flown around by the first man on the moon."

Brendan launched into a great imitation of Frank Sinatra's "Come Fly with Me." This was good. The moment called for upbeat music to take the edge off the sharp feeling of loss.

EPILOGUE

March 29, 2020
Amanituck, N.Y.

Over the past forty years, frequently recalling my extraordinary week with HB, I always think of the moment when he told the network people what the proof of his story would be: He would disappear. Imminently.

Disappearance made no sense to them as a proof. It proved nothing. It was certainly not the kind of concrete proof that would be useful in a public defense of the company, let alone a courtroom defense in whatever litigation might result from putting HB on television. The lawyer Delacore was exasperated by the disappearance idea and dismissed it on grounds that disappearance was easily faked. HB's calm reply was, "Not as perfectly as it's going to happen for real."

He got that right. When it happened he was up in the air with an American hero, flying through the night sky, checking out the moon and gazing down at the twinkling lights of McGill. After flying in lazy circles and dipping down for a closer look at some town landmarks, they found Cambridge Street. Neil flew above the street and brought the plane down low to make a close pass over 614, buzzing it and probably scaring the wits out of the Kumars. HB whooped in delight and gave Neil a happy thumbs-up sign and then he was no more.

"Just gone," Neil told me when he called later that night. "I was suddenly talking to an empty seat."

I knew it. I'd felt the ripple in the air. I squeezed Brendan's arm and he understood. Mike understood too. I was happy that it had ended sweetly but losing HB came down on me with a heavy hand. My face streamed with tears as we walked to our car.

In the morning we flew back to New York. A few days later Mike sent a clipping from the McGill newspaper. The reporter, who had not found out about the event at the church until it was over, struggled through the challenge of explaining the HB story but the headline writer had fun with it:

GOOD CITIZEN DIES–AGAIN

The moment HB vanished I dropped my last 1 percent of resistance about his authenticity. I'd started the week with absolute refusal to believe a word of his story. Then I moved on to a state of forgetting-to-disbelieve it. Finally I accepted it, finding the courage to believe the unbelievable. HB was not a hoax or a grift or a joke or delusion. He was what he said he was. That's my opinion and I'm sticking to it.

Near the end of his TV interview, HB said most people wouldn't believe him so his impact would be minimal. Again, he was right. The reaction to the interview and Creighton's subsequent flameout was explosive but short-lived. With HB gone, the story couldn't advance and deflated like a balloon. A month later it was barely remembered. As years went by, it sank to the lowest rung of public memory, a trivia question: "He said he'd returned from death to visit his granddaughter. What was his name?"

HB spilled enormous beans about mysteries that had caused head-scratching wonder for centuries, but he was a challenge to beliefs that were too entrenched to be tampered with. Most people dismissed him entirely rather than reexamining their notions of what if anything follows the end of life. I wished people were more open. I think there was insufficient awe for the opportunity of listening seriously to what HB Taylor had to say.

I regret that HB was frustrated by the difficulty of telling his story. I'm glad he got to discuss it with Neil Armstrong. I'm also glad that, to my knowledge, he was not ridiculed or disrespected. I think he radiated a natural integrity that made critics reluctant to belittle him. Of course there was considerable skepticism about him but I wondered if skepticism was also a shield against the longshot possibility that he was the real thing. It didn't matter. The result was inevitable. His impact was minimal.

About the time that HB and Brendan and I were flying to Ohio, Richard Creighton was swaggering into a board meeting where he arrogantly portrayed himself as the network's sole champion and protector of traditional values. He emphatically contrasted the board's "pusillanimous and embarrassing indecision" over preventing HB's appearance to his take-charge moral leadership in launching the already-legendary crawl, firing three people, causing both hosts to resign in anger, and putting on a madman show before much of the staff.

It was later observed that the word "pusillanimous" alone was enough to get him fired. The board was reportedly explicit in telling him to go fuck himself. Which he did, going deep into debt to stage a rally at Madison Square Garden to declare his candidacy for the Republican presidential nomination. Against Ronald Reagan.

Gary Warren and Gina Harkness received public apologies and were back on the job by Monday. Aaron Buehler received the official blame for permitting HB's TV appearance and his firing was not reversed. Wick Sorenson was suspended for not blocking the interview as a violation of network standards. He later resigned. Sonya Lester, who'd done nothing worth being fired for, was reinstated.

There was no white-collar investigation and no litigation.

HB's impact on the world might have been minimal but of course it wasn't minimal to me. A grandfather I'd lost when I was seven years old had returned and restored my positive outlook on life. I broke out of the blues that dragged me down after Doug's death. I loved New York again. I liked food more than drink again. I did a 500-mile bike ride in Scotland and came home vibrant and fit, no longer schlumping around like a blonde scarecrow.

And I came out of it with a good man, Brendan Leary. After Ohio we gave it a try as a couple. We had to battle through early obstacles but I kept HB's appraisal of him in mind and finally everything jelled. We lived together unmarried for twenty years and tied the knot on the millennial New Year's Eve.

Brendan never got his hoped-for foothold in luxury real estate but he had a knack for owning and running bar restaurants. His New York saloon never had a bad night. He opened a bar in Amanituck that became instantly lucrative and highly popular thanks to a blue-collar ambience that attracted a mix of the town's working people, slumming rich guys, and well-heeled literati. He became a major personality around town, a role he relished.

My TV career ended about a year after HB. TV is a young person's game and I got too old for it. But I jumped on a lucky opportunity and scored an excellent position as a speechwriter for the president of a New York educational institution. Not just one president but two of her successors.

I've lost touch with Jean Maxey, who got married and moved to Redmond, Washington, where she and her husband made a fortune working for Microsoft. Minnie Horch moved to India. The other summer renters of the past are long gone.

Brendan and I had dinner with Mike and Claire Deems when they made a tourist visit to New York celebrating his retirement as principal of McGill High School in 1998. Andy Shafer wrapped up a fine TV career and moved to Los Angeles. Gary Warren retired rich and now pilots his own airplane and flies around giving motivational talks. Wick Sorenson became a lecturer at Barnard College and published numerous academic articles. Aaron Buehler sued the network for firing him but later settled and took a seat of power more suited to his talents—the seat of a Caterpillar tractor on his family's farm in Connecticut.

A few months after the HB episode (perhaps during a shaky patch with Brendan) I wrote a letter to Burt Reynolds telling him the Ohio story. He replied with a nice but notably unflirtatious note. I never saw him again. He died in 2018.

Neil Armstrong died in 2012.

I tried to read *The Pickwick Papers*. I couldn't get into it but I keep it on my desk to remind me of HB. Next to it, nicely framed, is the little photo of HB and Sportie with Larry and Myrtle Lajoie.

Brendan and I gravitated back to the Amanituck house, which I have relieved of its Irish bachelor austerity and turned into a pleasant home. We know local people and have lots of boisterous company, sitting around schmoozing until late at night. It reminds me of HB's dinner table sessions in McGill, long ago.

As I write this in my small home office, we have fled the city in horror of the pandemic raging in New York. Today's death toll alone exceeded 200 people. We could not bear the wailing sirens of ambulances carrying infected people to hospitals and probable deaths.

We are seventy-eight and eighty-two years old, healthy and fairly vigorous but vulnerable. We are not morbid but we're hoping that each of us will be each other's last significant survivor, allowing one or even both of us to exercise the afterlife option of returning for a short visit. Which we will spend in Amanituck. You won't see us doing interviews on television.

Because of Covid, Brendan has temporarily shut down both bars. We are here for the duration. I need something to focus on. Maybe I will finish a writing project I've been working on for some time, a far-fetched tale about a grandfather who comes back from death.

It's based on a true story.

On some mornings here I awaken before daybreak and go outside, walking barefoot across the dewy lawn to the spot under the streetlamp where I first encountered HB.

I try my damnedest to reach out to him. I talk to him, out loud. I tell him how much I miss him and express my firm confidence that we will meet again in the afterlife. He clearly said that we cannot speak to the dead like this and we cannot be reunited in death—I can hear him saying, "That's not how it works"—but I do it anyway. We never learn, do we?

—the end—